TROPICAL CONNECTIONS

TROPICAL CONNECTIONS

Susie Vereker

This first world edition published 2009
in Great Britain and in the USA by
SEVERN HOUSE PUBLISHERS LTD of
9–15 High Street, Sutton, Surrey, England, SM1 1DF.
Trade paperback edition published
in Great Britain and the USA 2009 by
SEVERN HOUSE PUBLISHERS LTD

British Library Cataloguing in Publication Data

Vereker, Susie.
    Tropical connections.
    1. Women art historians–Fiction. 2. Islands–South China
    Sea–Fiction. 3. Love stories.
    I. Title
    823.9'2-dc22

ISBN-13: 978-0-7278-6787-2   (cased)
ISBN-13: 978-1-84751-154-6   (trade paper)

All Severn House titles are printed on acid-free paper.

Typeset by Palimpsest Book Production Ltd.,
Grangemouth, Stirlingshire, Scotland.
Printed and bound in Great Britain by
MPG Books Ltd., Bodmin, Cornwall.

ONE

Lonely in her new existence, Claire stood on the balcony staring into the oriental dusk. Even now the heat was oppressive, and she was still unused to the strange exotic smells – incense, spices, charcoal, overripe fruit and overripe drains. She took a step forward and smiled when she saw the good-natured chaos below.

The streets were packed with old grey buses belching exhaust fumes, ancient Japanese cars, open three-wheeler taxis and hordes of rickety bicycles. Pedestrians – some in colourful sarongs, some in western dress – strolled through the traffic to chat with friends or bargain at the noodle stalls. Occasionally a driver would hoot his horn, but no one seemed impatient or angry in this more or less permanent jam.

For a moment she thought of going down to join the crowds, but she felt too white, too conspicuous. Then whining mosquitoes began to home in on her fresh European blood. So many of them, everywhere. She was about to flee back into the air-conditioned apartment when something brushed against her legs. She jumped, rigid with irrational fears. Turning, she found herself looking down into the eyes of a small tortoiseshell cat.

She smiled in relief. 'How on earth did you get up here? Where did you come from?'

The cat indicated that it required her to open the French window.

'No, really, cat, I've just arrived. I can't cope with visitors.'

The cat stood its ground. Claire studied the access to the balcony. Could it have climbed up that fragile-looking creeper?

'Oh, all right then,' she said. 'I suppose it'd be too dangerous for you to go back whatever way you came. I'll just have to shoo you out the front.'

But the cat had other ideas. After a thorough inspection of the apartment, including all the half-unpacked boxes and suitcases, it disappeared into the large fitted wardrobe in her bedroom.

'It's filthy in there. Come out, cat, for God's sake.'

She peered in, but the cat had vanished. The wardrobe cupboard was large, and behind the hanging rail was a deep, dark space that sloped under the eaves of the building. Cursing under her breath, she crouched down on her hands and knees, but couldn't see anything. Where was her torch? God knows, somewhere in one of about fifty boxes and anyway it probably had a flat battery.

Blindly she felt around with her hand. 'Hope there isn't a dead mouse,' she muttered. Or a dead rat. Or a live one. Horrors! She wriggled quickly backwards at the thought, but as she did so her hand brushed something. Another unnecessarily scary moment – though it seemed to be just a rather solid bundle of paper. Whatever it was, she refused to check out this black hole again until she had plenty of light and industrial rubber gloves. The flat had been left pretty clean, mostly, but obviously no one had bothered with the nooks and crannies.

There was a sudden rustle, but it was only the cat, covered in cobwebs and unharmed.

'About time,' said Claire with a sigh of relief.

Evading her, it padded purposefully towards the kitchen where it sat staring pointedly at the fridge.

She smiled again. 'I'm not inviting you to dinner, if that's what you're hinting at. Where I come from, it's bad manners to feed other people's cats.'

The cat remained seated, patiently alternating its gaze between the fridge and the floor, obviously thinking her hostess as thick as a haddock. It was at this point that Claire remembered a long meandering note from the previous tenant of the flat, a former employee of her boss. She took the note out of the drawer. On page 4, paragraph 2, she read: 'Our maid left and we gave our cat, Grace, to the caretaker, but she may show up.'

'Grace?' ventured Claire. 'That's a very elegant name for a cat. So this is your flat? You must think I'm pretty inhospitable. How about some milk then?' She took a carton out of the fridge and poured a generous helping into a bowl.

Unimpressed, the cat wrinkled its black nose.

Claire sighed. 'Oh, all right. I'll feed you just this once. We've got something in common, I suppose – displaced persons. Will this hamburger do? It was going to be my supper, but I'm not very hungry anyway. No, you must eat it outside. I suppose you won't mind this plastic plate, madam?'

The cat weaved around her legs as she lured it to the front door and put the plate on the landing.

'You needn't think this is going to happen again,' she said as the cat devoured her dinner with delicate greed.

Shutting the door quickly, Claire returned to her muddled unpacking. She reminded herself that she was meant to be an organized and efficient woman – a mature woman who made career moves. She had left behind her old messy life and begun a brave new one, finding a new job abroad, an interesting job in her own field.

Damn it, why were these boxes so impossible to open and why had she brought all this unnecessary junk with her? She found the lost scissors again and ripped open yet another carton. Why had the removal men packed everything in six layers of paper, even a single worn-out flip-flop? Where was the waste bin, for God's sake?

Suddenly amongst her art books, she came across a photo of Leo. She stared at it for a minute and then dumped it in the bin beside the stray flip-flop. That was where it belonged.

It was dark now, so she drew the curtains and advised herself to pull herself together. A drink might stiffen her upper lip. Searching through the cupboards, she found some Mekhong whisky and a cleanish glass. She was about to turn on the kitchen tap when she remembered the warnings about typhoid, or cholera, or worse. She hadn't yet arranged supplies of bottled water, so it would have to be whisky diluted by lukewarm Coca-Cola from an unfamiliar Asian can.

She grimaced as she sipped her drink. She didn't even like Scotch, let alone this raw rice whisky. Of course, she'd rather have had a huge glass of wine, but apparently wine suffered in the heat and soon tasted of old socks if you didn't keep it in an air-conditioned store, or so she'd been told. And it was ridiculously expensive, taxed to the hilt, better stick to spirits, people said. Funny how many old Eastern hands had come out of the woodwork and proffered seemingly endless advice.

A small gecko darted across the ceiling, before stopping, motionless. Of course it wouldn't fall. They never do, but all the same she watched it out of the corner of her eye.

Shuddering, she remembered a much bigger monitor lizard she'd seen swimming lazily in an open sewage ditch. Harmless too, apparently.

She wandered slowly around the over-furnished yet alien flat – a flat generously provided by her new employer, a man she was yet to meet. It had all been arranged through colleagues on the old-boy network over the telephone, by email and letter. She had been employed to catalogue the Buddhist art collection of Jean-Louis Durant-Vandenberg, a rich, gay Swiss, a connoisseur, a cosmopolitan man of culture, and everybody at Sotheby's assured her he was a very good chap. Well, most people had said that. But it might have been wiser to have met him first, she thought. And was it really such a good idea to have travelled quite so far from England and burned every single one of her fragile boats?

Johnny Case contemplated tweaking one of his wife's swollen breasts but decided against the idea. She'd probably say he was unhygienic, or make one of her unpleasant little cracks about not knowing where he'd been. Instead, he would just drop in on that sexy-looking woman who'd moved into the apartment below. He assumed she was single and therefore very much available. He'd already found out her name. After a small tip, Mr Soi, the caretaker, had been forthcoming. Miss Glay Dow-ing, as he pronounced it, was English, had a six-month lease and was living alone. Johnny decided that a friendly welcome from an experienced expat Brit was just what Claire Downing needed. She'd have no idea about the subtleties of life in south-east Asia.

'Just going to do the right thing and say hello to the new neighbour, darling.' For a moment Deborah turned her large brown eyes towards him and then returned her gaze to the baby in her arms. Johnny resented the fact that she never looked at him with the same tenderness.

'Go ahead, honey,' she said. 'Claire seems like a nice person. I met her in the elevator and told her we'd like to invite her over to dinner. Why don't you fix it? If you have any free time, that is?'

'I'm sure I'll have time to be kind to Claire.'

'I'm sure you will,' said Deborah laconically.

Americans were reputed not to understand irony, but his

wife seemed to major in the use of it. Johnny often had the feeling that she understood too much about many things, especially his private social life. The thought sent a frisson down his spine. He wondered if he could really afford to pay for a flat for his new mistress nearer to the city centre. She probably wouldn't permit it anyway, he said to himself. These upper-class Maising career girls were so proud and secretive. They didn't like to admit to having a foreign lover.

He walked down Lotus Court's marble stairs past the dusty potted palms to ring Claire's doorbell. As he waited, he smoothed back his greying hair, which tended to frizz in the humidity, so he kept it short and neat. He tucked his white shirt into his well-pressed beige trousers and smiled to himself. He was confident of his own lean, dark good looks and had never found his lack of height a disadvantage – particularly with nice small women like Claire. He wondered if she had yet found a chap or whether she might like a discreet fling. He smiled again as he thought of how frightfully convenient it would be. Much easier than trailing to the other end of town to visit his current lover.

He was still smirking when Claire opened the door. After making the usual introductory noises and commiserating about the stress of moving, he insinuated himself into her sitting room and accepted a large whisky, only his third that evening. Rice whisky. Oh dear, never mind, she'd learn.

He launched into the long briefing with which he regularly honoured newcomers. His settling-in talk, he called it. He enjoyed giving advice, and when the recipient of his wisdom was an attractive and attentive female, his settling-in talk would last some time.

'You'll find it very different from the good old UK,' he began. 'But the locals are very friendly, at least superficially, and they're polite and cheerful, though it's hard to get to know 'em well. The ones connected with the Prince are pretty snobbish and grand. Luckily, my wife and I are right in with the set who went to university in England. I'm the Secretary of the Oxford and Cambridge Dining Club.'

He paused to make sure that Claire had absorbed the importance of all this information. Yes, he'd been right. She was quite a looker in a slightly prim sort of way. Apart from the mouth. Not a prim mouth, he thought. Early to mid-thirties, he reckoned. Fair hair, pretty colour, a bit wild though. Skinny figure, good legs. Smallish tits – just about enough, probably, to make it worth while.

He smiled and continued. 'I myself was born in this part of the world, Father having been an expat banker too, and so it's easier for a chap like me to understand what makes 'em tick. Very proud and independent like many island people. You see, they've never been colonized, in spite of being fairly near Indo-China. I suppose in colonial days the islands were too small and remote to be worth conquering. No decent harbour in those days either. Well, the Japanese were here in the war, of course, and now they're starting to invade the place economically, but basically Maising has stayed independent. Being Buddhist, they didn't want to join Malaysia when it was formed, and so they've always been rather poor and Third World.'

'Interesting,' said Claire, bending down to pick up a note-book from the floor.

Johnny revised his assessment. Not so skinny after all. A nice round bottom.

He shook his head. 'Point is that nowadays Maising is an up and coming place: the harbour's been improved. I'm sure you'd like to see round the port. The harbour master is a friend of mine. I'll fix it up.'

'That's kind. Is there a regular ferry service to the other islands?'

'Regular?' He wrinkled his long nose. 'Hardly. Not known for regularity in this part of the world. No, Maising city is pretty developed, even too developed, as you see, but up-country and on the other islands, it's very basic. Best way to explore the area is by boat. You must come for a sail.'

'Thank you.' Claire pushed back her hair. 'Did you say you were a banker? Which bank are you with?'

'Selby's. Not as affected as some by the world banking problems, luckily. But I don't suppose you've heard of us.'

She hesitated for a moment. 'As it happens, I have.'

'Well, then, as you know, we're pretty much concentrated in south-east Asia and the Far East. Now, where was I? Probably boring you about the history of the country. I expect you'd rather know about the local crafts and where to buy batik, and all about the good old International Women's Club. Deborah, my wife, she's American but quite Anglicized, almost normal,' he chortled, as he always did when making this little joke. 'She wants me to ask you to sups. She'll give you the low-down from the feminine point of view.'

'How kind.'

He shot her a long look from underneath his hooded eyelids and then tried a direct question. 'Do you have a husband or boyfriend coming out to join you then?'

'No,' she said shortly.

Bingo! Perfect – a beautiful, lonely blonde. And just the right age, not too young to be picky and not too old to be picked. Bit pale though. Could well be a genuine blonde, in fact.

'What brought you to this far flung part of the world, Claire? You don't mind if I call you Claire, do you?'

'No, of course not. As for the job, I'm going to work for a Swiss called Durant-Vandenberg. He's an art expert and dealer. I was at Sotheby's before I came here, you see.'

'Vandenberg? Really? What's a woman like you doing with a shady chap like that?'

'I am an art historian and he's an expert in his field and a very interesting man, I'm told,' she said defensively. 'I haven't met him yet.'

'You haven't? Well, well.' He grinned and rubbed his hands together. 'Very interesting man, if you like that sort of thing. Just be careful what you collect.'

Seeing her blank expression, he turned the conversation to the British Sports Club where he played squash and tennis. He would take her down there to join. She'd meet all the Brits. The club had an excellent restaurant where they served good old British food – like bangers with real baked beans. Great stuff. To join she would need two sponsors, but he would tell one of his chums to vouch for her. She could leave it all to him. He'd give her a head start in Maising expat society.

Claire murmured something about wanting to meet locals, but he assured her that the British Club was where she'd be most at home, no doubt about it.

Meanwhile, of course, she'd need a maid. Clear up this mess in no time.

When Claire also expressed doubts about that idea, he assured her that absolutely everyone had a maid, however low their salary. Best to ask his wife, she'd know what to do, hiring servants being women's work.

Eventually, when he thought he'd done enough ground-work, he stood up to leave. She hadn't responded to the more probing looks he'd given her, but then that reserved sort of woman rarely did at first. Might come through a few months later if he made the effort. Never know. Not that it was worth bothering with reluctant Western females on this island when there were so many local young lovelies who knew how to treat a man.

As he opened the front door, a cat dashed in. 'I know that bloody animal. Damn nuisance. Gets in everywhere, used to belong to the Haynes – disappeared in a sudden puff of smoke those people. Bit odd, but then I always thought he was a bit of a shady chap – wife was OK though,' he said. 'As for the cat, I should complain to the caretaker, his responsibility. Get him to dispose of it. Probably be glad to take it off your hands. They eat cat meat here, some of them.'

When she had finally managed to sweep Johnny out of the front door, Claire heaved a sigh of relief.

'Yuk, what a creep!' she said to the cat, who was sitting in the middle of the room, complacently washing its face. 'All right, Grace, you win. Wait here. I'll go and see Mr Soi.'

She found him eventually, squatting on the back doorstep and smoking a cigarette, or something similar. The caretaker bowed obsequiously. 'Yes, yes, you want to buy my cat, madame? Velly, velly nice cat. Good cat. Catch many mouse, rat, kill cockroach too. Good cat expensive, but I give you special price.'

Without bothering to bargain, Claire paid the sum demanded of her. Barely concealing his astonishment, Mr Soi counted the green notes and quickly put them in his pocket. 'You want more animal, madame? I get you dog, or nice bird. Have friend sell many special parrot.'

'No, thank you. Not even a special parrot. The cat will be more than enough,' she said.

Back at the apartment she found Grace sitting by the waste-paper basket, sniffing at the photograph of Leo. Treacherous bastard, what was he doing now? Claire could guess. She shook her head. No, no, she'd wasted enough precious years on him. She was now going to concentrate on more important things.

Meanwhile, Johnny's interruption had distracted her. The muddle and confusion – suitcases, boxes, and so much crumpled yellow packing paper – looked worse than ever. She began to undo three cases at once in an attempt to make the flat seem like home. Grace retreated to the sofa and, folding both paws under her chest, lay down on a pile of clean white sheets.

'Very helpful, madam,' said Claire, opening yet another box. She propped a set of English flower prints on the bookcase, but the room had a personality of its own which seemed to overwhelm her few possessions.

Whoever had developed Lotus Court had spared no expense. Everything from the lampshades to the panelled walls had been decorated with bows and curlicues – a modern oriental chocolate box. She had planned to put away the gilded lamps and the hideous puce rugs, but where? Ah. Under the eaves at the back of the bedroom cupboard, of course, once she had cleaned it out. On second thoughts, maybe it would be good to have a cleaner from time to time, but a so-called maid was out of the question, far too uncomfortable and archaic.

It was surprising that her artistic boss, who owned this flat, hadn't bothered to change the decor to a more minimalist style, but then he only leased it to his employees, so why bother? And the rent was very cheap.

She was exhausted, frustrated and, yes, lonely. More and more, she needed a kindred spirit to talk to, though not someone like pompous, oversexed Johnny. Was he a typical expat?

She'd meet her new employer tomorrow. An unnerving thought, but he was a cultured, educated man, bound to be different from the Johnny-type in most respects. At least he wouldn't make a pass. She had been informed by her London colleagues that, though he was said to have once been married, Jean-Louis Durant-Vandenberg these days preferred men. There was talk of a young Cambodian friend.

When the taxi delivered her to the compound set on the edge of the city near where the rice fields began, she found Mr Vandenberg waiting for her on the verandah of his large, romantic-looking wooden bungalow. Beaming and shaking her hand, he exuded bonhomie but his eyes were small and sharp. His nose was small and sharp too, and rested in the middle of his pale face as if pinched from a ball of dough. Short, plump and youthfully middle-aged, with thin grey hair tied in a neat pony tail, he wore black sandals and a Chinese-style shirt without a tie – a kind of sophisticated hippy.

He moved quickly, gesticulating with long, manicured fingers and talking a great deal, pointing out all his treasures, his office, hers – a large modern room with everything one could wish for in the way of computers and other equipment.

The house itself was an elegant blend of oriental and western, old and new, with ornate dark red inlaid cabinets offset by cream Thai-silk curtains and thick, luxuriant Chinese rugs. As for his wonderful collection of Buddhist art – the scale of it took her breath away.

Despite Jean-Louis' jovial manner, she felt uncertain in his presence: his playful smile seemed to her faintly sinister rather than reassuring. God knows why she felt like this – she'd met all sorts of artistic weirdos over the years and anyway he seemed extremely kind.

As he showed her around, he told her she must not think of coming to work full-time until she was truly settled *chez elle* and comfortable in her skin, as he put it.

As she was exploring the office, she came across a locked filing cabinet. When she asked Jean-Louis what it contained, he said smoothly, 'Those are my personal files, my dear. You need not concern yourself with them.'

He turned at the sound of the door opening. 'Ah, Pel, I should like you to meet Claire, our new colleague. You will find Pel a great help, Claire, as he is Cambodian and something of an expert in Khmer art.'

Dressed in hip Western gear, Pel was youngish and beautiful in his delicate Asian perfection, she thought. He smiled cautiously at her and made a bow, bringing the palms of his hands together as if in prayer. Claire remembered to respond in the same way.

'Welcome. I hope you will be happy here,' he said in reasonably clear English.

Claire gushed that she was sure she would.

The men smiled at each other and she felt oddly excluded by their complicity.

*   *   *

Later, back at her apartment, she pondered about Jean-Louis. Perhaps she was just too English to strike up an immediate rapport with a mega-rich, gay, half-French Swiss with a Dutch name. But her senior colleague in the Oriental Department of Sotheby's spoke very highly of J. L. Durant-Vandenberg. He'd supported her application for the job with Jean-Louis, so it must be all right, above board and a good thing.

Clearly, though, her new neighbour disapproved of her new boss, but then Johnny Case talked in a rather old-fashioned manner. In his masculine pomposity he reminded her of Howard. Perhaps expatriates who had stayed in the East most of their lives were a breed apart, their thoughts and attitudes pickled in aspic at the time they or their parents left the British Isles all those years ago. Or maybe they just acquired a new style of thought and behaviour from one another. They were certainly different from people one met in England, and that, too, must be a good thing. Travel broadens the mind, said Claire to herself, doubtfully.

One of these days she would telephone Howard – dear, sensible Howard sitting in Selby's Bank on the other side of town, doing whatever international bankers did. Howard was the only person she knew in Maising, but each day something had prevented her from calling him to say that she had arrived.

At her age, when unspoilt, decent single men were starting to become thin on the ground, it would be crazy not to take him seriously. She didn't like to admit to herself that kind-hearted, well-mannered and really rather nice Howard could be a long stop, a fall-back position. Just in case the brave new life didn't work out.

TWO

' I guess you need a friend, Claire. Just drop by any time you need anything.'

Deborah Case was so different from the reptilian Johnny that Claire wondered how they came to marry. Large and lovely with abundant natural charm, Deborah visited almost every day so that her neighbour would not suffer from what she called the 'newcomer blues'. In spite of her newish baby and demanding small boy, she seemed to have plenty of time to show Claire around the city.

Today Deborah had promised her an expedition to the tourist market. 'We'll take a taxi – they're very cheap out here,' she said. 'It's too hot to walk and there's nowhere to park a car in town. Sounds crazy to take taxis to go bargain hunting, but that's the way it is.' She talked continuously as they stood on the dusty pavement, explaining this and pointing out that – the orange-robed monks, the tiled pagodas, the modern office blocks, the dilapidated wooden shacks, the stalls selling purple and white orchids and elaborate jasmine garlands.

Claire thought she would never be able to assimilate all the sights, and the information and advice she received from every side. When they were finally settled in an ancient Datsun taxi with shiny seats that stuck to their legs, Deborah turned to her.

'So, you're single, are you? Forgive me if this is too inquisitive, but the caretaker gave us your mail by mistake and it said *Mrs* Downing.'

Claire sighed. These questions were always difficult, even though she found herself answering them a thousand times. 'Technically, legally, I'm a widow.'

'A widow? Oh, I'm sorry.'

'It's OK. It happened a long time ago.'

'You must have been very young.'

'I was, he was. We were in our early twenties. We weren't married long, only eighteen months.' To save further questions on that front, she added, 'It was a car crash.'

'That's just awful.'

'It was devastating, utterly, utterly devastating, but time does heal. You get over it. I did get over it. You have to.'

'No children?'

'No, sadly.'

Deborah digested all this information, then she said, 'I'm surprised you didn't marry again. You're very attractive. And still young.'

Claire smiled. 'Thanks. Very kind of you, Deb, but I'm not that young any more. One of these fine days I'll probably bore you to bits with my life story including my excessive caution and lack of success with blokes ever since, but right now it's a bit hot for this conversation. It's addling my brain, this heat. Sometimes I feel as if I'm breathing fifty per cent carbon monoxide.'

'Yes, I know, it sometimes takes a while to acclimatize – you'll get used to it. But tell me what you're doing here, of all places? Why did you pick Maising? Was it just the job with Vandenberg or is there a boyfriend involved?'

'Not really.'

'What do you mean, not really?' Deborah smiled widely.

'Well, there's a man I know in Maising, but he's not a boyfriend, just a friend.'

'And might he become the man in your life, this friend?'

Nosy old Deb, thought Claire. She smiled good-humouredly. 'No way. Life's quite complicated enough without men confusing the issue. I've decided I prefer to remain serenely single.' She waved her arm. 'What's that grand tower?'

'Just a hotel, another new one, the Intercontinental. New buildings all the time these days. Never stop knocking old wooden houses down and sticking up a modern concrete block.'

'Where are we? Are we nearly at the market? All these streets, it's so confusing.'

But Deborah was not to be distracted. 'What's his name this Maising friend?'

'Oh, he's called Howard Gillespie,' said Claire, staring out of the window, trying to memorize the route, though without much success.

'Howard?' said Deborah, after an almost imperceptible pause.

'Yes, d'you know him?'

'Sure,' said Deborah. 'Everybody knows everybody, and besides he and Johnny work for the same bank. We must get you two together.'

'No hurry,' said Claire quickly, as the taxi screeched to a halt in a narrow street which led to still narrower lanes, covered with blue awning, hot and damp, and smelling of sickly sweet fruit, strong spices and not altogether fresh fish.

She was relieved that Deborah abandoned the subject of Howard and reverted to enthusiastic advice giving.

They went on to examine the street stalls with rack upon rack of cheap beach clothes and garish shirts embellished with fake designer labels. Others sold leather-look handbags and purses featuring the name of Dunhill or Dior. In the increasing heat, Deborah bargained happily for five minutes or more over a yellow snakeskin belt costing less than five dollars. Then, as Claire complained of exhaustion, they entered small shops crammed with blue and green pottery, and intricate jewellery set with semi-precious stones.

'You like watch?' asked the vendor, thin, bright-eyed and smartly dressed in a white safari suit. 'I have Lolex, Cahtier, anything you want. You two nice laidee, I give you special price.' He led the way around the back of the shop, past a foul-smelling open ditch and unlocked the door of a corrugated-iron shed. Producing several large plastic boxes, he laid them on the table. 'Lolex? You like for laidee watch or man watch?'

He opened the box to reveal about fifty watches bearing famous European names nestling on dirty cotton wool. After much laughter and more bargaining, Deborah bought a Rolex copy and Claire selected one inscribed 'Cartier Genève'.

On their way home, Claire said with a smile, 'You know, I wouldn't dream of buying a fake watch on a London street. Very improper.'

Deborah laughed. 'You may find yourself doing other things you wouldn't do back home.'

Then the ever-hospitable Deborah asked her to a party. 'We usually like to have people Saturdays. Tonight it's just some folks from the bank and a few islanders, mostly business contacts of Johnny's – apart from Drew. He's a newly divorced Australian guy. I asked him along because he needs cheering up, I guess. Oh, and maybe Howard will look in. He often does . . . What to wear? Oh, anything you like. God knows if I'll fit into any of my clothes – I'm so damn fat after the baby. I'll just die if I have to wear a maternity dress.' She rolled her brown eyes upwards as she tried to squeeze in her waist with her large hands.

As Claire dressed for the party, she thought about Howard. Would he be there? As usual, she worried about her appearance.

She was pale and thin, but it was too hot to eat much and too hot to sunbathe on her city balcony – she'd tried, but the instant she sat down she was covered in sweat. Maybe she'd make it to the beach one weekend to get a healthy tan like the rest of the Westerners here. But even the most beautiful tanned blonde couldn't compete with the Maising island girls with their long black hair and lovely creamed-coffee complexions.

Grace padded into the room as she was staring at a heap of clothes on her bed. After a thoughtful pause, the cat leapt on to the dressing table to survey the scene.

'What do you think about this dress, pusscat? Yes, you're right. I look like a peeled banana in yellow. How about black? Too sad. I think I'll go for the blue. Deb said it was informal. She's nice, isn't she? But a bit inquisitive.

'Not the only one, of course – people often ask me why I haven't remarried. As if there's a massive queue of prospective suitors. Some hope. Thing is though, despite my so-called career and lovely life, maybe I ought to try and find a husband before I'm too old to pull the blokes. My mother certainly thinks I should.'

Grace gazed impassively, her tail twitching slightly at the end.

'Yes, I know some women can pull until they're seventy-five, but I'm not Sophia Loren. Anyway, you can't have babies when you're seventy-five. Well, you probably can these days, especially if you're Italian, but it isn't a good idea.'

Claire took off the blue and tried the black again. 'So why haven't I taken the plunge? Same old story. Because I'm over cautious and because, whenever I do throw caution to the wind, I've been compulsively going for the wrong type. To be honest, cat, I have – or used to have – a weakness for handsome men. But I've changed. I've made a new sensible resolution and that's partly why I'm here . . . Actually I think I'll wear the blue after all. Doesn't make me look quite so limp.'

After further doubts and delay about shoes, she arrived at the Cases' door and rang the bell, which had an irritating chime like her own. Deborah's maid, dressed up in a smart black uniform, ushered her into the room, already crowded and noisy. Howard was not there. She did not know whether to be relieved or disappointed as she looked around at the guests.

'Hi, Claire, great to see you. Sorry Johnny's late. He had to play in a tennis match.' Deborah rushed her around, introducing her to a sea of coppery faces, reeling off names so fast that Claire did not even try to remember them. Yes, she had just arrived, she found herself saying over and over again. Yes, she liked Maising. Yes, it was hot. Yes, she was working for Durant-Vandenberg. This latter point seemed to cause several raised eyebrows. Eventually Deborah whirled her out on to the balcony where she was presented to a dark-haired man who was standing by himself, staring down at the city street below.

As he turned towards her, Claire caught her breath, recognizing the sudden spark, the kind that was inclined to start a rip-roaring and inevitably disastrous fire.

She smiled up at him, trying to avoid transmitting her thoughts, but, she feared, not entirely succeeding. Their hostess rattled off again to attend to another guest.

'Hi, I'm Drew, the token Australian.' He was looking at her with interest. About her own age, he was thin, tall, and good-looking in a dishevelled, windburned way, but his dark eyes, sunk deep in their sockets, were tired and strained. His faded shirt was dark blue and, unlike the other men, who were all smartly dressed in tropical suits, he wore creased off-white chinos.

Pulling herself together, she said politely, 'I'm Claire Downing, the token new blood.'

'Always a good thing in these parts, new blood. This is a pretty incestuous society – all these expats in a small country socializing with each other and minding each other's business.' He gestured towards her empty glass. 'Can I get you a drink?'

'No, thanks, I'm fine.'

'Yes, you are, the finest thing I've seen in a while,' he said, smiling again. His Australian voice was low and musical. 'So, tell me, what brings you to Maising, Claire? Did you come here with your husband?'

Straight to the point, she thought, amused.

'No, I don't have a husband.'

'Divorced?'

'No, widowed in my twenties.' Claire resigned herself to cross-examination.

'Oh, shit.'

'A long time ago obviously. And to save you asking, I don't have any children.'

'Sorry again.' He looked very sympathetic as people did.

She smiled sadly. 'Me too, but there you are.'

'I know a little about the feeling. I'm separated myself.'

Good news. Not that she cared, of course. Aloud she said, 'Oh dear. And do you have children?'

'No, my wife didn't want any – bad for the career.'

It was hard to tell what he felt about all this. He seemed the laconic, buttoned-up type rather than an emotional new man.

'So were you married long?' he asked, and so she answered his questions calmly but briefly. She preferred to give as few details as possible.

'Sounds like you went through the mill a bit,' he said.

'Yes, but I survived. You have to.'

'Must have been very hard.'

'It was hard, but, as I said, it was a long time ago now. I'm absolutely fine these days.'

After a suitable pause, he asked, 'What about nowadays relationship-wise?'

She smiled wryly. 'Pretty dud, relationship-wise. No broken heart though.'

It was true. She'd always had a system of pretending she was OK about everything, until finally she'd regained her shaky equilibrium and genuinely *was* fine, more or less. She said jokily, 'So, go on, Inspector, what's your next question?'

'OK, Claire, so did you come here to (A) further your brilliant career? Or (B) to get away from a man? Or (C) to get closer to a man?'

She grinned. 'Well, A of course, with a bit of B on the side.'

'Ah. So tell me about him, this unlucky bloke you ran away from.'

'I didn't run away exactly, and he's not an unlucky bloke. God, why are we starting on this personal stuff?'

'But go on, tell me, is it really over? Perhaps he'll chase after you.'

'No, he won't. Definitely. Thank God.'

'How can you be so sure?'

For a macho-looking bloke, Drew managed to sound caring and thoughtful. Quite a feat.

'Because I am. One knows these things.'

He raised his eyebrows. 'So you've moved on?'

'Yes, moved on, literally.' She smiled ruefully. 'Now, enough. Please can we talk about the weather, or our jobs or something?'

'OK, OK, I was just checking things out.'

She smiled again. 'You don't seem to realize that the appropriate opening questions from the expat community are "How are you settling in, Claire?" Or "How do you find the heat?" or "Have you been out East before?" or "Have you joined the British Club?"'

'How about "Let me show you my Javanese etchings"?'

'No, no one's asked that, though there was a young British naval officer over there who invited me on board his visiting ship to see the torpedoes. As he looked about eighteen, I declined.'

He laughed. 'So tell me about your brilliant career instead then, Claire.'

'No, it's your turn to be interrogated. Tell me about yours, seriously, I mean.'

'OK, seriously, if you insist. I'm an Agricultural Adviser – under the auspices of the Australian Overseas Aid programme.'

'Aid to the Third World, development and all that?'

'Yes, you know, when rich countries give money and expertise to poor countries so that they can develop into something more like us.' He grinned.

'Not too like us, I hope. But what do you do exactly? D'you hand out money for tractors or something? Or are you one of those saints who rush in and help starving people?'

'I'm not involved in emergency aid, not directly. In this part of the world, we try to help people to help themselves. I deal with large projects like irrigation works and small ones like helping peasant farmers make better use of their resources. I'm a farmer myself, you see. Or used to be.'

'I must say you don't look or sound much like my idea of an Australian farmer.'

'What were you expecting? A bloke with corks round his hat?'

Claire was embarrassed. 'No, but . . .'

He broadened his accent. 'We Ozzies are a very sensitive and refoiyned people. You mustn't upset our delicate souls. Don't forget we brought the world opera singers, conductors, painters, writers – Joan Sutherland, Charles Mackerras, Sidney Nolan, Patrick White, not to mention Germaine, Dame Edna and Kylie.'

She laughed. 'I know, I didn't mean . . .'

'You were just bowled over by my sophisticated chat?'

'Yes, that's what it must have been.' She smiled up at him. 'Come on, this conversation keeps getting out of hand, let's talk about something safe like the view.'

'I'm very happy with the view in front of me,' he said.

They were silent for a moment – she felt a sense of expectation in the air. Another couple came on to the balcony talking in loud voices. Drew took a step forward and touched her hand. 'Too many people here,' he said quietly. 'Let's go somewhere else, a bar, restaurant, whatever.'

'Now? Well, I'd like to, but I've only just arrived at the party. It'd be rude to leave so soon. Deborah might think I'm not enjoying myself.'

'She won't mind. You're a free agent, aren't you?'

'Yes, of course, but . . .'

A hand tapped her shoulder and an oily voice boomed in her ear. 'Claire love, so sorry not to have been here when you arrived, but I've brought a little surprise for you.'

Tugging her by the arm, Johnny pulled her round and led her forcibly away from the balcony into the room. She looked back at Drew, but he shrugged and turned to stare at the night sky.

Johnny patted her hand. 'A little bird told me that far from being a bride of oriental art you have an ulterior motive for coming to Maising and here he is.'

Howard stood there, tall and solid. 'Claire, it's so very super to see you again.'

He leant forward and kissed her cheek. 'You can do better than that. Give her a big hug, old man,' urged Johnny.

Clumsily Howard did as he was told. Claire pushed him away, laughing in what she hoped was a relaxed manner.

Oh God, what now? She turned towards the balcony door for a moment and saw Drew standing there with a sardonic expression on his face. 'Let's have a little drinkie to celebrate your reunion, you sweethearts,' said Johnny. He put his arms around them.

'Do leave us alone, Johnny. We've got a lot of catching up to do,' said Howard, smiling happily. He gazed at Claire in wonderment, as if he could hardly believe she was really standing in front of him.

'Of course, of course,' said Johnny. 'Cupid's done his stuff. Here, go into the study. It's got the best air con in the flat. I'll see no one comes in. Take this bottle of champers to smooth the way.' He leered as he left, closing the door behind him.

'Wow, well, it really is terrific that you came to Maising,' said Howard. He put the champagne bottle down on the red leather desktop and then picked it up again. 'Oh dear, Johnny didn't give us any glasses. I'll just get 'em. Don't go, don't run away, will you, Claire?'

He rushed out, leaving her standing awkwardly in the middle of the room. It seemed a long time before he returned. She noticed a photograph of Deborah in bridal attire standing under an arch of roses. How slim and glamorous she looked in those days. Hearing the door open, she quickly put the frame down.

'Couldn't find any clean champers glasses so we'll have to use these tumblers. You don't mind, do you?' He poured the champagne so quickly that it bubbled over. Wiping the table with a large handkerchief, he almost spilt the drinks again as he turned to hand her the brimming glass.

'Cheers, Claire. It really is terrific to see you,' he repeated yet again. She smiled and sipped her champagne.

He said, 'How about a belated toast? Let's drink to our reunion.'

She took a step back and said light-heartedly, 'Sure. Good to see you.'

'So what are you doing in Maising?' He looked puzzled, yet hopeful.

'I came here to work for Vandenberg.'

'Oh?'

He sounded disappointed so Claire rattled on. 'Just luck, really. I wanted a change of scene and here I am.'

'Wonderful.' Howard smiled more confidently. 'Let's go out to dinner to celebrate your arrival. Johnny hopes to join us later when the guests have gone.'

As they left the party, she looked around for Drew, but he had disappeared. Just as well. That kind of man, above all, was the type she was determined to avoid in future, attractive but haunted and not to be trusted one inch.

Suddenly she realized Howard was asking where she wanted to eat. 'Oh, anywhere, I leave all decisions to you, Howard.'

THREE

Claire had admired Howard's decisiveness when she first met him, just as she acknowledged his other strengths: he was a single, straight man, gainfully employed, a few years older than herself – crucial qualities, her more practical girlfriends would say. The older the woman, the rarer such uncomplicated, unencumbered men became, or so was the prevailing wisdom.

Claire hadn't quite come around to that way of thinking because she wasn't looking for a new relationship, let alone a husband. Despite the dread biological clock, she didn't consider herself on the shelf. What modern woman did? Completely un-PC to think that way. In fact, when she first met Howard she was still involved with Leo, though the relationship was fragile.

She'd gone alone to stay the weekend in a big, cold house in Hampshire for a young cousin's eighteenth birthday. A nightmare party. She felt like Mrs Methuselah and only old men with false teeth or spotty youths seemed to want to dance with her. But then Howard, another guest, strode across the dance floor like a knight in shining armour and saved the evening. He explained his aunt was a neighbour, an old friend of the family, whatever, and he too felt out of his depth. They saved each other.

Though handsome in a solid, sandy-haired sort of way and obviously a good man, at first she decided he wasn't really her type. She didn't mind the big chin, it was more

his old-fashioned Woosteresque vocabulary that seemed a
little odd. 'Golly, what a strange lot the uncouth youth of
today are' or 'Jolly good show'. Sometimes he sounded more
like eighty than forty, though maybe he was just being ironic.
When he expounded on his expat lifestyle, she was amused.
She could just picture him as a colonial officer dispensing
justice to the locals in a jungle clearing. However, it turned
out he worked for an international bank – a respectable solvent
one, he assured her – on some island out east and was in
England on leave. So it was just a brief but not romantic
encounter, she thought.

But Howard obviously had other ideas. In an extremely
gentlemanly manner, without so much as a kiss on the cheek,
he made it clear he was smitten. He was very keen to see her
again. No harm in accepting his invitation to lunch in a pub
and then, the following weekend, a picnic in Kew Gardens.

Howard talked a great deal in the pub, but Claire liked to
listen, and she was genuinely professionally interested in south-
east Asia and its art. He seemed surprised she had even heard
of the area and chatted happily on, while gazing at her in
obvious admiration. She noted he had good manners, opening
doors left, right and centre. And she gave him brownie points
for being kind to his frail old aunt when they called on her.

A week after they met, as they wandered along the grassy
avenues among the daffodils and ancient trees at Kew, Howard
obviously had something on his mind. He steered her towards
the elegant Japanese pavilion, but Claire said she was tired
and did he mind if they went home now. As they turned
towards the gate, Howard opened and shut his mouth several
times. They walked on.

Amused, she suspected he was about to suggest a wicked
weekend in Brighton, which she thought she would turn down.

But, tugging her by the arm, he blurted out, 'Actually, I
was planning to ask you to marry me.'

She assumed it was a weird kind of joke. Smiling, she said,
'It's a bit old-fashioned. You've only met me wearing a long
frock or trousers or jeans. You can't ask people to marry you
when you haven't seen their ankles. I mean, I might have legs
like tree trunks for all you know.'

'That sort of thing doesn't matter a damn. Why – have you
got bad legs?' he asked as an afterthought.

She grinned. 'No, they're OK, quite good in fact . . . But that's not the point – you don't know anything about me.'

He shook his head. 'It's a question of instinct.'

'Honestly, Howard, life isn't that simple.'

'Why not? Seems perfectly simple to me.'

'As I said, you don't know me.'

'I know enough to know you are the right person. So is it yes or no? I want to take you back to Maising with me, you see.'

She shook her head wonderingly. He *was* serious. Hesitantly, she began, 'Howard, I'm very honoured and touched by what you say, but I can't make a decision about something as important as this just like that, on the spot. I have a job, a flat, another person in my life.'

It appeared that he'd been so busy with his own concerns, he hadn't thought of hers. His eyes widened in shock. 'What sort of a person?'

She shrugged. 'A bad-news person mostly.'

'So there's hope for me? Claire, I love you, I need you to decide,' he said earnestly.

'But, as I said, I don't know you.' She mustn't hurt his feelings.

He continued doggedly. 'I haven't time for anything else, that's the thing. I have to go back to Maising next week when my leave ends.'

'Oh, I see, that's difficult.'

A group of chatty middle-aged ladies wandered across the lawn towards them.

'So is it yes or no then?' asked Howard urgently.

The whole scenario – colonial chap from jungle seeks instant English bride – now reminded her of a Somerset Maugham novel.

She wasn't used to being stuck on a pedestal and adored, but after Leo's rough and casual behaviour she found a bit of worship and generosity of spirit soothing to her fragile ego. It was difficult not to be flattered, but of course she couldn't take off with a strange man she hardly knew. Very gently, she told him so.

Once back in Maising, Howard wrote numerous emails apologizing for rushing her and describing the wonderful luxurious life out East: sun, sand and sea (photos of beach attached). Sometimes Claire replied, in brief friendly terms. Then she heard about the job with Jean-Louis just when her relationship with Leo hit the rocks. Seemed like Fate with a capital F had intervened. She made a sudden wild decision. Chuck Leo, chuck England and seize the day. It probably wouldn't work out with Howard, but he, knight in shining armour again, had inspired her to act.

Howard, too, was sure that Fate had intervened. Here, miraculously, was Claire in person on the island – the most wonderful woman in the world, the one he'd been waiting for all his life. She was so suitable in every way (so beautiful, so kind, so intelligent) and he was taking her out to dinner. It must mean something. Johnny Case seemed to think it did. He must have deliberately invited them both to the party. He was a good friend, old Johnny.

Howard experienced yet another large pang of guilt about the night he'd spent with his good friend's wife.

FOUR

'Marvellous party, darling.' Johnny rolled off his wife's comfortable body and moved to his side of the bed. After a snuffle or two, he began to snore gently.

Deborah lay awake, staring at the patterns of dark and light on the ceiling. Headlamps from passing cars illuminated one corner and then all was momentarily dark again. It was weeks since they had made love and tonight's efforts had not made her any happier. Johnny had been drinking heavily at the party. These days he only seemed to want her when he was smashed. Perhaps no man would desire her now that she was so overweight.

She wriggled out of bed and crept across the room. Gently shutting the bathroom door behind her, she switched on the light and stared at herself in the mirror tiles that Johnny had installed behind the bath. They reflected a tall young woman with classic Mediterranean features that she had inherited from her grandmother: wide eyes, full lips and high cheekbones.

Deborah did not care for her own style of looks. Her colouring was striking enough in England and the States, but here, where every woman had long dark hair, hers wasn't special any more. The Maising were small and neat. Deborah felt like an untidy elephant beside them.

She took off her nightdress and stared at her heavy breasts and generous thighs. She sighed. If she weren't feeding Jojo, she wouldn't even have those big tits to compensate for the rest of the flab. At least the kids love me, she thought. Tears came into her eyes. After parading around the party doing her goddam perfect-hostess act, she was too exhausted to sleep. She wandered through into the chaotic sitting room. Pima had cleared some of the debris but had been sent home before the late-stayers left. Deborah picked up a tray and mechanically began to collect the dirty glasses and brimming ashtrays.

She thought about her neighbour. Claire was delicately pretty, blonde – so damn thin. And she was a great person. Unfortunately.

Until tonight, Deborah had held the notion that Howard was in love with her, but too gentlemanly to say so. The thought of this secret passion she inspired had consoled her a little through the vagaries of Johnny's behaviour – her husband had been brought up in south-east Asia and liked to go to massage bars. She had tried to be sophisticated about the whole thing. She was a diplomat's daughter and had travelled all around the world. She knew that people had different customs in different countries. But Johnny's I-only-go-for-the-massage routine was pretty hard to believe. During Deborah's second pregnancy, he had promised to give up the massage bars, but he often went out alone, allegedly on business. She found his behaviour unnatural and suspicious. If they made love more often, married life might be OK, she thought, like it was in those first sexy infatuated times. But Johnny just didn't seem to want her much now, even when she wasn't pregnant. Not being wanted was hard to bear.

Then there was the drinking. It was during one of Johnny's binges last year that Deborah had been pushed into an act of vengeance. In a wild and unpremeditated fling, she had spent the night with Howard. She had known and liked him for a couple of years. He was the sort of man who took trouble with children. He'd play with Sam at the beach and even listen to what he said. Howard would pay attention to her too, in his gallant, old-fashioned and apparently harmless manner.

A faithful woman at heart, Deborah normally stopped at the flirting stage. But at the Selby's Bank beach house there had been a party. Johnny, roaring drunk and abusive, left without Deborah, announcing that he was going to the Paradise Club. She'd stayed at the party, dancing with Howard, drinking far too much, and finally walking with Howard to the far end of the beach. Despite the alcohol, Howard's love-making had been thorough, efficient, and extremely satisfactory. There'd been such tenderness between them that she thought, half-anxious, half-happy, they might be going to fall in love. But the next day he had avoided her, and the next, until finally he had come furtively round to say that she was a wonderful woman, but he was terribly, terribly sorry to have, well, done it with a friend's wife. She wouldn't tell Johnny, would she? He hadn't meant such a thing to happen and she could rest assured that it would never happen again. He had avoided being alone with her ever since.

The only repercussion, or possible repercussion, was Jojo. Deborah was not certain whether she was Johnny's child or Howard's. She and Johnny were dark, and Jojo was very fair, but babies often were. Even someone as naive as Howard must have considered the possibility of paternity, but he never raised the subject of Jojo's origins, and neither did Deborah.

Despite his avoidance tactics, from time to time she had caught him unawares, staring at her as if he hoped for some sort of sign. Just when she was on the point of responding, he would look away.

But all that was obviously over now that Claire had arrived on the scene. One look at Howard's face when he saw Claire told her everything. Since his glances had turned elsewhere and Johnny's eye still wandered far and frequently, Deborah felt even more unloved and uncertain.

At least I have the children, she repeated to herself. She crept into their rooms. How delicious they were, all quiet for a change. She gently kissed each fat, round cheek, inhaling the smell of clean baby. Turning out the lights, she went back to lie down beside her snoring husband.

*   *   *

'I wanna go swim,' insisted Sam, tugging at her skirt with both hands.

'OK, honey, just wait. Jojo's nearly finished.' She glanced down at the baby nuzzling at her breast. Towards the end of her feed, Jojo's small face took on the glazed and satisfied look of a drinker about to pass out.

'Now, go swim now, *now*!' Sam jumped up and down, jealous for her attention. 'Mummy, now.' In a moment, he would start patting the baby in a semi-aggressive manner.

Deborah said gently, 'Why don't you just run and ask Pima to get your things ready? Then we'll go.'

But it was another half an hour before everything was assembled: the towels, the change of diapers for the baby, her sterile bottle of water, spare sets of clothes. Sam needed armbands and also insisted on packing goggles, flippers and snorkel – ridiculous on a three-year-old but apparently essential gear – along with two plastic ducks and a pink water pistol.

She knew she should be taking the children round to her mother-in-law's pool, but the atmosphere at Poppy's was so much more relaxed. Besides, Muriel's house was the other side of town and Poppy's was within walking distance, if a person wanted to walk with a pram and a small child in that heat, pollution and dust, which Deborah did not. So she drove the three hundred yards.

'Deborah, sweetie, how marvellous to see you all.' Poppy put down her cigarette and kissed them. Her thin crimson lips left a smudge of lipstick on every cheek, but Deborah did not mind and Sam did not notice.

'I swear you've got bigger since last week, Sam,' said Poppy.

He beamed up at her as she inflated his armbands and helped him into the pool. Deborah sat beside her sleeping daughter and watched them. She knew Poppy must be well into her fifties, though she looked ten years younger. When asked how she'd kept her figure and complexion when so many European women looked like corrugated paper after years in the East, Poppy always said, 'Darling, I smoke a packet of cigs a day and I never go out in the sun.'

Her husband Jock was the recently appointed area manager for BP and hence they occupied a magnificent white colonial-style mansion in a ten-acre compound. But Poppy did not behave like the other expatriate memsahibs who took their husband's status as their own. She had invited Deborah to tea after a chance meeting at the British Club, and since then she'd treated her more and more like a substitute daughter and loved the babies as if they were her own grandchildren.

Deborah felt relaxed and soothed in these grand surroundings. She enjoyed watching the teams of languid gardeners patiently watering the lawns and the spiky bottle-green shrubs, and she liked the way the uniformed maids appeared and disappeared, whisking Sam away to play. Her own part-time maid usually wore a loud T-shirt and jeans, and had little time for anything except keeping the disorderly household clean and half-tidy. But still, as Deborah reminded herself, she was damn lucky to have Pima. Back home no one had help in the house. Maising had its advantages.

Poppy waved her long crimson nails. 'Deb, sweetie, sorry to leave you in the lurch, but I've got a big bridge tournament this afternoon. I'll just take Sammy inside on my way – Lita is dying to see him. You and Jojo stay out here and rest.' Poppy believed in rest. 'Stay as long as you like,' she continued. 'I should just warn you, Alex may appear. He's on a gap year between school and university. Seems to involve sleeping all day, though he usually surfaces about this time.'

'Who's Alex?'

'You know, sweetie, Jock's son from his first marriage – to Mary the earth mother who went off with someone else and then died, poor thing. Alex is a nice boy, but he doesn't really approve of me. Thinks I'm fast, or shallow or both. His ma was one of those large, cosy, arty women who didn't care about clothes, you know the type. Extraordinary creature, used to make her own bread in this climate, can you imagine? No wonder she popped off before her time. Did far too much. Don't giggle, Deborah. It was very sad about poor Mary.' Poppy shook her head. 'Now be careful, dear, the sun is coming round and you won't be in the shade much longer. You're looking very pretty today, by the way.'

'But I'm so fat.'

'Nonsense. You're just right. Skinniness isn't attractive to men. Jock is always complaining about my bones. Anyway, you've lost quite a bit of weight since I last saw you, haven't you?'

'Well, some, maybe, but not enough.'

'Nonsense. You, sweetie, are a perfectly lovely young woman. Say that to yourself every day. Now, really, I must go.' With a final wave of her hand, she rushed off.

From behind she looked like a young girl in her red swimsuit. Deborah smiled and, as she closed her eyes, tried to feel just a little bit lovely.

Some time later she woke up. A startlingly handsome boy was standing between her and the sun. When she smiled up at him, he flushed as if he had never seen a woman before.

'Hi there, I'm Deborah. You must be Alex. Poppy told me how great it was to have you around. D'you plan to stay here long?'

'Yes, well, no. I don't know.' He seemed confused rather than reassured by her friendly manner.

'How do you like it? Have you been here before? Do you mind the heat? Pretty steamy, isn't it?'

'Er . . . which question shall I answer?'

'Take your pick.'

'Well, this is my first trip to Maising. But I've been to this part of the world before, and I'm into swimming and sailing and stuff, so I expect I'll like it here.'

'Sure you will.' Deborah smiled at him, trying to ignore his looks and the fact that she could find a teenager sexually attractive. He'd only just left high school, for God's sake. He was a well-made boy, tall and very slim, almost a man but not quite. His dark blond hair curled at the nape of his neck in small damp tendrils, and his eyes were a pale blueish green under thick black lashes.

He said, 'I hope you don't mind if I ask a question too, but where do you come from? You sound a bit American, well, not quite English.'

'No, I'm not quite English, as you put it, only by marriage. I was born in the States, but I sometimes feel I'm not a true American. I've got this weird nowhere accent because I've been to school in Switzerland and London, and I've lived abroad so long I sometimes wonder if I'm quite anything.'

'Well, if you're married to an Englishman, you must be British, so that's all right.'

Deborah laughed. 'Actually, I have a US passport and being American is fine with me.'

'I didn't mean that I thought it was better to be British.'

'Sure you did. But don't worry, my baby is British.'

'Baby?' He sounded surprised.

'Yup, over there in the shade.'

He crept over and peered at Jojo. 'It's very small, isn't it? But quite human-looking.'

'She – not it – is beautiful, the most beautiful child in the world.'

He laughed and came back to sit beside her on the edge of the pool. As they talked she became aware that he was staring covertly at her breasts, which were inadequately concealed by her old and saggy black swimsuit.

She slipped into the pool and began to swim up and down. Alex watched her every move. It was almost a relief when Sam came rushing out on to the terrace clutching a large piece of sticky chocolate cake that he wanted to share with his mummy.

FIVE

'I just got a letter from Mom. She's afraid I'm losing my American culture. Today, just for Mom, I need to do something American, and you need to meet people, so I'm inviting you to the International Women's Club luncheon,' announced Deborah on the phone. 'You can take the afternoon off, can't you?'

'Thank you very much, Deb, but that sort of thing is just not me,' began Claire.

'You'll love it, really. There's a Beautiful Colour Revival speaker – well, I know it's not new, but there's no harm reminding ourselves again.' She sighed. 'I guess I need something more than colour to make me beautiful. What I really don't need is food, but they said there'll be a special low-cal option. So, what d'you say?'

'Well . . .'

'It'll be a great experience for you. I'll meet you in the lobby of the Hotel Splendid at noon. Don't be late now.'

The Splendid was Maising's newest and most magnificent

hotel, a concrete palace, its grandeur contrasting oddly with the traditional wooden shacks and shophouses which surrounded it.

Claire felt a little overwhelmed as she paid the taxi driver and walked up the marble steps to the entrance. Two doormen wearing gold and green uniforms with white gloves bowed as she walked through to the orchid-filled lobby. The discreet muzak could hardly be heard above the sound of water cascading down a curious circle of rock pillars which loomed in the middle of the reception area like a tropical Stonehenge.

She looked around. The guests appeared as rich and glamorous as the interior decor. A tall, well-dressed vision detached herself from a group of women seated on a gilded sofa.

Claire smiled. 'Deb, you look terrific. I didn't recognize you.'

'Well, I still clean up OK, I guess. When I first met Johnny, he told me I looked like a messy version of Catherine Zeta-Jones. Nowadays he calls me Sumo. Nice, isn't it? But let's go. We need to get a seat.'

She led the way to a queue of elegant multinational women, who all expressed rapture at seeing her. Claire longed to escape, but Deborah dragged her on, introducing her to what seemed like fifty women at once.

'Doesn't this look just great?' said Deborah, ushering her towards one of the many large round tables which filled the ballroom. 'You don't mind if we join you, do you?' She addressed two smartly attired elderly Maising women sitting opposite. They smiled timidly in welcome.

She leaned towards them. 'I'm Deb and this is Claire, a new member.' The ladies twittered some polite words in English and then resumed their own whispered conversation.

After studying the menu and saying it was all too fattening, Deborah enquired about Howard.

'He's fine,' said Claire.

'Yes, but how is it with you two? How are you getting along?'

'Fine, thanks.'

'Do you date him a lot?'

'From time to time.'

'Claire, will you quit stalling. I should go all out for him, if I were you. He's the most eligible bachelor in Maising. Is it serious or are you two just good friends?'

'Just good friends, platonic.' Claire decided to distract her. 'Look, who's that woman waving at us?'

Deborah looked around. 'Lord, my mother-in-law, good old Muriel. Sorry, honey, but she's homing in on us. Pray to God she doesn't want to join our table.'

A short, fat, overdressed woman came waddling towards them, towing behind her an unhappy-looking girl. 'Good morning, Debbie, or is it afternoon?' She patted her purple-red hair and smiled.

'I guess so. Hi, Muriel.' Deborah kissed the air beside her mother-in-law's plump cheeks. 'This is Claire, my new neighbour.'

'Pleased to meet you, dear. And this is Lucy. She's a new bride, aren't you, dear? Just recently married, ever so romantic. Her husband is at the Embassy, the British Embassy – he's rather a senior chap. You may have met him, Debbie. Martin Williamson, the Economic Counsellor. My friend Helena – that's the Ambassador's wife, Claire, in case you didn't know – has asked me to introduce Lucy to some young people. I'm sure you'd both love to look after her. Now I must tootle back to the top table as Helena likes me to help with the local bigwigs.'

She smiled complacently and then turned to her daughter-in-law. 'Do bring the babies round soon. Their grandad and I love seeing you all. And the kiddies just adore their gran. It's such a very special relationship.' Her expression grew misty for a moment, then she blinked her blue eyelids. 'Now I must love you and leave you. You'll be all right now, won't you, Lucy? I'll pop into the Embassy to see you next time I'm at Helena's. She often asks me to call at the Residence. We're great chums, on such a lot of committees together. I can see her looking round for me now, so I'd better dash. Bye-ee for the time being, dear.' Waving her hand, she turned and waded away around the tables.

'Shame she couldn't stay,' said Deborah with a grin.

Lucy stood awkwardly beside them. In her late twenties, she was very pale, with stringy mouse-coloured hair and a thin mousy face to match. She wore a shapeless blue dress which hung from her astonishing breasts in crumpled folds.

Claire thought she had never seen such an enormous bosom stuck on such a skinny and unvoluptuous girl. It just didn't belong.

Deborah smiled at the newcomer. 'Hey, sit down next to me, Lucy. Welcome to Maising. Great to meet you. How do you like it here?'

Lucy smiled back nervously. 'Oh, thank you, fine, thank you.'

Claire began to make the usual conversational overtures, but Lucy was hard work. She seemed to have nothing to say. Deborah, inspired no doubt by a larger audience, embarked on major friendly advice-giving and chattered incessantly throughout the first two courses.

How lucky I am to have a good-natured, cheerful neighbour like her, thought Claire once again, wondering how many other newcomers had cause to be grateful for Deb's kind efforts.

The dessert was a long time coming. The overzealous waiters hovered anxiously, glancing towards the kitchen door from time to time and rearranging the empty plates. Claire began to feel she could no longer bear the babble of a hundred and fifty women in one room and decided to escape to the Ladies. It would be an excuse to explore and to avoid any more of Deborah's cross-examinations about Howard.

She hardly knew herself what she felt. Howard was such a good man, pleasant-looking, generous-hearted and prosperous. Prosperous wasn't normally the kind of quality she worried about, but it was a plus all the same. Just the kind of bloke a woman of her age should go for. She'd had some pretty dud relationships. Howard was highly eligible, as Deb said. But was her heart in it? Did that matter at her stage in life? With the dread biological clock ticking away towards thirty-five, she was unlikely to get a better offer from a better man. That is what the entire world would say and they would be right.

Having repaired her make-up in the coyly named Little Girls' Room, she padded along the red-carpeted corridors and out into the garden where she found herself wandering among a series of S-shaped fish ponds curling around miniature red pagodas and baby temples flanked by luxuriant tropical shrubs which had already grown surprisingly large in their new environment.

'Not bad for an instant jungle, eh?' said a voice in her ear.

Claire jumped. Beside her stood the Australian she had met at Deborah's party.

'Hello, Drew.' Ridiculously pleased to see him, she felt the colour rise to her cheeks. Searching quickly for a topic of conversation, she waved her hands about. 'You said you were an agricultural expert – tell me the names of these plants and flowers.' To her own ears, her voice sounded light and over-girlish.

He smiled and took her by the arm. 'I'm a farming man. Don't know much about tropical botany, but I'll do my best.'

They walked over a miniature Venetian-style bridge and came across a small round pond where a stone cherub perched spouting water from its penis.

'Quite a mixture of landscape design,' said Claire, laughing. She stepped back so that Drew would have to let go of her arm.

'Yeah, it's popular to borrow from the Europeans and the Indians, and the Japanese and jumble it all together with their own ideas.' Once again he touched her hand lightly.

Rather tactile on such a short acquaintance, she thought.

'Look, Claire,' he said, 'you're not seeing the real Maising hanging around joints like this. Why don't you come out with me this arvo? I'm just on my way to a farm project up-country. Not too far. We'll be back tonight.'

'I'd love to, but I can't. I'm meant to be at a ladies' lunch with Deb.'

'Oh, she won't mind. She'll have plenty of other women to yak away to.'

'Yes, but it's rather rude. I haven't even had my "crushed mango sorbet with sauce de lychee" or whatever.'

'Oh my God!' He rolled his eyes. 'You haven't even had your ice cream. Terrible for you. Tell you what, Claire, I'll buy you dinner on the way back tonight and you can choose whatever dessert you want. OK?'

Claire smiled. 'All right, all right, it's a deal. I'd love to come. I'll just go and tell Deb.'

'Must you? Don't want to be too late at the project.'

'Yes, I must – otherwise she won't know what's happened to me. She'll probably send out search parties.'

When it came to the point, she decided, for some reason, to tell Deborah a little white lie and said that Jean-Louis had called her back to the office.

SIX

Bumping around in Drew's battered Land Rover in her best suit, Claire worried that she was seriously overdressed for an up-country expedition. She was rather pleased to have come across the local expression 'up-country' – it made her seem like a tropical expert. When she mentioned that she might be a nuisance tottering around the farm in her straight skirt and high-heeled strappy sandals, he insisted on stopping at a market stall and buying her what he called sandshoes.

'Freaky footwear,' she said, putting on the purple and orange sneakers, the only ones that fitted.

He smiled. 'No worries. Farmer Lek isn't a fashion man.'

They drove on past flat rice fields, empty apart from the occasional water buffalo, and began to climb into the higher, more arid country. The road deteriorated into a rutted dirt track and she was thankful when they eventually arrived at a small group of bamboo houses.

Mr Lek greeted Drew like an old friend. Short and scrawny, with skin like a dried chestnut, he wore long blue shorts and a sweat-stained indigo shirt. He bowed politely to Claire and made a small speech, smiling a great deal and nodding his head. Not having progressed very far with her language lessons, she understood nothing.

'He's pleased that you're English. He says he wants to show you all around because part of this irrigation project has been paid for by your great queen,' translated Drew. 'The section donated by you Brits is only half an hour's walk.'

She groaned. 'Oh my God, I don't think I can last ten minutes in this heat.'

'Do you good,' said Drew, taking her arm to help her up a steep bank.

Claire was acutely conscious of his touch. She broke away quickly and began to ask Drew questions to translate about irrigation and rice crops and other matters which did not really interest her. Mr Lek talked a great deal more and Drew listened to him with great patience and politeness.

Inland there seemed to be very little wind and the hard-baked red earth reflected back the heat. Eventually, to her relief, the tour ended in the shade of the palm-thatched hut.

'Mr Lek wants to know whether you would like Fanta or Sprite,' said Drew.

'Oh, I don't mind. Anything. I'm dying of thirst.' She regretted her vagueness when she was presented with a revoltingly sweet red drink that tasted of cherries boiled in old Rugby socks.

Before they left, Mr Lek insisted on unlocking a dilapidated shed to show them some gleaming stainless-steel machinery.

'Brand new dairy equipment – apparently the Danes gave it to him,' said Drew. 'It's worth thousands of dollars. He's very proud of it. Can't actually use it, of course, as one part went wrong and no one here can fix it. Anyway, he's only got six cows.'

'What a waste. Shouldn't someone do something?'

'Yeah, but that's up to the European Community. It's part of their aid. I can't interfere. I only work for the FAO and, of course, Oz projects.' He laughed. 'You'll get used to international bureaucracy one of these days.'

To Mr Lek's evident delight, Drew took several photographs of him with Claire. Then he shook hands with the farmer and his quiet wife who had appeared from the fields where she had evidently been working all afternoon.

'We'd better go, Claire,' said Drew. 'Need to get to the restaurant in good time. Don't want to miss the sunset.'

Clinging to the seat, she closed her eyes as they raced along the highway. When she opened them again, Drew was manoeuvring down an increasingly narrow road full of potholes. She saw that the rice fields had given way to dismal shacks and a row of concrete shops. Parking behind a malodorous warehouse, he helped her down from the Land Rover and, continuing to hold her hand rather longer than necessary, led the way around the corner. There, much to her surprise, was the sea and, reaching out into the clear shallow water, a magnificent old wooden pier.

'Trust me,' he said. 'The scenery gets better every step you take.'

She was not disappointed. At the end of the pier was a traditional outdoor restaurant, plain dark wooden tables and chairs, white cloths, pots of frangipani, oleander and small fronded palms. A few prosperous-looking islanders sat sipping drinks at the long bar, but otherwise the place was quiet and empty.

A smiling girl in a tight batik skirt ushered them to a table overlooking the sea.

Claire sat and stared. The sun, dark orange, was balanced on the horizon. She watched entranced as it sank into the water, illuminating the sky and the sea with dramatic shades of crimson, scarlet and pink. Quite quickly darkness fell and a candle in a glass globe was brought to their table.

Drew had remained silent during the sunset. Now he smiled across at her. 'Hope you like fish. It's all they serve. Shall I order for you? I know what's good. They do a great seafood dish here with island veggies and lemon grass.'

Normally she disliked men who offered to order for her, but tonight she watched contentedly as he negotiated with the waitress. 'I'm impressed by how well you speak the language.'

He grinned. 'When you've had a few more lessons your-self, you'll realize how bad my accent is. And I don't go much for grammar either. Not too good on verbs. But I get by, after a fashion. I communicate.'

She smiled back at him. 'Yes, you communicate well. I liked the way you talked to Mr Lek.'

'Ah well, he's a mate, a good bloke.'

'He seemed to think you were a good bloke too. Tell me about your work. What else do agricultural advisers do?' she asked, sitting back in anticipation of a long male monologue, but Drew said he wanted to know all about her. As she talked, she was aware that he was watching her intently, studying her face with his dark eyes.

Eventually they fell silent. She could hear the sea lapping below them in the darkness. The night was warm and she'd been sipping her wine more steadily than she'd intended. She felt the sexual tension between them grow. She smiled to herself. Oh dear, she thought. Watch it. Wouldn't be a good idea.

They did not speak much on the way home. Back in the city he parked outside Lotus Court and switched off the ignition.

For a moment Claire looked at her hands. She'd more or

less decided not to ask him in, but then heard herself say, 'Would you like to come up to my apartment – for a drink, I mean.'

Well, at least she'd managed a casual, unprovocative manner. He wasn't the type to pounce uninvited so she was just being polite, really she was.

'I'd like to see where you live, but, uh, better not tonight. I'm off to Rome for a conference tomorrow. The flight leaves at five a.m. God-awful time, so I need to pack and sort out a few papers. I'd originally planned to go straight home from the farm, so I'm not organized.'

'Goodnight then and thank you so much for a lovely day,' she said quickly, and began to open the door.

'Don't rush away. I need your phone number,' he said.

Yay, thought Claire, mollified. She scrabbled in her handbag and gave him her card.

'Thanks.' He shoved it in his pocket. 'I'll see you to your apartment.'

'Not necessary, really. Bye-bye. Have a good trip to Rome.' She jumped down from the Land Rover and hurried up the steps. After a hearty goodbye wave of her hand, she closed the heavy teak door of Lotus Court behind her and took the lift to her apartment. Throwing her clothes in a heap on the chair, she lay down on the bed. But after a while she turned on the light again – she just couldn't sleep, so she got up and paced about for some time.

Ensconced comfortably on the sofa, Grace the cat lay watching her.

'Not my type at all, Grace, actually. Most unsuitable. What do you think?'

Grace yawned, showing her sharp teeth.

'You're right. Not an interesting subject. I'll shut up. Don't worry. I'm going back to bed straight away.'

Suddenly the telephone rang, very loud in the silent flat.

'I've finished my packing.' Drew's voice was low.

'That was quick,' she said, smiling to herself.

'Could I come round for a beer or a coffee after all? I know it's late, but . . .'

'That was quick,' she repeated when he appeared at her door fifteen minutes later.

'Yeah, not much traffic at this time of night. It's very late. But you're still dressed. Though you're wearing something different.'

'I got dressed again when you rang.' She did not describe the panic as she'd raced around the flat, tidying, adjusting the lighting and the music, persuading the cat to go out, choosing something suitable to wear and then discarding it for a dress even more demure and high-necked.

She led him through into the sitting room. Oh God, that music was too sultry and the lights a little too low. She turned on an extra lamp. 'Do sit down,' she said formally. 'Black or white?'

'What?'

'Would you care for black or white coffee? Or perhaps you would prefer a drink? There's whisky, I know. Oh, yes, you said beer. I think there's one in the fridge, maybe you'd . . .'

'White coffee, please.'

She went to the kitchen and returned a few moments later with a tray. 'I'm afraid it's instant. Do help yourself to milk and sugar. Sorry I don't have any cream.'

'Are you always this socially polite?'

'Oh, yes, always. I like to do the right thing,' she said, still smiling but keeping a distance between them.

He sipped his coffee. 'Me too. That's why I've come.'

'Oh?' Claire raised her eyebrows.

'Yeah.' He spoke rather quickly. 'I came to tell you that I'm a bit of an emotional wreck after I split up with my wife last year, and I'm not into committing myself in any way as far as women are concerned . . . and I thought that if I spent the night with you, you might expect some sort of commitment. Oh God, I'm not putting this well.'

'We hardly know each other. I didn't invite or expect you to spend the night,' she said sharply.

'I know, but I wanted to, and you knew I wanted to. I still want to, for that matter.' He grinned suddenly. 'It's tough behaving like a gentleman.'

'Perhaps.'

He looked up. 'Perhaps what?'

She didn't return his smile. 'Perhaps I don't know anything. Look, Drew, I think you've made your position pretty clear. And you're right. I'm not the type for a one-night stand, never was. Now we both know where we are, you'd better go home and get some sleep before you go to the airport.'

He stood up slowly. 'OK, I get the message.' He took a few steps and turned. 'Before I go, will you tell me about that bloke Howard?'

'What about him?'

'I mean, what's the situation between you and him?'

'No situation. We're just friends really.'

'So how do you feel about him?'

'I like him. He's a nice man.'

'So you just have a cosy relationship, you and good old Howard?'

'None of your damn business,' she said evenly.

He walked to the door. 'Yeah, sorry, I had no right to ask. I'd better go before you kick me out.'

Trying to breathe normally, she accompanied him to the hall.

'G'night then,' he said.

'Goodnight, Drew. And thanks for the lovely present.' She waved her hands at the purple and orange sneakers.

'Don't mention it.'

She smiled. 'Shall I put away the coffee or will you be phoning in an hour or so to say you're coming back for another cup?'

'Tempting invitation. You're such a nice polite English person.' He looked at his watch. 'But if I don't go straight to the airport, I'll miss the bloody plane. You're in luck, Claire. You've got shot of me at last.'

He kissed her gently and quickly on the lips, his arms encircling her waist. They stood in the doorway. She thought he would kiss her again and was about to reach up to him, but then with a sudden goodbye, he left.

Claire closed the door. Eventually, restless, excited, uncertain, she went to bed.

SEVEN

Claire and her common sense had a long dialogue over the next few days and she told herself that common sense had won. Drew was not for her. Everything was against him, most of all, of course, was the fact that he was newly divorced and still heavily caught up with his ex. He'd actually said so himself. She was too mature and sensible and, let's face it, too old to waste time with the wrong sort of man. She would slowly explore the possibilities of her relationship with Howard and, more important, concentrate on her work.

At first she'd been apprehensive about working in such a small organization, more of a household than a business. Jean-Louis was still charm itself in a distant and slightly creepy sort of way. She was also intrigued by Pel who turned out to be a lot more than a so-called toy boy.

At first he'd regarded her with some suspicion. He must have considered her a rival, not in a sexual sense obviously, but as a person who took up too much of Jean-Louis' attention. He used to spend a great deal of time whispering to Jean-Louis, as if determined to exclude her from the conversation. But apparently reassured by her unassuming and businesslike approach, he had accepted her presence.

Pel did not seem to have a great deal to do. He spent hours swimming lengths in the pool and practised some form of oriental martial exercises each morning. She liked to watch him surreptitiously. Small and lithe, catlike, he was extremely attractive with his thick black hair and fine eyes. His skin was a pale creamy brown and he always wore a gold cross around his neck which glinted in the sun.

She supposed him to be yet another object of beauty in Jean-Louis' collection. But then one day, when she came early to work, she saw him in the garden shooting at a series of targets with a small black revolver. He did not miss a shot. Perhaps there was more to Pel than met the eye.

The turning point in her working relationship with Pel

occurred when he discovered he was older than she was. Age and respect for age were important to Cambodians, the younger person should respect the older one, he explained with a smile. Claire was mystified, but surmised that maybe he'd feared she would displace him in the hierarchy now she'd become Jean-Louis' special assistant. So she trod a cautious path, asking Pel's advice whenever she could, and this tactful approach seemed to be working. It wasn't hard to be nice to Pel because he was such a sweet and gentle person, much easier to deal with than the demanding, volatile Jean-Louis. Sometimes J-L was charm itself and other times her presence would suddenly seem superfluous or inconvenient. He'd shut the door in her face and had long telephone calls in one Asian language or another, she couldn't tell which.

But he was a generous employer and continued to provide her luxurious apartment virtually rent-free. He even offered to find her a maid, but Claire thought that if she ever changed her mind and took such a step, she'd rather find someone unconnected with Jean-Louis. A maid produced by him would seem like a spy.

'What do you reckon, Grace?' Claire asked the cat one weekend. 'Maybe we should have a maid or rather a part-time cleaner after all. It's very hot for housework, even with the air-conditioning, and you'd have someone else to boss around.'

Grace gazed at her in a bored manner, half-closing her green-grey eyes.

'But as it's Saturday I think we should have a domestic-goddess morning and get things straight before we even think of a maid. I'm going to put those naff lamps and vile rug away in the cupboard under the eaves – I've been meaning to do it for weeks – and I'm going to put you on the balcony before I do.'

Grace was not impressed by this move. While the cat glared at her through the balcony window, Claire hardened her heart. She was rarely in the mood for reorganization and didn't wish to be distracted by interference from Grace, who tended to ignore her completely when Claire needed company, but, on the other hand, liked to pad about on the computer keyboard at most inconvenient moments.

Already hot and bothered, Claire found the hoover and, propping up her torch, began to clean out the eaves cupboard. 'Damn, forgot that pile of newspaper, hope there's nothing worse.' The hoover clunked on something behind the newspapers. She cursed again and, rearranging the flickering torch, got down on her hands and knees. There wasn't much space, but she could just about see two boxes right at the back of the cupboard. Quite heavy as she dragged them forward. No point in not opening them, so she did.

Blimey.

In each box were two ancient bronze Buddha heads. It was clear from the shiny metal at the neck that they had, relatively recently, been severed from their respective bodies.

Blimey, she muttered again. How strange that the former tenants had forgotten something as valuable as these Buddhas. What to do – she had no address, no email, no way of contacting them. Jean-Louis was away, so she decided, after some thought, to ring Pel, who said, to her surprise, that he would come round right away.

Pel examined the Buddhas and then looked grave. 'I believe these may be stolen,' he said in a matter-of-fact voice.

Claire's heart sank to her bare feet. 'Stolen?'

'We must return them to their owner.'

'But hadn't we better call the police?'

'That is not a good idea.'

'But surely it's the right thing to do.'

'What may be the right thing in your country is not always the right thing here. If you as a Westerner have stolen property in your apartment, then the police may blame you.'

'But it is nothing to do with me. I just found them,' she stuttered, suddenly afraid.

'I know, Claire, but you may not be believed.'

'But Jean-Louis will explain. He will vouch for me.'

'It isn't always convenient for Jean-Louis to take a different view from that of police.'

She stared at him. 'So what shall I do?'

'Pack them away again and when I have found out to whom they belong, I will come and collect, and restore them to their owners.'

She clutched his arm. 'Can't you take them now? I don't want them here, I really don't.'

'No, that would not be wise. The caretaker watches everything by day. By night, he is often sleepy with whisky, so moving them one evening will be more discreet.'

She gulped. 'But they're just boxes. He won't know what they are.'

'Best to be careful,' he repeated solemnly.

'OK. Are you sure this is the right way?'

'Yes, I am sure. Discuss this with nobody. You don't have a maid yet, you said?'

'No.'

'Well, don't hire one until I have moved the parcels. It will take a day or two.'

'All right,' said Claire, uncertain, reluctant and scared.

After he had gone, she began to go over and over the situation in her mind. She trusted Pel. Everything about him seemed totally honest, but still the situation worried and frightened her. She was tempted to search for the words 'stolen Buddhas' on the computer, but what if that was unwise? What if someone somewhere knew what she was looking up?

On Monday Claire returned to the office first thing. Jean-Louis was still away, thank God. She paced about in an agitated manner until Pel appeared.

'Well?' she demanded.

He smiled in a not altogether reassuring way. 'I have found the owner, an important man. I shall collect the boxes tonight. Better if you are out to dinner.'

'But who will let you in?'

'Jean-Louis keeps a spare key to your apartment. I shall use that. Don't return before eleven o'clock.'

'OK,' said Claire in a small voice, only half reassured. Of course Jean-Louis was bound to have kept a key, but the thought made her uneasy.

At dinner with Howard that evening she floated a general kind of idea about how the island worked. Were, for instance, the police highly regarded? Not really, he said absent-mindedly, usually best to solve your own problems. That's what people do. Not such a bad idea, luckily they're not a violent people, but mostly they deal with problems direct, a lot to be said for that.

Then he went on to talk of other matters.

Howard saw her to the lift of the apartment block. She knew he wished to be invited in for coffee, and no doubt coffee was all he would expect. But she was anxious to be alone, although in some ways his presence would have been reassuring.

Warily she opened her front door. The flat was calm and empty, and Grace was still sleeping on the balcony.

Claire rushed immediately to the bedroom and checked. Yes the boxes had gone. And that was that, she hoped. Thank God, the crisis was over. What a relief.

In need of comfort, she went to fetch Grace and sat for a long time on the sofa stroking the cat. The event had all been upsetting, unsettling and peculiar. The idea that she could have been held account for stolen antiques that were nothing to do with her offended her sense of right and wrong. The darker side of these paradise islands evidently. She longed to discuss the whole matter with somebody. Deb might be at home, but of course she wouldn't be the best person in the world to confide in. Far too indiscreet. No the thing to do was just shut up and be thankful for Pel.

And Howard. He had asked her to go sailing next weekend. How normal, how reassuring. Maybe she could talk to him about the Buddhas, but, then again, maybe she had better keep quiet. As Pel said, the only way to keep a secret is to tell no one.

EIGHT

It was too hot, in Deborah's view, to move from her sunbed under the beach shelter. A place in the shade under one of the four giant thatched mushrooms was much in demand among the less active members of the yacht club. Not even pretending to read, she rested her book face-down on her still too round stomach. She was observing: watching Sam drive his toy cars into the wheels of Jojo's pram, watching her baby daughter's quick gentle breathing, and watching Claire.

She could see that Claire, in turn, was watching Howard as he and Johnny rigged the Hobie Cat and hoisted the rainbow-coloured sail until it shivered in the faint breeze. One or two boats had taken to the calm water, but most yachtsman sat by the sea's edge waiting for a worthier wind.

Deborah gazed at Howard too. He was a pleasant-looking man to observe as he competently went about his business. Though she had often fantasized about him in the past, now that she suspected Claire was the centre of his attention, Deborah thought it better to find a new hero for her dream world. A candidate had not sprung to mind, except sometimes, as now, she thought of the boy, Alex. When this happened, she quickly pushed the thought away.

She closed her eyes and opened them again to see three-year-old Sam moving purposefully towards a small girl digging a sandcastle under the next mushroom. He picked up a large plastic spade and looked as if he were about to bring it down on the other child's head. Deborah leapt to her feet, but before she could reach her son he sat down suddenly and began to help with the digging.

'Did you see that, Claire? That's the first socially positive thing Sam has done in his entire life. He actually changed his mind about hitting Lisa. I'm so happy.'

Claire laughed absent-mindedly. Deborah sensed that she was not paying attention. The point about women friends is that they should be willing to listen to inconsequential remarks and take part in trivial conversation.

Deborah tried again. 'Claire, how do you like my new swim-suit – do you think this cut makes my thighs look any slimmer?'

'Oh, yes, much,' said Claire vaguely, looking round. 'Not that there was anything wrong with your thighs in the first place.'

Deborah smiled. 'What's on your mind, honey?'

'Oh, nothing.'

'How's the cat?'

'She's fine, in complete charge, both of the flat and me.'

'And is your job going OK? I always thought that Jean-Louis guy was kind of creepy.'

'Oh, he's all right to work for.'

'You never told me what you actually do.'

'I'm sure I did. I'm just numbering and cataloguing all his

antiques, where they're from, how old they are, you know. For instance, I measure the height of the Buddha statues, basic things like that.'

'Interesting, but I'm sure it's more tricky than you make out. Sure you can describe a Buddha by size and whether he's standing, sitting, reclining, whatever, but how do you judge his age?'

'Either I know or I guess – it's to do with things like the shape of the head, the eyes and the finial – that's the topknot. Then I check with Jean-Louis or in the reference books.' Claire waved her arm. 'Um, what else do I do? I feel I ought to work out a better way of keeping track of all the deals he does. You know, buying stuff from Thailand, Laos and Indonesia, and all around here, and then selling it on to dealers in London and America. His records and accounts are a bit of a muddle. I'm trying to sort them out, but there are certain records that Jean-Louis prefers to keep to himself.'

'Mm. I wonder why he lives here rather than in one of those bigger countries, if that's where his stuff comes from. Maybe he likes the casual way this place is run: no taxes, no rules. Johnny's heard some dubious things about him.'

'I don't suppose he is Johnny's type.'

'Not exactly. So how do you get on with the toy boy?'

Claire appeared to hesitate for a second. 'Pel? He's great, rather sweet and so handsome. Pity he's gay, really.'

'Maybe he likes girls too. But, seriously, Claire, I'd be kind of careful around Jean-Louis – business-wise.'

'As I said, he's OK. And he's got plenty of friends in high places. They're always coming to dinner, the police chiefs and other bigwigs, so he can't be that dubious.' Claire stretched her arms again. 'Look, my love, it's too hot to talk about work. I mean, I need to concentrate on my suntan. Will you put some cream on my back?'

Deborah paused to rub in the lotion and then, returning to the shade, she broached the subject that was uppermost in her mind. She summoned up a carefully casual tone and asked, 'How are you making out with Howard, Claire?'

'Fine.'

'Do you like him?'

'Yes, of course. Unusually considerate and reliable for a man. And very kind.'

Deborah ran some sand through her fingers. Then she plunged on. 'How about passion? You don't sound too passionate about it.'

'Howard is just a friend. Anyway, I'm not into passion at the moment,' said Claire lightly. 'Causes too many problems.'

'Like with that guy in England – the one you told me about?'

'Yes, he was a problem. Plenty of passion but not much else good. Bit of a bastard, really, the kind of charming bastard that women go for. Anyway, it's over. I've made a resolution to avoid newly divorced men, far too many hang-ups and worries with their ex. The ex always seems to hover over the relationship like a murky mist, even if she was the one who wanted the divorce in the first place.'

'Yeah, stick with a nice, easy-going, uncomplicated guy like Howard,' said Deborah. 'He's so sensible. What you see is what you get.'

Claire opened her beach bag and as she did so, two chunky key rings fell on to the sand.

Deborah picked them up. 'Why do you have two sets of hotel keys?'

'Oh, I'm looking after Howard's while he's sailing.'

Deborah stared at her. 'Well, well, well. Two keys.'

'Subject's closed. Back off, Deb,' said Claire with a grin.

'OK, OK, sorry. But you seem kind of made for each other.'

'You think so?' Claire leant back in her chair and grinned. 'Well, who knows what may happen? You'll just have to contain your curiosity, Deb.'

Claire put on her beach shoes and walked across the hot sand towards Howard and Johnny.

Howard was sitting glumly on the edge of his boat in the shade. 'Not enough wind for a sail,' he said.

Claire smiled at him. 'Shall we go for a walk then?'

'A walk? In this heat?'

'Well, why not?'

'Rabid dogs, dead cats, voracious insects, snakes, open sewage and slightly strange people not too far from this area. You name it why not. It's not all beautiful paradise beaches here, you know.'

'We could stick to the path. I like the palm trees and the

bougainvillea and we might see some unusual birds or something. What are those intense blue ones, or how about the
amazing yellow ones? Then I'm told there's a bird who behaves
like a mini peacock, so cute – what's that one called?'

'Claire, I have to disappoint you, but I'm not well-informed
about nature, sadly. I'll take you to a bird-spotting place
another time. Let's just go for a swim. I'll buy you a book
about wildlife as soon as we get back to Maising. God knows,
sometimes I think there's too much bloody wildlife in this
place.'

He took her hand and led her towards the quiet sea.

Deborah watched them and thought, why am I pushing her
at him, when I'd rather be there myself? I must be some kind
of crazy post-natal masochist. Or maybe it's just a way of
telling me that I should stick to my husband however big a
shit he is.

She looked towards Johnny. His attention was directed elsewhere, as usual. He was staring hard at two newcomers. In
particular he was staring at the girl, pale, thin and plain. It
was Lucy, the Embassy bride with the astonishing bosom
which now loomed out of a thin multicoloured T-shirt. Johnny's
eyes were fixed on the fish motif swimming across the front
of this T-shirt.

Deborah took Sam by the hand and went over to welcome
the new arrivals.

Johnny had ushered them all over to the bar where he was
giving advice as usual. 'Mustn't stand in the sun if you've
just come from the UK, and keep your shirt on even in the
shade. Terribly burning sun, gets reflected off the sea and the
beach.' He droned on about the numerous cases of sunburn
he had seen.

Deborah greeted Lucy and her husband. Poor Lucy, thought
Deborah, as Martin brayed about what kind of boat he might
want to buy. A widower approaching fifty with a long sad
horse-face, he must be twenty years older than his new wife,
and was said to have grown-up children whom he never saw.
Why did Lucy marry the guy, grey-haired and dull? The poor
girl was pretty silent herself, but what did they have in
common?

For the rest of the day, when Deborah was not watching

Claire and Howard, she studied the newcomers. They were an undemonstrative couple who sat side by side in the club-house; Martin reading a serious-looking paperback and Lucy absorbed in an old Maeve Binchy. Neither seemed interested in watching or participating in any sailing. Maybe they were afraid of sunburn, but they didn't seem to be having any kind of fun.

Pushing the pram, Deborah walked with Lucy and Martin back to the hotel in the late afternoon. She noted that even in the quiet lane, they did not hold hands or even touch. Quite strange for newly-weds.

As usual Johnny had remained behind drinking at the Club with the Germans, who always began early with the beer. Summoning up all her reserves of patience, Deborah went through the ritual of putting the hot, tired children to bed. It was always an exhausting performance at home with Pima's help, but, single-handed, after a day at the sea when the kids were always extra grouchy, Deborah found it an effort to keep from becoming grouchy herself. Jojo never even sat in the sand, but she seemed to have it in every crevice. And Sam was a little sunburnt on the back and shoulders which made him yell when she poured water on his hair.

She washed through the beach clothes and then had a shower herself, luxuriating in the feel of the cool fresh water on her skin. Once the children were at last asleep, she summoned the hotel babysitter and went down to the garden longing for her evening drink.

It would have been nice to have a husband to drink with, but of course Johnny was still at the Club. To cheer herself up, she ordered the most expensive cocktail on the card and sat down. Then she saw the new couple walking down the steps to the garden. They did not see her. Lucy's pale face was flushed and Martin was gazing down at her smiling, a certain expression on his face. They both looked extremely pleased with themselves.

Deborah knew immediately that they had just come down-stairs after making love. She was both reassured by and jealous of their mutual happiness.

NINE

Lucy's happiness was not unclouded. The intimate side of her marriage was indeed a success, as Deborah had perceived. Lucy had been an amateur in this field, as in many others, but sex was a great deal nicer and easier to cope with than anything else, she thought.

Quite apart from the culture shock of suddenly finding herself a married woman, she was now living on the other side of the world where the complications of her new, elevated status seemed almost overwhelming. Nothing in her previous quiet existence had prepared her for her role as the wife of a senior official – nor the enormous house with its vast unfriendly rooms and the ubiquitous patrolling servants. She was bewildered by the dull and formal parties, and the making of diplomatic conversation. And nothing had prepared her for the Ambassador's wife.

She had been summoned to Mrs Blackerstaff's drawing room on her first day in Maising. 'Do call me Helena,' had been the first command, as difficult to obey as the many that followed. Helena was tall and thin with dyed black hair cut in a straight fringe, a style obviously unchanged since her days at Girton.

She said, 'We're pleased that Martin has married again. It's so important for a Counsellor to have a wife, particularly when he's Deputy Head of Mission. Of course, no one will expect you to do everything that Belinda did.'

'Belinda?'

'Belinda Crew, the wife of your husband's predecessor. She was terribly active in the Embassy, such a tireless worker. We were a little disappointed when Martin arrived without a wife, so it's a good thing he rectified matters during his home leave, though, I must say, my dear, you do seem a little young. But perhaps you are used to helping your parents entertain? I was just saying to the Ambassador that these days rather few new entrants or their wives come from families used to formal entertaining at home.'

'No, er, we led a quiet life, my mother and I. She, my mother, was ill. I looked after her.'

'Very commendable, my dear,' said Helena in a dismissive tone. 'But,' she went on, 'unfortunately, hardly good experience for diplomatic life. Still, I expect you went on a Going-Abroad course. The Foreign Office does so much to help people like you these days.'

'No, I didn't go on any courses,' said Lucy. Then she added shyly, 'There wasn't time.'

Helena raised her bushy eyebrows. 'My dear, I feel you should have made time. Never mind, I expect you'll make up for your lack of experience by trying frightfully hard, won't you? But I advise you not to take on too many tasks at once.' She smiled in a manner intended to be kind.

Her teeth were rather yellow, Lucy noted.

Helena continued in full flow. 'For instance, no one will expect you to be in charge of the Wives' Group during the first month or two, as you'll be too busy organizing your staff and giving a few parties to meet people. It's terribly important to get to know the locals – their names and faces may seem a little similar at first, but you'll soon learn not to mistake Mrs Ong for Mrs Ong-Li. Mrs Ong-Li is the one who's terribly good about helping – we've had lots of fun organizing bazaars. You will run a stall at my bazaar next month, won't you? I'm giving you an easy one, the cake stall. All you've got to do is telephone a few awfully nice people and ask them to make cakes.'

Lucy shifted uneasily in her chair. 'But I don't know any one,' she said tentatively.

'My dear, as soon as you say you are Martin's wife people will be only too willing to help. Anyway, the Counsellor's wife always does cakes. I dare say Belinda left a file of notes about how to organize the stall. She was so efficient. Good, that's settled.' She picked up a large navy blue notebook. 'I'll just jot it down – Lucy to do cakes.'

Having read several novels in which the young heroine married a widower, Lucy had been prepared to live with the shadow of Anne, Martin's first wife. Martin, who refused to discuss 'relationships' even in general terms, was particularly silent about her. Lucy thought other people would try to be equally discreet, but they might inadvertently talk about poor dead Anne from time to time, and that it would not be easy. But no one spoke about Anne at all. Instead they raved on about this Belinda woman, this paragon of a diplomatic wife.

Martin laughed when she complained about the Belinda syndrome and told her that everyone in the Service had to live with tales of their predecessor at post.

'But it's nearly two years since she left,' moaned Lucy. 'And as soon as I say who I am at the Embassy, people ask me if I know her and say how wonderful she was. And Somjit won't do anything I tell her. She just does things Belinda's way. She arranges Belinda's favourite flowers by her favourite chair. We eat according to Belinda's menus. I even have to keep my underwear in the same drawer as Belinda did.'

Martin laughed again. He seemed to regard her struggles with intense amusement, as if she were a soap-opera heroine, an entertainment to him. 'Well, I never met Belinda Crew, but she does sound like an efficient woman and Somjit certainly has been well trained. If I were you, I'd enjoy myself and just let the servants get on with it. You'll have plenty of scope to do housework your way when we go home.'

But Lucy was one of those unusual young women who actually liked domesticity. During all the years she lived in the Salisbury flat tending her ailing mother, she had been dreaming of a house of her own, ideally a country cottage with a garden, and, of course, a loving husband and a baby in a pram under the apple tree. Married life with Martin lived up to only one of these ideals. He certainly loved her, even more thoroughly than she'd anticipated. Thoroughly, though, it seemed, spasmodically. When he remembered she was there, he was kind and attentive. But Martin was not a companionable husband. On the rare evening that there was not an official cocktail party or dinner, he would retire to his study to read or write. When he did sit and talk to her, he tended to discuss island politics or international affairs. And if she gently turned the conversation to her own concerns, he would merely say she'd get used to Maising. Everything was bound to be different from Salisbury and living with Mother.

Her mother was another of Lucy's worries. She was so far away. Were they looking after her properly at the nursing home? Mother was now too ill to write, but the matron sent reports about her patient being a little unsettled. Lucy felt full of guilt. Martin said she'd be fine eventually, but Lucy knew that nothing would ever be fine again for Mother.

When Lucy was born, her mother had been over forty, and when she had later been afflicted by multiple sclerosis, Lucy's father had disappeared, leaving the only child, teenage Lucy, to cope.

Martin didn't understand about any of that. He said he did, but she could tell that most of the time his mind was elsewhere. Not that she resented this. Lucy felt it was proper that men should concentrate on the world's problems, which were far more important than her own concerns, daughterly or domestic.

The Number One, as the senior maid was customarily called, always had an anxious frown on her flat beige face. She was the only gloomy islander that Lucy had met, and the only unbeautiful one.

Today Somjit looked self-important as well as worried. 'Sir say you give big cocktail party on twel' June, madame,' she began, blinking through her thick glasses.

This was the first that Lucy had heard about any such party. Why did Martin arrange these things without consulting her? Red in the face, she rummaged in the drawer for her diary, but could not find it. 'I'm not sure about that date, Somjit. I forgot to write it down,' she lied. 'I will check with him.'

'Cook want to know what food you like for party.'

'I will talk to Nee myself.'

'Nee she say she no understand madame. Madame speak too fast.' Somjit smiled, baring her protruding teeth like a sorrowful chipmunk. 'Better tell me, madame.'

'I'll talk to my husband, then I will speak to Nee.'

'Sir alway say he like food same Missus Belinda like. Everyone say Missus Belinda choose velly nice food. Better I tell Nee you like food same Missus Belinda. Then she no make mistake.'

Lucy gave way immediately. She did not want there to be any mistakes in the catering at her first big party.

Later that evening as they were changing for dinner, Martin was only faintly apologetic. 'Darling, don't get in such a state,' he said. 'Of course we have to give parties. It's my job. And Somjit knows what to do. Just leave it to her. That's the advantage of these older servants, bossy though they may be. Sorry I forgot to consult you before I mentioned it to Somjit. But I don't have any choice about the date. H.E. asked me to give this reception for some visiting agricultural chaps.'

'But I won't know anyone. I'll get the names all muddled if I have to introduce people.'

'No one expects anything of you, but to cheer you up you can ask some of those people from the yacht club like those girls you met, Claire and Deborah. Always good to have pretty women at a party even if they're not useful contacts for the British farmers. Now stop fussing, darling.' He smiled. 'I must say, you're looking rather sexy this evening. Is that a new dress?' He took her in his arms and began to kiss her ear.

'Go away,' muttered Lucy, averting her face.

But, as he nuzzled her neck, she felt herself sinking towards him. He began to unzip the dress she had just put on.

She pulled back, giggling. 'Teddy bear, it's nearly dinner time. You know Somjit always likes to serve the meal promptly at seven thirty, that's when Belinda had dinner.'

'To hell with Somjit and to hell with Belinda,' he murmured as Lucy's dress fell to the floor.

She felt guilty about the martyred expression on Somjit's face when they eventually strolled down to dinner after eight fifteen.

TEN

Claire had been surprised and pleased to receive an invitation from Lucy and Martin. The Counsellor of the British Embassy and Mrs Martin Williamson requested the pleasure of her company at a reception, which according to the impressively stiff card, was being held to mark the visit of a United Kingdom agricultural delegation.

She was looking forward to visiting the Embassy. Set in a park-like compound, it had been constructed at a time when Britain still had influence in the world and wished to demonstrate the fact, according to Lucy. Each of the three houses was large, white and imposing. The first building held the chancery and consular offices. The Ambassador and his Deputy lived in respective splendour in the other two.

The guard at the gate would not permit her taxi to enter the Embassy grounds, so Claire walked nervously down the drive and rang the bell on the great front door of No.2 House. A manservant in a white uniform ushered her along a marble-floored verandah into an enormous room full of people.

Martin and Lucy stood by the door shaking hands. Dressed in floral silk in a rather unbecoming shade of green, Lucy looked less plain now that she had acquired a suntan, but she had such a strained expression on her face that Claire's heart went out to her. She hoped that Deborah was right about their hosts' happy marriage.

Claire shivered. With powerful air-conditioning and two huge ceiling fans, the room seemed cold compared with the tropical air outside. She looked at the impenetrable crowd of noisy dark-suited men, punctuated here and there by a few decorative women. The only people she recognized were Jean-Louis and Pel, both conspicuous in unconventional colourful clothes, Pel particularly resplendent in a bright red shirt. As she had no desire to talk to her boss, she began to wander around the edge of the room and soon found herself cornered by one of the visitors. He was a large middle-aged man with a Norfolk accent and a red face who announced that he was the sales director of a firm called Taurus.

'What do you actually sell?' asked Claire, to make conversation.

'Semen,' he said in a matter-of-fact tone. 'Bull semen, that is. And it's been a good evening because I've just done a deal to flog litres of the stuff to that bloke with the glasses.'

'Oh.'

He took a large gulp of his beer and laughed at her expression. 'I expect you're wondering what he's going to do with all that semen.'

'Well, I . . . I suppose it's for cows.'

'Brilliant! You certainly catch on quick. I've known young ladies puzzle for hours over that one. You must be a farmer's daughter if you're familiar with AI.'

'Artificial insemination? I don't know the first thing about it, and I hope you won't mind if I say I don't really want to be enlightened any further. But why don't you actually sell the bull himself?'

He moved closer towards her and leant forward. 'I expect you think it'd be nicer for the little Asian cows to meet a real Hereford bull, eh?'

She backed away. 'I don't think I have an opinion on the way animals feel about these matters.'

He laughed again, so heartily that his fat cheeks trembled. 'To tell the truth, I don't think they care one way or t'other. They don't react much, don't cows. Bulls, though, that's another matter. I could tell you a thing or two about bulls.'

'Are you staying here long?' interrupted Claire, wishing to change the subject. 'Maising isn't a great place for sight-seeing, but there are some impressive temples.'

'Not much of a man for temples, prefer something a bit more meaty, I do. Now, a bloke I know told me the nightlife's quite exciting here. Quite exciting, he said. Why don't you show me round the town tonight? I'm sure a pretty woman like you knows her way around.'

Claire declined his invitation politely and made a quick retreat. Aiming for the opposite corner of the room, she weaved her way through the crowd looking for someone she knew. Howard had been invited and was taking her out to dinner afterwards, but he said he would be late. Maybe she could try to find Deborah.

Then she saw the person she had subconsciously been searching for. Drew was standing talking to three men. He had his back towards her, but, as if he sensed her presence, he suddenly turned round.

Detaching himself from the group, he came towards her. His face creased into a delighted smile, causing her knees to shiver. In a dark suit, he looked lean and elegant, and had somehow grown even taller than before.

'Nice surprise! Good to see you, Claire, all blonde and brown and lovely.'

She smiled. 'Have you been back from Rome long?'

'No, only a couple of weeks.'

Two weeks, thought Claire, and he hasn't bothered to ring. It all went to prove he wasn't really interested. She said aloud, 'I hope you had a successful trip.'

They talked for half an hour. Claire kept telling herself that she should move on, circulate, find Howard. But Drew's eyes held hers and she stayed.

'Shall we go now?' he asked eventually.

'Go where?'

'Out, you and I. We've got some catching up to do.'

'But I've arranged to meet Howard here.'

Drew smiled his unsafe smile. 'Just tell good old Howard you're having dinner with me instead.'

'But he's a friend. I can't just stand him up.'

'Always the polite English person. Just do what you feel like for a change. Thought you were pleased to see me.'

'Yes, I am, but I can't go out with you tonight.'

'But I need to see you now, this evening.' He took hold of her hand.

She pulled away. 'For God's sake, Drew, why didn't you phone in advance? I hardly know you. I can't keep every night free in case you should deign to appear.'

'That's what I want to explain when we're alone.'

'Go ahead, explain here and now,' said Claire.

But as she spoke a tiny, beautiful Maising woman in a tight blue dress came up and took Drew possessively by the arm.

Obviously discomfited, he muttered, 'Uh, Claire, this is a colleague from the Ministry of Agriculture, Mrs Liana Son. Liana, this is Claire Downing, an art historian.'

'Privileged to meet you,' said Liana. Her English was good, with strong American-style overtones. Immaculately coiffed and smartly dressed, she smiled, drawing back her glossy red lips to display a set of perfect teeth. 'Hey, Drew, one of the delegates is just longing to speak with you. Will you excuse us, Ms Downing?'

The woman buzzed around him like a shiny little beetle. Claire stood staring after them. She had been on the island long enough to know that modest Maising females were not in the habit of clinging on to the arms of business associates. Liana's appearance explained everything that Claire wanted to know about Drew and a lot she did not. Her instincts had been right. He was a mistake of the type she'd made in the past and would not make again. All that sob-stuff about his ex-wife, and now this woman. She should have known, should have steered clear from the very beginning.

Grabbing a glass of wine from a nearby waiter, she went in search of Howard.

Howard was gratified when, rather than go out, Claire offered to cook him dinner after the Embassy cocktail party. She had never before been enthusiastic about inviting him to her apartment. The omelette she prepared was leathery, the toast slightly burnt, and the wine Bulgarian, but Howard didn't mind these shortcomings. Apart from her cooking, she was perfect in every other way, as he had known the moment he met her.

But he had lost confidence – she hadn't appeared to take his proposals of marriage seriously. If he talked about the future, she always changed the conversation.

And she was physically cool. Howard wanted to touch her and kiss her. He very much wanted to make love to her, but she always kept him at arm's length. It was hopeless really. He should have taken her polite hints.

Tonight she seemed more desirable than ever, her arms so smooth and brown and languid, her bare legs so slim under the short skirt, her toenails pink in the gold sandals.

A small, strangely coloured cat weaved about her ankles and then came to inspect his shoes. He stroked its white chest. 'What a beautiful cat,' he said tactfully.

Claire smiled indulgently at the animal and he had the feeling he had passed a small test.

Leaning over and displaying a discreet amount of tanned bosom, she poured him some brandy that was slightly better than the wine but not much. He was surprised when she gulped down a glass herself – she was normally a modest drinker. It occurred to him she had also drunk quite a generous amount at the cocktail party before he arrived. One could say, if one weren't a polite sort of bloke, that she was just a tiny bit pissed.

Claire put on some soul music and invited him to dance. He was glad of the excuse to hold her in his arms. Howard's method of slow dancing consisted of rocking from side to side, more or less on the spot. Tonight, to his surprise, Claire danced close to him. He noticed anew how small and light she was, so slim but seductively rounded in the right sort of places.

She put both her arms around his neck. He found that his

hands, more or less involuntarily, had come to rest on her bottom. Amazingly, she danced even closer. It became obvious, even to Howard, that she wanted him to kiss her and so, willingly, he obliged. He kissed her for a long time. She kissed him back, enthusiastically, until his head reeled and his desire became impossible to disguise.

Murmuring something he did not catch, she took him by the hand and led him along the corridor into the bedroom, where he found himself sitting on her narrow bed. She smiled at him, a mischievous, expectant expression in her blue eyes.

At that point he knew that his earlier suspicions had been correct. He hadn't dared to hope, but she had now made matters quite clear: he was being seduced. In a blaze of lustful happiness Howard gave his full cooperation.

The morning after Claire awoke late to find the cat miaowing indignantly. 'Yes, I'm pleased to see you too and I'm sorry I kept you waiting for your breakfast.' Her voice sounded bleary and thick. Let's face it, she wasn't feeling her best.

She opened a tin of cat food for Grace, and poured herself a large black coffee which she took to the bathroom. After her shower, she felt a little better but not much. Thank God it was Saturday. She plonked herself down on the sofa with another cup of coffee.

Grace came to inspect, and, after some thought, decided the most comfortable place for her after-breakfast nap would be Claire's stomach. She sprang up and then paddled about a bit before settling down.

'Please don't dig your claws in and, please, don't purr too loudly. My head is buzzing enough as it is.'

After a pause she said, 'Grace, yes, I do like him . . . Yes, the sex was fine, if you must know . . . But it was nice just to be held, that's what you miss when you're single: normal human contact.' Claire stroked the cat's shiny tortoiseshell back absent-mindedly. 'Have I done the right thing? Probably not, I don't know. As I said, he's a very nice, kind man, but . . . Do you think I am protesting too much? Don't stalk off again when I am talking to you, pusscat. It's important, love and sex and marrying the right man. Don't want to make a mistake. As I told you, it's better to stay serenely single than go for the wrong person.'

ELEVEN

There being little to do after dinner in Maising, Lucy and Martin had also made love that night. After the stress of the party, Lucy found it hard to relax. As soon as Martin had given his final groan, signifying that it was all over as far as he was concerned, Lucy returned abruptly to the subject on her mind.

'Was I OK?' she asked.

'Lulubelle.' He patted her bottom. 'You're always very much OK.'

'I don't mean cuddles in bed,' she said crossly. 'I mean the party. Was it all right? I was absolutely terrified. I'm sure I was the most hopeless hostess. I didn't introduce a single person, not one. I could hardly remember the names of the people I knew perfectly well. And that dress was a disaster. I looked like a dead cabbage.'

'Now, we've been through all this once already. You looked fine, not a cabbage in sight. People had enough to drink. The food was OK and it was served as efficiently as one can expect in this country. Everything worked well.'

'That's because I didn't make any of the arrangements, you and Somjit did.'

'But you were the hostess. The agricultural chaps were very pleased with the party and the Ambassador said something polite about you when he left.'

'Did he? I don't believe you. He hardly bothered to speak to me, and Helena looked bored and fed up the whole evening. There must have been something wrong.'

'Nonsense. Everything was absolutely OK. Stop fussing about nothing, silly girl. Now, I've got a busy day tomorrow. Goodnight, darling.' He turned his back on her and, quite soon, began to breathe deeply. Oh goodness, he'd sounded annoyed. It was almost a quarrel.

She loved Martin, but again and again she reflected that he did not take her seriously. No one did. She was just Martin's wife and everyone saw her in that role, except for people like

Johnny Case who saw her as the girl with the big bust. At least Martin protected her from lechers, just as Mother had done at home.

For years Lucy had hated her breasts. She would have given anything for them not to have been part of her. They were always in the way and attracted the wrong people. But she had learnt to hunch her shoulders and dress in smocks. And avoid men. Mother had helped her avoid men.

Mother had obviously thought Martin too old to be a threat, and when she had finally noticed something in the air, it was too late. Her daughter had fallen in love. She had tried to warn Lucy that marriage to a much older man, to a stranger, was an enormous risk, but Lucy had, for once, ignored her advice.

Maybe I should have listened to her, thought Lucy in her darker moments. People had such old-fashioned attitudes here. In England she had mattered as a person in her own right. To all the professionals involved with her mother's health, Lucy was a carer, someone who was in charge of another. In Maising she was not even in charge of her own house.

If only she had a baby, she could have something of her own to cherish.

Keeping as far from Martin as possible, she tried to get comfortable in the hard official bed. She would like to have gone downstairs for a drink of milk, but she had read in *Woman's Way* that to encourage conception one should lie still after love-making. She had also read that it was difficult for older couples to conceive. At 28, she might not be old in child-conceiving terms, but Martin certainly was. She had used the Pill during their honeymoon, but it made her feel strange and puffy, so, without telling Martin, she had abandoned it.

She couldn't talk about such a delicate matter with him. He had once said that he didn't want any more children now his sons were grown up, but she was sure he'd be pleased if she became pregnant. She wanted to present him with a child to love, particularly as he didn't seem to get on with his sons very well and never saw them.

But why hadn't she conceived? Four months had gone by and each month brought disappointment, and an increasing unease that something might be wrong. She would have liked to share her worries. Consulting a strange foreign doctor was out of the question, too embarrassing. She had no close female friends she could confide in. Claire, being unmarried, was presumably more concerned about avoiding pregnancy. And Deborah was surely too talkative to be discreet. If only, Lucy sighed, she could talk it all over with Mother.

Some weeks later, as part of her official duties, Lucy visited an Embassy wife who had just had a baby. She was enchanted by the miniature creature and touched by the expression on the new mother's face. She described the scene to Martin at lunchtime, but his mind was clearly on the conference he was about to attend on the other side of the island.

'Well done, Lulu. Must've been a bit of a bore for you having to go over to the hospital. Glad you did your stuff,' he said absently.

'No, I loved it. The baby was so gorgeous. You should have seen its sweet little nails.'

'Not my cup of tea. Thank God I'm over that stage. Ghastly business, all that screaming in the night and endless nappies.'

'But we might have a baby ourselves one day.'

He frowned. 'No, darling, I remember being rather specific about that. I thought we'd come to an agreement in the beginning. I really don't want any more children. Quite enough trouble with the first two.'

She stared at him. 'I hope you're just teasing me as usual.' Tears came into her eyes. 'If we have a baby, I'll look after it all by myself. I promise it wouldn't be a nuisance to you.'

'With the best will in the world, babies always disrupt the whole damn household.'

'But the baby and I could go and sleep down the other end of the house. You wouldn't hear a word. The air-conditioning is so loud – it drowns out all other noises and . . .'

'You're not pregnant, are you?' he asked suddenly.

'No.'

'That's a relief. Seriously, Lucy, if we had a baby I'd be over sixty by the time he was due to go to Marlborough, and the FO pension wouldn't pay for that sort of education.'

'Don't you see I wouldn't want to send my child away,' she said passionately. 'He – or she for that matter – could go to a local school. If we were short of money, I could get a job or something.'

'What as? Be realistic, Lucy, you're not really qualified to earn much – unless you sell your beautiful body,' he said, laughing at his own joke. 'Now I must go, darling. The car will be waiting. Is my suitcase ready? I'll be back for lunch tomorrow. Bye now.' He kissed her quickly and left.

Lucy ran upstairs so that Somjit would not see the tears cascading down her face.

After lecturing herself all night about the need for a full and frank marriage, Lucy promised herself that she would discuss the matter with Martin when he returned. She knew he loved her, he really did, so he was bound to change his mind. Today she would go out and forget the whole problem. That would be what the self-help gurus would advise.

Rather than spend too much time in her own house getting in the servants' way, Lucy had taken to sightseeing with the Women's International Club tours. She was not especially interested in archaeology, but Martin approved of her 'joining in'. As the club was mostly run by Americans, it was enterprising and efficient.

The Excursions Chairwoman, as she called herself, was a handsome but frightening New Yorker named Bethany. This morning the decrepit coach hired from the Maising Bus Company was unusually punctual and Beth ticked off the members one by one on a list attached to a leather clipboard. It was always a relief if the ladies all turned up and if they all paid their dues promptly. Then Beth would be in a good mood and the excursion would be a success.

The ruined temple was found in its correct position several miles east of Maising's only major highway and the site was considered by all to be suitably beautiful, interesting and photogenic. Souvenirs and refreshments were available – rather too available – but Beth soon dealt with the importunate small boys hawking trays of pottery shards supposedly excavated from the ruins, but probably manufactured and antiqued yesterday.

All went well until the group leader became dissatisfied with the barely intelligible version of English spoken by the local guide. A one-sided argument ensued, with Beth talking loudly and the guide looking embarrassed and puzzled. Finally he was dismissed and she gave permission for members to wander around the ruins on their own provided that they took their official club tourist handbook with them, and that they returned to the coach punctually at noon.

'Oh God, I've forgotten my handbook,' said Deborah to Lucy. 'Please let me share yours or Beth will make me walk around with her and study every significant stone in the site. I'd prefer to wander quietly with you.'

After an hour of clambering among the crumbling terracotta pinnacles and admiring the rows of Buddhas, Lucy and Deborah were exhausted. They sat down in a small patch of shade beneath the tallest of the stupa and watched a young man who was taking measurements on the edge of the site and then photographing the ground.

Deborah grinned. 'Cute, isn't he? I usually find the island guys either too delicate-looking or too bucolic, but that one is something else,' she whispered. 'He's kind of like a young bull-god among all these stone phallic symbols.'

'A pretty human god, if you ask me. I thought we were here to study old stones rather than young men,' said Lucy primly, but she continued to watch him.

Eventually he looked up and wiped his brow. Then he sauntered towards them. 'Good morning, ladies. Awfully warm, isn't it?' he said in faultless English.

They smiled back and agreed that it was indeed hot. In reply to their questions, he explained that he was an archaeologist and was planning a new dig.

'Wow, maybe you'll discover some hidden treasures,' said Deborah.

He smiled. 'I doubt it. Most items of value have been looted over the years and sold abroad. But of course one always dreams of a significant find.'

Deborah insisted on taking a photograph and then, in turn, he insisted on photographing the two girls, rather to Lucy's surprise. Afterwards he offered to show them over the ruins, but they declined politely, saying that they could not bear to spend another moment in the sun.

'Well, maybe you'd like to see a peasant village instead. I'm just about to go and try to get hold of some coolies to help dig the first layer or two. It's only fifteen minutes' walk – mostly a shady path.'

Before Lucy could express any doubts about the wisdom

of going off into the jungle with a strange man, Deborah sprang up and said she'd just adore visiting an unspoilt local community.

As they walked along under the palm trees, Lucy comforted herself with the thought that the jungle was really just a tropical wood and that both she and Deborah were bigger than Meng, their new friend. He informed them that he had studied at London University. He had even been a guest at the Maising Oxbridge Dinner, and claimed to have met Deborah's husband. Lucy was reassured by this information, though she still distrusted his flashing smile and handsome good looks.

They soon arrived at a clearing where a dozen or so bamboo-thatched houses stood on stilts. A fat grandmotherly woman was sitting at the bottom of a ladder, pounding something on a stone, and a group of older men were lying in the shade chewing rhythmically, their teeth red with betel nut. A couple of goats were enclosed within bamboo palings and bedraggled chickens foraged amongst them.

As soon as she saw Deborah and Lucy, the old woman cried out. Then several more women and children appeared. Laughing and exclaiming, they ran forward to pinch Lucy's pale skin and finger the skirt of Deborah's dress.

'They are interested in you,' said Meng unnecessarily. He spent some time talking to the grandmother while Lucy and Deborah stood awkwardly, surrounded by chatter and curiosity.

'They say your visit is most auspicious. They want to show you their prize possession,' said Meng.

The women pulled them towards a life-size black statue on the edge of the clearing. Lucy could see that the figure was covered in garlands of flowers, and sticks of incense burned at its feet. As they drew near she was astonished to recognize not an eastern god, but a plump, elderly Queen Victoria seated on an ornate throne. In full regalia, including crown and long flowing robes, she was a magnificent sight.

Beside the statue squatted a thin old woman, dressed in a white blouse and black sarong. As if to compensate for her plainness she wore a great deal of silver jewellery, and an elaborate headdress covered most of her scrawny hair. The villagers bowed to her and she inclined her head, smiling a little and displaying the discoloured stumps of two lonely teeth.

'She is Girah, the Spirit Woman, she looks after the statue,' said Meng. 'These people found it fifty years ago. It must have been looted from Singapore by the Japanese. It's been here ever since.'

'But shouldn't they give it back?' asked Lucy. 'Surely it should be at some Embassy somewhere.'

'I believe there was an official British investigation into the matter and the decision was to leave it here. You see, the village women regard the Queen as a fertility symbol – they make her offerings when they want to become pregnant. She's very efficacious, I'm told, particularly if taken with one of the Spirit Woman's potions. In fact, they have a whole secret fertility ceremony which takes place at night involving Queen Victoria and numerous other dead spirits.'

'Fascinating!' breathed Deborah. 'But it doesn't sound very Buddhist.'

'No, these people are animists. They like to invoke the good spirits to help them in their everyday life, and then there are other malevolent spirits who have to be placated. For them Queen Victoria has become an honorary good spirit.'

Deborah laughed heartily, but Lucy stared at the statue. Apart from the incense and flowers, offerings had been made in the form of money and food placed in a dozen or so small copper bowls which sat around the queen's feet. As the others returned to the centre of the village, Lucy reached quickly in her purse and dropped some coins into an empty bowl. The Spirit Woman gazed at her without moving. Something about her eyes made Lucy shiver.

Then she heard Deborah shouting, 'Quick, it's nearly noon. We must hurry back. Beth will get mad if we're late.'

Sweating and exhausted, they reached their rendezvous to find the bus with doors closed and engine running. Beth was standing beside the driver. Looking extremely displeased, she opened the door for them.

Lucy had hoped to avoid any further contact with Meng, but, during the furore created by their late departure, he pressed a card into her hand.

'Telephone me if you want to return and consult the Spirit Woman,' he said quietly.

Lucy jumped quickly on to the bus without saying goodbye, but she put the card into her pocket.

TWELVE

When Deborah took the children to swim at Poppy's the next day, she regaled her hostess with an account of the sightseeing trip and the encounter with the handsome archaeologist.

Poppy showed small interest in antiquities, but she was delighted to talk about Meng. 'Sweetie, you're so right. Some of the islanders are simply divine.'

She was wearing such a glamorous poolside ensemble – one could hardly call it a swimsuit – that Deborah felt a pang of envy. It really was unfair that a fifty-year-old managed to be so damn thin.

'Mind you, I never had a Maising fling,' continued Poppy. 'Although I was tempted by a member of the Royal Family – a long time ago.'

'Tell me more,' urged Deborah, hoping for juicy revelations. Poppy often hinted about past lovers but seldom delivered.

Poppy pursed her red lips. 'One just doesn't talk about these matters. It'd be fearfully indiscreet. I will tell you that Jock got very jealous. But he needn't have been. I showed enormous restraint in the face of great temptation – the princeling was ten years younger than me. I've always fancied younger men, and a title does add that extra frisson,' she chortled. 'Talking of men, how's that husband of yours?'

'Much as usual,' said Deborah shortly.

Poppy raised her eyebrows. 'Still playing around?'

'Reckon so.'

'Oh dear. Perhaps you should consider taking a lover yourself, sweetie,' she said seriously. 'How about that young chap, that archaeologist you just told me about? He sounds most appetizing.'

'Not my type – he was strange, too smooth and sophisticated,' said Deborah, with a smile. 'Anyway, I think he preferred Lucy. He kept gazing at her bosom, like everyone does.'

'Poor child, yes. She is rather top-heavy. Trouble is, her shape's so amazing that one can't help staring. But you are much prettier, and wasted on that tiresome Johnny, spoilt by his mother. I always thought Muriel was a fool. Question is, I've often wondered, dear, why did you marry Johnny? I suppose because he's rather good-looking. So many women marry for looks and it's such a mistake. Far better to marry for money as I did, both times.'

Deborah laughed. 'I think I married Johnny because he was kind of different, my first older man. I met him when he came to work for Selby's Bank in Geneva. I had a dull, respectful Swiss boyfriend at the time. Johnny was exciting. Well, he wouldn't take no for an answer. I was plump even then, but he really seemed to like me. It was flattering, you know. And my parents didn't approve – that made him all the more desirable.'

'Oh dear, how often that happens.'

'But he's not that bad, Poppy. I guess our marriage is no worse than a lot of others,' said Deborah, feeling she had confessed too much.

When they had first met, it was Johnny's all-demanding sensuality that had attracted her. He had taken her to bed on their second date and kept her in sexual thrall until they had been married two years, when she had discovered that he liked to spread his talents around other bedrooms. She should perhaps have left him then, but youthful pride had made her cling on to her marriage. She was sure that he loved her, that he would change, reform, quieten down, but he had not.

Poppy, who considered herself an expert on the male sex, was still giving advice on the subject. 'Nevertheless, you need to bring Johnny to heel or find a better husband. As I said, I'd suggest an affair. It would give you a lift. In some regards, having a baby seems to be rather a lowering experience. All that animal earthiness – my friends say it makes one feel like a great fat cow rather than a desirable woman. To raise your feminine self-confidence, what you need is a sugar daddy. Someone who'd really appreciate you. I'll put my mind to it.' She waved her fingers again. 'Look, I'll have to go now, my sweet, another bridge tournament. If there is a pause between hands, I'll try to jot down the names of a few prospective lovers for you.'

Deborah laughed. 'A kind thought, but . . .'

'Just what every girl needs to get her over the seven-year itch. Now, if I find you a sugar daddy, will you do something for me? Take young Alex with you next time you go sightseeing. He sits around here all day doing absolutely nothing but reading. Drives Jock mad with his apathy and laziness. They get on each other's nerves most frightfully. Jock's always correcting the way he speaks and going on about how he's paid for him to go to one of the best schools in the world and why does he talk like a dustman. Most unfair, really. Alex sounds like any other teenager, but you know how pernickety Jock is. Always writing to *The Times* about grammar.'

Deborah smiled. 'Maybe he *is* kind of old-fashioned.'

'Old-fashioned? Prehistoric is the word. And then he goes on about how it's a wonder Alex has the energy to get up in the morning. And how is he going to manage when he gets to Oxford and why isn't he studying more? Though of course Jock disapproves of psychology – that's what Alex is going to read. He thinks Alex should be studying something sensible like economics. But I said to him, "Jock old thing, just be thankful the boy hasn't insisted on art school instead." Alex is quite arty, you know. Did I tell you his mother was a painter of sorts? She used to do rather murky, watery water colours, quite nice if you like that sort of thing.'

'But you didn't.'

'Not much. I put most of her paintings in the attic. Jock never noticed.' Poppy laughed. 'Well, anyway, about Alex. Jock thinks I ought to take the boy about more, show him some island culture, but, as you know, sweetie, I do try to be a good step-mama, but I'm not keen on native art and things, and I am so fearfully committed to my bridge – you would have thought a husband would understand that after all these years of marriage.'

'Yes,' said Deborah, thinking more about the attractions of Alex than Jock's general insensitivity.

'Of course, I'm keen on social life and I did make the effort to introduce Alex to some of the young people here,' continued Poppy plaintively, 'but he just said they were boring. I'm at my wits' end. If you could just inspire him, chuck a tiny bit of culture at him, see some of the less tedious sights, sweetie, I'd be eternally grateful. I know he likes you and the children.'

During the weeks that followed, Deborah did as she was asked. She took Alex with her around the city. They visited the museum, the four biggest temples and the bird sanctuary. Sometimes she took the children along too, but mostly she did not. Alex was an attentive and charming companion. Too attentive and too charming at times, thought Deborah. She knew he had a crush on her and was flattered. Of course, he was too young to take seriously, but it was kind of nice to be on the receiving end of so much admiration. It was admiration that would have to be kept at a distance.

All the while that she was telling herself to stand back, Deborah was letting herself grow closer to Alex. The sightseeing trips became more and more lengthy when he decided to take up sketching the scenery. He hadn't painted for a year, he said, but she inspired him. He even insisted she sit for a pencil portrait, but in the end he refused to show her the result. She took the children to swim at Poppy's pool three or four times a week, and Alex was always at home. In the company of others, she treated him in a friendly casual manner, but when they were alone she would sometimes find herself acknowledging his unspoken desire. Not with words or touch, just with longish looks from underneath her eyelashes. She hoped that nobody had intercepted one of these looks because, broad-minded though Poppy was, she obviously would not care for her eighteen-year-old stepson to be seduced by a married woman.

It was even possible that Alex was still a virgin. 'Did you have a girlfriend at school, Alex?' she asked him one day.

He smiled. 'There aren't any women. It's a boys' school.'

'Yes, but there must have been girls around. Didn't you meet any girls in the town?'

'Not really.'

'How about that girls' school nearby you told me about? You must have met a few of those girls. Didn't you have a special one?'

'There were some I liked, but no deep meaningful relationships, if that's what you're trying to find out.'

'I don't believe you, Alex. You're a very good-looking boy, you must have a girlfriend.'

'Maybe I'm a late developer,' he said with a lazy smile.

Then one evening he came around to her apartment with a plastic duck that Sam had left behind. Deborah did not say that Sam was always leaving toys at Poppy's and that normally they were retrieved at the next visit. She invited Alex to have a drink.

Accepting a beer, he gulped it down. 'Where's your husband?'

'Oh, he's not home yet.'

'Is he coming back for dinner?'

'No, I guess not.'

Alex began a long earnest, excited talk about the meaning of life, the future and the origins of the universe.

Either he never speaks or he won't stop, thought Deborah, as she sat and listened, watching his mobile face. No doubt his clothes were the despair of Poppy's immaculate maids. He wore torn faded black jeans and scuffed sneakers. His white T-shirt was shrunk tight over his muscular arms and chest.

More than anything Deborah wanted to touch him. As if he read her thoughts, he stood up and began to move towards her.

Quickly she forced herself to ask a polite question, something, anything to distract him. 'D'you have to do much reading to prepare yourself for your psychology degree?'

He stared at her and then sat down again. 'Well, yes, there's a reading list and I bought about ten books with terrifying titles. Trouble is, if you can't understand the titles, you don't feel you've got much hope with the text. Still I'm learning the jargon; like in cognitive science you study the mind through the use of computers. I mean, if you know how computers operate, it may help you to study how the brain works.'

'Right, so in a year or two, you'll be analysing us all.'

'Well, not exactly. I'm not doing psychoanalysis in the way you think. Psychology is the study of the mind and human behaviour, as opposed to psychiatry where you're a doctor curing sick minds.'

Deborah smiled. She liked his impassioned way of speaking.

'I'm not going to be a doctor,' he went on. 'Or cure people's minds – just study them, and do research. Though some clinical psychologists go in for psychotherapy, I suppose, but that's just not me.'

'But you must eventually make use of your studies – to give advice, in your job, I mean – if only to work out what makes people buy a brand of detergent.'

He looked offended. 'I'm not interested in the psychology of soap.'

'So what are you going to be? Are you going to be an educational or maybe an industrial psychologist?'

His shoulders tensed. 'Don't you start! That's what's nice about you. Normally you don't ask those sorts of questions. Dad and Poppy are constantly banging on. I just don't know what I'll do eventually. Maybe I'll just drop out, paint, whatever.'

'Before you drop out, you may as well study a bit. Now just tell me what you've read about so far, in those psychology books, I mean.'

'Do you really want to know? Dad thinks it's a very phoney subject. He says it's just chaps sitting about doing crazy experiments to prove something that's common sense anyway.'

'I really do want to hear about it. Maybe because I'm American and we have all sorts of crazy ideas. It sounds pretty interesting to me.'

So she sat and listened some more, telling herself that she was doing the right thing in drawing him out, letting him talk in a relaxed kind of way.

'Did you know,' he said earnestly, 'that there's been some research about happiness in marriage? Some statistics that prove—'

'Hard to measure with statistics,' she murmured.

'Yeah, but the findings were that marriage is good for men – married men are the happiest, most contented. Divorced and single men aren't happy at all. But it's different with women. The majority of married women are less happy with their marriage than men are. So marriage is better for men than it is for women. Surprising, isn't it?'

'Mm, I think I read about that survey,' she said. 'Maybe it's a generalization that's true, or maybe women spend more time sitting about wondering whether they're happy or not. And people sure don't seem to like being divorced as much as they think they're going to – not that I've done a whole lot of research.'

'Yes, and according to a book I've read on child development, children of divorced parents . . .' He went on to tell her some more facts and figures.

She let him talk on, sometimes tempted to agree with his father about psychologists going to a whole load of trouble to prove the obvious. But Alex's enthusiasm for his subject was so sincere that she refrained from cynical remarks.

Eventually, after listening to a dissertation about toddler behaviour, she said, 'D'you know, I think I could have written that book myself. *A Case Study of Two Kids* by Deborah who researches all day and all night.'

He laughed. 'Yes, but I bet you didn't know that even a five-week-old baby can recognize his mother's photograph among several others and can call it up on a screen by learning a pattern of sucking and gestures.'

'Hey, that's amazing. But you can tell me more another time. Poppy must be expecting you at dinner.'

He looked at his watch. 'They were going to a cocktail party first. But I suppose I'd better leave. Dad gets very uptight about mealtimes.'

She led him to the door. 'I don't really want to go,' he said suddenly, his eyes fixed on hers.

'I think you'd better. Goodnight, Alex.' Deborah quickly shut the door behind him.

She lay awake that night for a long time, thinking.

Apart from her brief encounter with Howard, she had not been unfaithful to Johnny despite the years of provocation. She felt she had every excuse to take a lover, but Alex was not the right person. As she had already told herself, he was too young, too vulnerable. He might become too emotionally involved, and it was immoral to seduce the young. She'd feel guilty. That would be descending to her husband's level of behaviour. So she would have to put a stop to the whole thing, before anything happened.

But week after week she continued to meet Alex and he would tell her how much he liked talking to her, how important her friendship was to him, how she was the only person who listened. She could discuss everything he cared about and she was the only one who really understood his artistic efforts. Day after day, she basked in this flattery, and as he gazed into her eyes with increasingly meaningful looks, she began to wonder who was slowly and expertly seducing whom.

When Johnny went off to Hong Kong on business later that month, Deborah accepted an invitation to stay at Poppy's beach house. It'll be nice for the children, she told herself.

Though Poppy's beach house was much smaller and rather less luxurious than the city mansion, there was no question of roughing it. Only two maids were taken to the seaside, but there was a resident caretaker who prepared the barbecues and looked after Jock's motor boat, assisted by the chauffeur.

'We just camp here – and it's rather selfish because only my bedroom is air-conditioned, I'm sorry, sweetie,' said Poppy as she showed Deborah to the guest quarters, a separate wooden bungalow in the grounds.

'Oh, it's wonderful to have a sea breeze after the city fumes,' said Deborah.

But it was very hot that month before the monsoon. Deborah kept the children in the shade of the palm trees, and anointed them with suncream every half hour.

'I feel like I'm basting two little chickens,' she said to Alex, as he lay sprawled on a sunbed nearby. 'Be careful, Alex, your back is getting red. I'll baste you too.'

She poured a little cream on to his shoulders and began to rub gently. Then she massaged his back. His skin was warm and quite smooth, apart from the golden hairs that covered his long brown legs. She continued to massage for several minutes, when suddenly she stopped, embarrassed by her own feelings.

'Go on, please,' he said in a muffled voice.

'You can reach the rest yourself, lazy boy,' she said heartily.

'Then it's my turn. Let me put some stuff on your back.'

'No, I'm going for a swim.' Abruptly she put down the bottle of Ambre Solaire and ran into the sea. As she turned towards the shore to float on her back, she saw that Alex was swimming towards her.

She smiled. 'What are you doing in the water? I just put all that oil on you.'

'I know, but I was hot. I needed to cool down.'

'I guess you did,' said Deborah, laughing and swimming away from him.

He followed her and, grabbing her around the waist, pulled her towards him. 'Deborah.'

'Let go, Alex,' she spluttered. 'I'm too old for seaside games and too old for you.' With the palm of her hand, she splashed some water at him. 'Anyway, look, your step-mommy is calling you. I guess it's time for you two to go to the yacht club.'

Alone in the house after lunch, she put the children to rest. Jojo was fractious and Sam cross and balky. If he slept all afternoon, he would be up late tonight, but at least it would be cool. Against her principles, she gave him a cookie to take to bed.

Why wasn't there a breeze this afternoon? She went to her own room for a siesta. Closing the door behind her, she took off her tight uncomfortable swimsuit and lay down naked on the bed. The buzzing fan was rotating like a whirlwind, but it made no appreciable difference to the temperature in the room. It was almost too hot to think, except that her desire for Alex was on her mind. Her eyes closed.

A little later she opened them again. Alex stood in the doorway gazing at her. Deborah flushed but made no attempt to cover herself. 'I thought you went sailing,' she said.

'I changed my mind. I came back.'

'And Poppy?' asked Deborah lightly.

He took one step forward. 'Oh, she's still at the club playing bridge. She'll be there for the rest of the day.'

'And the servants?'

'They're off duty, down in their own quarters.' He took another step forward and then stopped. 'What about the children?'

'They'll both sleep for a couple of hours.'

'They don't wake up?'

'No, they sleep like logs in the afternoon. Usually I have a problem to wake them.' She smiled again. 'Are you just going to stand there, Alex?'

'Well . . .'

'Why don't you come in and close the door behind you?'

He cleared his throat. 'Right.' He shut the door, and then locked it, but he remained standing on the other side of the room.

'I have an idea,' she said eventually. 'Maybe you'd kindly

rub some more suncream on to my back. I guess I am a little
sore on the shoulders too.'

'Oh, are you going down to the beach then?' asked Alex.
His voice sounded hoarse and low.

'Not just yet. Maybe later. But you could put the cream on
now, if you want. Use that body lotion, in the white bottle.
It's very soothing.'

Slowly she turned on to her stomach and pressed her face
into the pillows.

'Right, er, OK,' he said.

He walked over to the dressing table and picked up the
lotion. Kneeling on the edge of the bed, he tentatively pushed
away her long thick hair and, very gently, stroked a little cream
on to her shoulders, and then her arms. He hesitated and then
began to anoint her feet, moving, very slowly, to her calves
and thighs. Appearing to lose courage as his hands approached
the generous mound of her bottom, he skipped over it and
began to massage the small of her back and up again to the
nape of her neck. The pressure of his fingers became more
intense.

'Shall I turn over now?' she whispered shakily.

He gulped. 'Oh, yes. Yes, please.'

THIRTEEN

Claire was not particularly offended that Deborah paid
her less attention these days, but she was surprised
about how often she bumped into the boy Alex creeping
furtively up the stairs of Lotus Court. When she mentioned
these visits, Deborah had hurriedly explained that she was
coaching him in French literature. Claire knew that Deb had
studied at Geneva University and was a qualified language
teacher – indeed she still taught English to Maising students
– but it was intriguing to observe that Alex's lessons always
took place on evenings when Johnny was out of town.

Could it possibly be a love affair? It seemed unlikely and
yet Deborah had been looking different – somehow younger
and slimmer, with a new happier glow on her face. And she'd

been wearing some snappy new clothes recently. Claire found the situation fascinating and longed to know the truth. She kept her suspicions to herself, for Deborah's sake.

It was one of many secrets that she did not wish to share with Howard. She was very fond of him, but he seemed to want to take over every aspect of her life, while Claire still preferred to remain as independent as possible, at least in thought.

It was entirely her own fault – she should never, ever have slept with him that night, breaking all her own personal rules about not sleeping with a man you don't really love and not encouraging false hopes in a man that loves you. And why hadn't she backed off at the time, why had she allowed the relationship to deepen?

Must be loneliness and the need for love, warmth and human contact, dammit. And the hope that if she got a bit closer to Howard that she might convince herself she loved him after all.

She went over and over the situation in her mind. One major plus about Howard was that he didn't mind her various imperfections. He accepted her just as she was. He never asked any jealous questions about her past, never mentioned her long-ago marriage, never mentioned her recent affair with Leo. Another huge advantage about Howard was that he didn't have an ex-wife. Leo's ex was trouble. She was the main cause of the bust-up, always phoning him, always emailing, always needing his advice about this and that. Could Leo come round and fix the outside light? The ex couldn't possibly manage it herself and he was soooh good at that sort of thing. Too darn good. Main problem was that Leo still loved his wife and what was worse, it had turned out that they still slept together. Claire had caught them in flagrante.

'Only now and then,' confessed Leo.

'Now and then?' screamed Claire, and that was the end of Leo.

But she had loved him passionately all the same, or thought she did – trouble is, she didn't feel the same way about Howard. Maybe that was a good thing. Too much passion was too much danger, and her fondness for Howard might grow into sensible mature love, with time. And it was sensible and mature love that lasted and weathered all the storms. But then . . .

Howard, ever faithful, didn't know about her doubts. Ignoring her plea to take things gently, he would tell her every day how much he loved her. He even mentioned marriage occasionally, not in a demanding 'you must marry me' sort of way, but in a warm, loving 'you'd make a wonderful wife' sort of way.

'I told you – I don't want to get married to anyone again,' Claire would say lightly. 'Too battle-scarred for all that.'

'Nonsense, you're young and lovely,' Howard would say soppily.

At the same time, he had begun to refurbish his house, making her choose some new curtain material for the sitting room on the grounds that that sort of thing was a woman's job.

He did not nag. He just seemed to assume that one day they would marry and everything he did was based on that assumption. He was drawing such a kind and gentle web of security around her that Claire knew it would be difficult to break away from him, even if she wanted to.

As for Drew she had put him to the back of her mind. She had not seen him since the Embassy party, the night when he had disappeared with – or allowed himself to be appropriated by – the bright and sexy Maising colleague who was all too clearly his mistress, the night when, in consequence, in a fit of pique and hurt pride, she had taken Howard to bed.

A day or two after that evening, Drew had telephoned and asked her, quite casually, to join him on a business trip to Bangkok.

She'd often thought about their conversation – OK, more accurately, she went over and over it in her mind in an obsessive manner.

She had adopted a cool matter-of-fact tone, but couldn't help smiling to herself. 'We've had precisely one date together and you're asking me to go away for the weekend?'

'That's right,' Drew said. 'You complain I don't call in advance. Well, now I have. We could stay at the Oriental or somewhere else luxurious. My treat. I can just about afford separate hotel rooms, if that's what's worrying you. But maybe not at the Oriental, on second thoughts.'

'What about your friend, Liana Son? Is she coming too?'

'Why should she? I invited you, not her.'

'But won't she mind?' asked Claire.

'Look, Claire, there's plenty you don't understand. If we spend the weekend together, we can talk. I won't lay a finger on you. But, there again, if you drag me into your room and insist on having your wicked way with me, then I might not be too strong willed.'

She was trying not to laugh.

'How about it?' he asked.

'How about what?'

'Will you come? I've booked two tickets.'

Claire smiled to herself again. 'You have, have you? What if I can't make it?'

'Then I'll have to cancel. But, give me a break, please come.'

'I'll think about it,' she said, and put the phone down.

After much heart-searching about loyalty to Howard, and several hours telling herself that she'd never, ever two-timed, and besides Drew was hopelessly casual and unreliable, and absolutely not her type, she decided to accept his invitation. In her entire proper, well more or less proper life she had never behaved this badly. Must be something to do with the heat.

She dialled Drew's number early one morning before she went to work. A Maising female voice speaking good English with a strong American accent answered the phone.

Claire hesitated. 'Liana?' she ventured.

'Yes, this is she. To whom do I have the pleasure of speaking?' purred the voice.

Claire had quickly replaced the receiver. In a rage, she sent off an instant email: 'Thank you, but no. Never. C.'

She had not heard from him again. Not that she wanted to.

Naturally Drew was another subject she chose not to discuss with Howard. Anyway, there was nothing to discuss, for whatever it was she had had with Drew, it was clearly all over before it had started. She would put him out of her mind, concentrating on Howard and on her job. It was better not to have much time to brood.

Fortunately she had plenty to occupy her, for she needed to finish Jean-Louis' catalogue and prepare it for printing. It was now developing into a lengthy publication, more of a book than a catalogue. She was gratified that he allowed her to continue her work without much supervision. Indeed their relationship seemed to be excellent these days. She remained on good terms with Pel too. He said nothing further about the stolen Buddha heads and so Claire thought it wiser not to bring up the whole dubious and scary subject.

As they talked one day, she told him she was envious of his command of French. He confided that his mother's father had been a French colonial officer and that he had been brought up a Christian. His English improved still more as he chatted with her regularly. He told her he wanted to practise the language so that he could help Jean-Louis with his English work, as she did.

'But you do help him. For instance, you make all the arrangements for the import of the works of art he buys from Cambodia. You know a great deal about Khmer art.'

'Yes. Naturally.'

'By the way, Pel, why do so many Thai antiquities come to us via Cambodia, rather than direct?'

He smiled as if he did not understand. Then he said, 'Pose your questions to Jean-Louis.'

But she knew Jean-Louis did not care to elaborate on the methods by which he acquired his treasures. Besides, she had already guessed the answer. He was probably smuggling goods out via Cambodia to avoid the numerous Thai export restrictions against works of art leaving the country. She had no proof of this theory, and as respectable galleries in England and elsewhere bought the items, she sometimes felt her suspicions must be unfounded.

She certainly would not dare to confront Jean-Louis on the subject. She thought it wise to confine herself to general questions about Buddhism and south-east Asian art. For instance, she was attracted by the teachings of Buddha on the suppression of earthly desires. How much easier her life would be without them.

Jean-Louis professed to have adopted the Buddhist faith. Christianity, he said, was too aggressive. He seemed to find it amusing that Pel held to the religion.

'Do you believe in reincarnation, then?' Claire asked Jean-Louis one day.

'Why not? I have no trouble in accepting the idea that life

is continuous, like a wheel going round and round. Then one does not fear death.'

'But if you don't make sufficient merit in this life, then you could be reincarnated as a dog or even a mosquito, I believe.'

'The Lord Buddha taught that all life forms are important. That is why one must not kill the lowliest of creatures.'

Claire raised her eyebrows. 'Then one shouldn't even use fly spray?'

He smiled. 'Ah, well, one is not killing the fly directly. One is merely spraying the air.'

'So killing is all right if it's indirect. You don't differentiate between zapping a mosquito and, say, arranging a murder or killing people with bombs?'

'I am Swiss, a pacifist. Nevertheless, in some senses, one should not attach too much importance to human life, for there is always rebirth.'

Claire was not always sure he meant what he said. He often had a mocking expression in his small round eyes.

'But why,' she persisted, 'if Buddha taught that even the death of an insect is wrong, have there been so many wars in this part of the world?'

'Man is imperfect, alas, but at least wars have not been fought in the Lord Buddha's name, whereas man has created havoc in the name of Jesus Christ – and still does.'

'True.' She paused. 'But, tell me, does the everyday-man-in-the-paddy-field Buddhist really want Nirvana, nothingness? I mean, you have surrounded yourself with beautiful things. I can't see you as a self-denying monk.'

'I, too, am imperfect, but one has to strive. Like Christians, Buddhists believe that one should not constantly covet the possessions of others. Selfishness and craving result in suffering.' He smiled. 'But I do admit to the sin of covetousness as far as antiquities are concerned. Now, let us strive to identify this piece of pottery, Sawankalok or Ayuthia, would you say?'

At that point they were interrupted by the arrival of a visitor. Jean-Louis introduced him as Professor Meng, a local archaeologist, who was also a collector, a semi-professional photographer and a gourmet.

'A man of many interests,' said Claire, smiling at the handsome islander.

The visitor was perhaps even more beautiful and certainly more powerfully built than Pel, who was standing on the edge of the group looking uneasy. It occurred to Claire that Meng might be another of Jean-Louis' lovers – except that he glanced at her in an appreciative manner and began to ask her questions about her life in Maising, flashing his dark eyes at her and smiling a great deal. After a while, Jean-Louis said briskly that he and Meng had private business to discuss.

When they had departed Claire asked, 'Who's that, Pel? What's the matter?'

'Nobody, nothing,' he said and went to his room slamming the door.

During the weeks that followed Claire worked hard on her project, determined to meet her self-imposed deadline. Jean-Louis was out late one afternoon when she was unable to guess the origins of a fragment of bas-relief. In the hope that Pel might be able to help, she called him in from the pool. Shaking the water from his long hair, he wrapped a towel around his waist and came into the office.

'Do you have any idea where this came from, Pel? It must be Khmer.'

He ran his hands over it several times. 'Maybe Angkor Wat.'

'From Cambodia? But I thought . . .'

He shrugged his shoulders. 'Who knows what happens in that country even now, so long after the war.'

'Does Jean-Louis have any records in those files about that sort of thing? I'm worried it's not legal.'

'Pose your questions to him,' he said uncomfortably.

'Do you have the key to that filing cabinet over there, Pel?'

His eyes travelled towards a green jar on the bookcase. 'Pose your questions to Jean-Louis,' he repeated.

She put her hand on his arm. 'Don't you mind that your country is being raped of all its antiquities?'

He stared out of the window. Then he spoke slowly. 'What does it matter? What does it matter about pieces of stone? Many much more terrible things happened. Many, many people were killed. My grandparents . . .'

He looked as if he were about to cry. She was stricken. 'I'm sorry. What about your parents?'

Tears began to roll down his handsome face.

She put her arm around his shoulders. 'I'm so very sorry. I didn't mean to pry. I know you must have suffered. How every one in your country suffered.'

He was silent and then he spoke. 'The only thing I have of my parents is a bird of ivory. That is all I have of them. It belonged to my mother.'

'An ivory bird?'

'Yes, it is quite small, delicate.'

'Will you show it to me?'

'Perhaps one day. I keep it in my room. Sometimes, some-times I pray to it. It is white, like bones.'

They remained with their arms about each other for several minutes; Pel sobbing quietly and Claire rocking him gently as if he were an unhappy child.

The door opened. 'A charming scene,' said Jean-Louis. He marched in, his small dark eyes angry. Pel jumped and ran from the room as if he were guilty of some crime.

'Is it not time you went home, my dear Claire? You must not work so hard,' said Jean-Louis, without smiling.

'We were talking about . . .' began Claire awkwardly, wondering how best to explain why Pel had been in the office in his swimming gear and why she had put her arms around him.

'As I said, it is time you went home.'

'But I wanted to tell you that . . .'

'There is nothing to say,' he said coldly, and left the room.

As she walked to her car, she heard Jean-Louis shouting and the sound of Pel weeping again.

When she returned to work the next Monday, there was no sign of either of them. The maid, full of excitement, told her that Pel had left in a rage and had not returned. She said that the master had told her to pack all Pel's belongings and then an unknown driver had arrived to collect them.

Claire found a note from Jean-Louis telling her he would be away for a day or two. During the course of the day, it occurred to her to look in the green jar for the key of the cabinet. She found the key, but when she unlocked the cabinet it was empty.

Curiouser and curiouser.

FOURTEEN

Next weekend at the seaside Deborah opened her eyes early in the morning when she heard her son's piping voice. He was talking to Pima, who was beseeching him to be quiet and not disturb all the mothers and fathers still asleep in the hotel.

Deborah lay back listening to the muffled noises. After twenty minutes or more, all was quiet. Pima must have dressed the children and taken them down to the beach. Such luxury, she thought, to bring a maid at the weekend to take care of both kids now that Jojo had been weaned at last.

Johnny was snoring with his mouth open, his greying curls spreading over the pillow in damp clumps. Deborah dressed silently in a bikini and white T-shirt. Carrying her sandals and a beach towel, she crept across the room and out into the tropical dawn.

Dawn was her favourite time at the yacht club because then she could have the view to herself. During the middle of the day she enjoyed watching the sailors and their colourful boats, but with all the bustle it was not much more peaceful than the city. Similarly, in the evening, one always had to share the spectacular sunsets with others, all of them drinking and talking. At dawn she could be private and selfish. The pale light reminded her of Europe. She might even feel a little chilly. It was a rare treat to be cold enough to pull on a sweater.

That morning the sky was not yet blue, but a glow rising in the trees behind her promised the inevitable long, hot day. The sea scarcely rippled as it spread towards the three dark islands on the horizon where a solitary fishing boat was making its way to port. She saw that the tide was ebbing away, leaving a shiny expanse between the edge of the sea and the line of seaweed and driftwood thrown up during the night. Above the tidemark the yachts sat on the dry sand, their sails neatly furled.

Alex would like to paint this, she thought. He'd been drawing more lately, moving away from landscapes to spend time sketching her face over and over again. Smiling to herself, she dried one of the dew-soaked rattan chairs on the verandah and sat down. Across the slope of spiky grass, a gardener stood clipping back the purple bougainvillaea which formed the boundary hedge beneath the tall palms. Otherwise there was no one to be seen, not even the children. Pima must have taken them around the headland to hunt for shells.

It was now six thirty. Breakfast at the club would not be served for another hour. Not that she particularly enjoyed breakfast here; the toast was always soggy and the coffee tasted of old cardboard. Only the tropical fruits – pawpaw, mango, pineapple and banana sprinkled with fresh lime juice – made the meal worth waiting for.

She opened her book. The novel concerned an affair between a female tutor and her young male student, with graphic sex scenes. Arching her back and stretching, Deborah thought of Alex again. He was too much on her mind. She should end the affair before it became public knowledge, before it ruined her friendship with Poppy, not to mention her own reputation. What if her mother-in-law should somehow find out? Their relationship was cool at the best of times. She could just imagine those thin pursed lips. The never-ending stream of criticism would become a torrent. If Muriel became upset about Deborah's toilet-training methods, or lack of them, what would she say about a love affair with a teenage boy?

As for Johnny, she definitely did not want him to know about it. At the very least, he'd sneer and make the affair seem sordid and banal, whereas to her it was a secret, special delight.

Alex didn't like the secrecy. 'Why don't you ever phone me, and why won't you let me phone you?' he would say as they sat side by side on the edge of Poppy's pool, a discreet distance apart, hands by their sides, fingertips just touching. 'I need to talk to you, even if I can't see you every day.'

'You see me two or three times a week.'

'Seeing you like this is no good. I need you. I want you now. Let's go up to my room. Poppy's out.'

Deborah smiled. 'You're crazy. The maids are all over the house.'

'I can give them all the morning off.'

'No, absolutely not. They're far too conscientious to accept such an order from you anyway. But next week, on Tuesday, Johnny'll be away. Come at seven thirty, if you want to.'

'Of course I want to, but I can't wait till next week.'

'You just have to.'

This type of conversation went on every time they met. Deborah grinned, recalling his insistence, the excitement, the passion, and recalling some of the risks they took: making love in the sea, in Jock's boat and, once, dangerously, in the pool-house while the gardeners wandered about outside. Surely one day someone must guess, even if she and Alex weren't actually caught in the act.

But to hell with everyone else. Addicted to Alex, she was flowering again after a long dormant period. As a feminist, she was reluctant to admit that this lusty passionate love – from a mere boy – had restored her faith in herself.

Though she had remained outwardly unchanged, cheerful and exuberant, her self-esteem had sunk lower and lower during the years of Johnny's philandering. His indifference during her pregnancies, his lack of interest in the babies, had hurt her in a way she hardly acknowledged. During the earthy process of childbearing, she'd become merely a fat, fertile animal, a milk-machine, a nursemaid, hardly a woman at all. Now, miraculously, she felt desirable and feminine again.

She turned the page of her book. Yes, it was an appropriate choice of novel, she thought. The fictional student consoled and sustained his tutor who also had an unhappy marriage. Deborah smiled when the tutor/heroine confessed that though she was behaving very badly, it sure was a whole lot of fun.

Continuing to read, she looked up now and then, but the children and Pima were still out of sight.

Some time later, she heard Sam's voice. He was running up the beach towards her as fast as his little, fat legs would carry him. Pima was hurrying after him, Jojo in her arms. Deborah smiled, wondering what new shell or cuttlefish bone Sam had found to show her.

'Mummy, I got tell you.' His brown eyes shone.

'Yes, honey, what?'

'There's a dead man on the beach, just round there.'

Deborah felt instinctively that he was speaking the truth.

'Oh God, let me just talk to Pima a minute.'

'Pima's scared. I'm not scared,' he said excitedly. 'Pima said not touch him, so I didn't.'

'Good boy. You did the right thing to come straight away to tell mommy.' She gathered him in her arms and held him tight, but he did not seem to be in the least perturbed by his experience.

Pima's pretty round face was grey with fear. 'Oh, madame, very bad. Man dead. Madame no go look.'

'OK, OK,' said Deborah as calmly as she could. 'We must get hold of the manager so he can call the police. Is the dead person a white man or an island man?'

'Pima don't know. Not white man. Maybe not Maising man. Maybe Thai, Vietnam. Very bad. Madame no look,' she repeated as if Deborah were about to rush down and gape at the corpse.

'Please go wake the manager, Pima. You know where Mr Kahn lives.'

'Pima don't know.'

The girl, usually quite sensible, seemed to have gone to pieces.

'Well, find one of the maids or a gardener and tell them to get him,' said Deborah.

Eventually the manager, an expatriate Pakistani, arrived on the verandah, rubbing his thin hands in an agitated manner.

'Oh my goodness, Mrs Case, what a terrible thing! We must make sure that the club members are not disturbed by this matter. I am calling the police now and they are promising to be very quick and quiet in removing this object from our beach.'

To her surprise, a silent police ambulance appeared within fifteen minutes and left with a covered stretcher soon after. Sam had wanted to help them find the body, but she'd restrained him with the promise of food. Alerted by the drama, all three waitresses arrived on time that morning and breakfast was soon ready to be served. Deborah ordered French toast for Sam as a treat and he tackled it with his usual gusto, covering his face and fingers with honey and generally behaving as if nothing in particular had happened.

While they were eating, a police officer came to interview them. He wore a skintight khaki uniform and a black holster containing a large revolver. Under his peaked cap, he had a haughty, withdrawn expression.

Mr Kahn acted as interpreter. 'Mrs Case is having nothing to say and her little child is too young to be of assistance. Mrs Case is not the type of lady who would know anything about such a matter, I assure you, Sergeant. The maid of Mrs Case is a simple girl who knows nothing either.'

But, as far as Deborah could gather, the policeman seemed mainly concerned that the matter should be kept as quiet as possible, as dead bodies were bad for tourism.

Mr Kahn bowed up and down. 'I am agreeing with you there, Sergeant. But I am sure that Mrs Case is not the sort of lady who wants to discuss such indelicate matters at breakfast time. And I am sure she will not consider it a suitable topic to mention to the other ladies and gentlemen members of our club.'

Deborah asked, 'Does the sergeant know who the dead man was?'

'The sergeant is of the opinion that the deceased was an Asian foreigner having no connection with Maising. A Thai pirate, no doubt.'

'How does he know? I mean, he could have come from one of the beach houses round the bay or a yacht or something. Pima said he was sort of well-dressed.'

'The sergeant has advised your maid not indulge in specu-lations. He wishes to tell you he is leaving now and thanks you for your cooperation. Pray continue with your breakfast. On this occasion, I should be most delighted if you would accept the meal with my compliments.'

Deborah was concerned that Sam might be adversely affected by this traumatic morning, but he seemed to have taken it in his stride, whereas Pima was unusually nervous for days after-wards. Eventually, however, she recovered her composure and seemed to forget the whole incident as completely as Sam had done.

A few weeks later, however, something jogged her memory. As had happened many times in the past, Poppy telephoned to ask if Pima could kindly come and be an extra party wait-ress that evening. Before she left for Poppy's, Pima suddenly said that she remembered seeing someone resembling the dead man once before, maybe when she had been hired previously to serve drinks at the Embassy or the bank compound. She was not sure if the man had been another waiter or a guest.

'Perhaps you'd better tell the police,' said Deborah.

The maid looked worried. 'Pima not remember well. Police say Pima a stupid peasant woman.'

Recalling the contemptuous way the sergeant had spoken to the girl, Deborah thought it likely that the police would say exactly that, so she let the matter rest, though, of course, she knew that Pima was far from stupid.

FIFTEEN

As the days passed, there was no mention of Pel and no sign of his return. Afraid that she had been the cause of their quarrel, Claire wanted to reassure Jean-Louis about the innocence of the scene he had witnessed, but, even when he was at his most affable, she had never dared to discuss personal matters. Now his manner towards her seemed to have chilled, she could not bring herself to raise such a subject.

Jean-Louis began to spend less and less time at his house, leaving her to work alone, proof-reading the catalogue. He told her that other affairs required his attention and he would be operating from his company offices in central Maising. She was careful to appear incurious about his business interests. These days, even when she asked him the most innocent of questions, he would gaze at her coldly for some time before answering. The skin around his small eyes was pale and dry, and when he was angry his nose appeared sharper and longer. Increasingly he reminded her of a fat bird of prey about to pounce on its victim.

She became convinced that he would dismiss her as soon as the catalogue had been printed. She wondered what she would do then. She would probably have to return to England as it would be difficult to find another suitable job in Maising.

An alternative would be to marry Howard. She was in her thirties, after all. It was unlikely she'd meet anyone else as nice as Howard. Yes, it seemed a sensible, even attractive, idea, but much as she liked him, she could not persuade herself that she was madly in love. In some moods, she felt that that didn't matter. As she had told herself before, at her age, mutual affection was more important than lust – she liked Howard, he loved her and there was no reason to suggest they wouldn't be more or less happy ever after. Judging by her own recent experience, true mutual romance was an illusion that didn't last, or even if it did exist, it was a rare luxury she herself could never possess for long. Even in her youthful marriage, she'd worried she loved her husband more than he loved her. Maybe that wouldn't have lasted either. After he'd been killed, she'd converted him into a saint in her mind. But he was no saint. How could he be? Let's face it, nobody was perfect, but some men had fewer drawbacks than others.

Talking about men with drawbacks, there'd been a while, only a very short while, when she'd thought Drew might be the man for her, but of course that had been just lust, yet another illusion.

So there was Howard. They were happy together in a quiet sort of way and her first impressions of him proved to be correct. He continued to be kind, reliable and generous, both in and out of bed, where she found herself appreciating his worshipful love-making.

Though he did not share her intellectual interests, he didn't complain or feel excluded when she sat working with her reference books strewn about, and he didn't seem to mind her untidiness or other domestic shortcomings. Instead, he pronounced himself gratified to have a career woman as a girlfriend, and he hoped that she would always keep up her art, as he put it. Claire was pleased to be regarded as a career woman, though she guessed that his experience of the species was limited.

Howard himself still displayed no doubts that their future lay together. As her past life had been full of heartache, she appreciated his steadfastness. She knew there was a danger in undervaluing love that was offered so freely and uncondi-tionally. Sometimes, however, she felt a sense of suffocation, almost as if, like a Jane Austen heroine, she was being forced into a situation by the pressures of society. In London, her private life had been private, but on a small island she and Howard were a couple, invited to parties together and spoken of together.

Extraordinarily anxious about old-fashioned proprieties,

he didn't press her to move into his house, but he assumed
they would spend most evenings together and that she would
act as his hostess when he entertained his business clients.
His house was seductively comfortable: modern but with
attractive verandahs and a small tropical garden, all tended
by efficient staff. The sort of place one could sink into and
just exist without too much effort. As he often pointed out,
the expat lifestyle here was good, sea, sun, and sand, with
complete freedom from domestic chores, so much better than
the chilly, damp old UK.

'Just as long as I don't have to play bridge,' said Claire,
not always totally convinced about the wonders of expathood.

Tonight Howard had told her he was obliged to take some
visiting Australians to the red-light district as they had insisted
on a full-frontal tour.

Claire laughed. 'I hope you know all the seamiest places
then.'

Howard looked worried. 'Well, I tried ringing Johnny Case
to get some advice, but he's out of town, so we'll just have
to plunge in and find our own way around.'

Howard's bland face was illuminated alternately green and
pink as he stood under a flashing neon sign promising 'Girls!
Girls! Girls!' Claire felt oppressed by the atmosphere.

The narrow streets were crowded with night people – slim,
bejewelled boys, flashily dressed older men and gaggles of
garish women with silicone bosoms and short, tight skirts.
Loud music blared from competing speakers, assaulting their
ears with a mixture of European pop music and wailing
Maising ballads.

'I'm rather at a loss in this area,' said Howard, looking
around in a bewildered manner.

'I don't believe a word of it. You must be an expert night-
clubber, Howie,' said Sharon with a grin.

'Yes, you've lived here for years, mate. Must know where
to go,' agreed her husband. They were a good-looking young
couple who evidently enjoyed the seedy surroundings.

A white-suited youth approached them. 'You like li' show?
I give you li' show at Go-Go Club. Velly good, velly nice,
sexy.'

'How much?' asked Howard. The youth named an ex-orbitant sum.

'No, far too expensive. They must be offering massage as well as a Live Show, whatever that is.'

'Massage extra. You like massage? I show you.'

'No, no,' said Howard. 'No, we don't want anything like that. Please go away.'

'You like ping pong?' persisted the tout.

'Ping pong?' said Claire, laughing. 'What can he mean?'

'Ping pong ball, cigarette, velly cheap, sexy. You like. I show you.'

'How much?' asked Howard again.

The tout mentioned a lower amount.

'Let's go for it,' said Brian. 'Sounds fun.'

Pocketing the notes proffered by Howard, the tout led them into a narrow side street. They passed two clinics offering to cure all forms of venereal disease. Very handy, as Brian remarked.

Claire held on tight to Howard's arm as the tout opened an inconspicuous door and led them up some evil-smelling stairs into a small bare room. Red walls and flashing lights were the only attempt at decor. A girl wearing an extremely in-adequate sequin bikini showed them to one of the eight tables. Two mournful-looking customers were sitting next to them, but otherwise the place was empty. Howard bought everyone a Tiger beer, at four times the normal price.

The pop music was then interrupted by a half-hearted fanfare. One of the waitresses ambled into the middle of the room with a bored expression on her face. Without ceremony or lascivious gesture, she removed her bra top and dropped it on to the floor. Then, retaining her air of drugged indiffer-ence, she unfastened the strings on one side of her bikini pants, leaving the garment to dangle lopsidedly from one hip. Claire thought the performance extraordinarily unerotic, but she noticed that all the men were fascinated. She did not care for the look on Howard's face.

After a few desultory wiggles, the girl took a couple of table tennis balls from a basket and began to stuff them up between her legs and thrust them out again as if she were laying eggs. Claire was nauseated.

The same listless performance was repeated with different

girls and different items. Rotating her pelvis, one smoked a cigarette in her vagina and another inserted razor blades, apparently coming to no harm.

'I don't think I can take any more of this. It's disgusting,' announced Claire suddenly.

Brian slapped her on the back. 'Where's your sense of humour, girl? Let's have another beer.'

'Actually, if I stay any longer I may throw up,' she said.

Howard hurriedly asked for the bill.

For some days after the nightclub evening, Claire remained in a bad temper. This was partly because she could not dismiss the degrading scene from her mind and partly due to the depressing prospect of having to entertain Howard's clients for the rest of her life if she married him. But mostly her gloom was due to the fact that she thought she had caught a glimpse of Drew in the crowded streets and he had seemed to be avoiding her. She had almost convinced herself that he meant nothing to her. Seeing him, however, brought back the heart-thumping longings she thought she had conquered. She reminded herself that she was a mature woman, no longer prepared to hanker after untrustworthy unsuitable men. But daily she thought about Drew and these thoughts gave her no peace of mind.

Howard, cheerful as ever, ascribed her black mood to lack of fresh air, inevitable in a tropical climate. What she needed was a weekend away.

He suggested a trip to the National Nature Reserve in the highlands and, with his usual efficient enthusiasm, made all the arrangements. Deborah and Johnny Case were invited, along with Lucy and Martin. Howard hired one guest house for the Case family and one for the rest.

As they drove up into the mountainous region through lush tropical forests, Claire did begin to feel more light-hearted, particularly when they had successfully negotiated a tortuous unsurfaced road and emerged on to a high plateau. The trees seemed even greener and more luxuriant than in Maising and the air cooler and fresher, as promised. However, the chipped wooden gates marking the entrance to the National Park were unpromising and when they finally stopped outside a pair of dismal bungalows Claire's heart sank again.

Inside, the paint was peeling from the grey walls and a squadron of flies buzzed angrily around the cobwebs hanging from the ceiling. Though the floors had obviously been swept fairly recently, it was not the kind of sweeping a Maising maid would think adequate. Claire peered dubiously into the bedrooms and was relieved to see no visible signs of animal life on the damp mattresses. With some trepidation, she pushed open the bathroom door. The lavatory, the Asian squat variety – a white china hole in the ground with ridges for feet on either side – was yuk but passable (she'd seen and smelt worse), as were the washing facilities, a huge earthenware jar of water with a small green plastic pouring bowl and a drain in the floor. Moving on to the kitchen, she saw an enormous red cockroach scuttling underneath the greasy cooker. The elderly refrigerator had been turned on and a small jar of coffee stood on one of the shelves. These were the only sign that their arrival had been expected.

Having earlier pronounced that it would be fun to dispense with maids for a weekend, Howard looked crushed. 'Probably a bit short of staff up here,' he said. 'I'll go and get hold of the game warden, but I don't know if he'll be able to send a cleaner at this hour.'

'Don't worry, we'll do it,' said Lucy briskly.

In no time at all and with the minimum of fuss, she had made the place bearable, if not immaculate. Deborah was busy with the children, so Claire tried to help in the kitchen, but she merely got in the way. The three men sat outside drinking gin until Lucy announced that the meal was ready.

'Well done, girls, good show, delicious,' said Martin in his toneless voice as they sat round the rickety wooden table.

'Yes, terrific,' said Howard absent-mindedly. 'Now, Martin, what is the situation about the bus contract? At the Bank we . . .'

'Lucy did most of the work,' interrupted Claire. 'Come on, you blokes, give her a big hand and tomorrow it's your turn to do dinner.'

'We expat chaps have not been brought up to cook. Deb can do it,' said Johnny, helping himself to yet more gin.

'But she has the children to put to bed.'

'I'll cook,' said Howard. 'You'd be surprised at my culinary skills. I seem to remember I once made spaghetti – about eight years ago, I think. It was quite acceptable.'

But Lucy said she loved cooking and would adore preparing another meal. Everybody hastily agreed that that would be the best idea.

'You're not much of a feminist, are you, Luce?' asked Deborah with a grin. 'Wait till you've been married a bit longer.'

Lucy laughed. 'No, I don't believe in that sort of thing.'

Dear Lucy, so old-fashioned but so efficient, thought Claire, wondering yet again if the poor girl could possibly be happy with baggy old Martin. But then when he remembered to look at his wife, he seemed delighted that she was there and his face became pinker and almost glowed. A dimmish sort of restrained civil servant glow, but a glow none the less. And he wasn't that bad looking, in a grey sort of way. He just looked totally out of place in the jungle, an intelligent codfish in shorts. Better than the lecherous snake Johnny anyway. Why did darling Deb ever fall for him in the first place? Claire knew the answer to that – the wrong lust at the wrong time.

Next day, as Johnny disappeared with a camera leaving his family alone, Claire persuaded Howard that they should accompany Deborah and her children on a visit to the waterfall, one of the highlights of the park, according to the guidebook.

When they reached the gorge, Howard offered to carry baby Jojo down the precipitous wooden steps. Claire went ahead, picking her way carefully, brushing aside the green foliage for Sam who had adopted the expedient of crawling down backwards. She reached the bottom first and looked back at the others. In the jungle scene, Howard made a handsome picture, like some latter-day Tarzan, large and fair, carrying the small child with blue eyes. Claire noticed anew how blonde Jojo looked beside her dark brother.

The waterfall was tall and spectacular, but the children were afraid to go near the roaring cascade of foam. No sooner had they sat down to admire the view from a safe distance than Sam started to whine that he was hungry and Jojo's nappy started to leak. So they were forced to return to the bungalow, Deborah apologizing profusely for the inconvenience of kids in general and hers in particular. But Howard said, generously in Claire's view, that the children were very good and no trouble.

Indeed, he genuinely seemed to like them, especially Jojo. Claire wondered if he was trying to impress her with his fatherhood potential.

The others returned from a long trek, having seen little of the promised wildlife except for the leeches that covered their legs. After a long discussion about leech prevention (thick socks soaked in tea), the horrible creatures were all removed.

'Never mind,' said Howard, still playing the part of hearty expedition leader. 'Tonight we can go on the game warden's safari lorry. They shine a powerful searchlight into the jungle so we'll see all the nocturnal mammals. We leave at ten o'clock. That's the best time to see animals, they say.'

In a rare paternal gesture, Johnny Case offered to look after his children so that Deborah could go on the night safari. He went out soon after dinner, however, to 'inspect the local watering holes' and by a quarter to ten he had not returned. Feeling that her need for solitude was greater than her desire to see a mouse deer, Claire volunteered herself as a substitute babysitter.

Alone in the secluded bungalow and aware of every unusual noise, she began to regret her kind offer. There certainly did seem to be more wildlife around at night. She kept hearing a sinister scratching noise outside the window and occasionally even on the roof. Then there was a thump outside the front door and it suddenly sprang open, but there was nothing in sight. Her heart beating, Claire wedged a chair behind the door.

A little later there was a loud bang. To her relief, she heard Johnny cursing. When she opened the door, he rolled in, dishevelled, sweaty and quite drunk. Pouring himself a tumbler full of neat whisky, he sat down beside her on the small sofa.

'Well, well, well, if it isn't the lovely Claire.'

Standing up, she smiled politely and said that she'd now be going back to her own bungalow.

He barred her way. 'Have a little drinkie first.'

Claire decided that it was better not to argue and accepted the large tot that he poured her.

His eyes shone as he examined her legs in the pink shorts. 'Always fancied you, you know,' he said with a leer.

She did not reply, but gulped her drink with a view to escaping as quickly as possible.

He looked at his watch. 'The others won't be back for an hour, so there's plenty of time for you and me to get to know each other a bit better. Always promised to come sailing with me and you never did.'

'Johnny, I have to go now.'

But he grabbed her by the wrist and forced her to sit beside him.

'You're hurting my arm, you moron,' she said sharply. But she couldn't pull away. He was much stronger than she was.

'Isn't that what you women like, a bit of rough stuff?' He licked her ear, breathing fumes of whisky over her.

She turned her head away. 'No, it damn well isn't. Look, Johnny, what about Deborah?'

'What indeed? What about old Deborah? I suspect my dear wife is up to something. I think she's having a bit on the side. What do you think, Claire?'

'I . . . I don't know what you mean.'

'I bet you do, but never mind about old Deb. I'll sort her out myself.' He patted her thigh. 'Did you know that there's no law against rape in Maising? The islanders know a thing or two about sex, about how badly women want it.'

Claire took a deep breath. 'I thought I heard Sammy crying. He may come in.'

Johnny turned his head to listen. The thought of his son seemed to sober him, but then he put his face close to hers again. 'We could go to your cabin and lock the door,' he said.

She tried to remain calm, but her voice was full of disgust. 'Johnny, you bloody fool, if you don't let me go, I swear I'll scream.'

'No one to hear you, my lovely.' He pulled her towards him and tried to jab his knee between her legs.

She pushed and turned, beginning to panic. 'Yes, there is, there's Sammy. He's already restless. He came in – just before you got back. He couldn't sleep – bad dream – did you hear that? He called out. You must've heard it. Johnny, you heard Sammy, didn't you?' she asked desperately.

'Sam . . . Sam,' repeated Johnny, his face close to hers. Then he suddenly released her. 'Well, maybe we'd better make it another time. You just give me the signal, Claire.'

She ran to her own cabin and locked the door. Shaking with rage, she paced about until the others returned.

Howard laughed at her security precautions. 'There are no bears or tigers on the island, you know. But in fact you didn't miss much because the passengers on the truck made so much bloody noise that all the animals had obviously buggered off to the other side of the forest.'

'Not quite all of them,' muttered Claire. She almost burst out with the whole story, but somehow managed to restrain herself.

On the damp lumpy mattress, she found it difficult to relax that night. She refused to make love with Howard, whispering that the walls of the cabin were so thin, and anyway she was tired. He did not protest and turned away to sleep. She lay back, wide awake. She would not tell Deborah about Johnny. She would tell no one. He had probably been too drunk for anything more than a quick grope, but whatever his intentions the incident had upset her a great deal. Everything she saw seemed to point against the idea of married happiness. Deborah and the drunken creep Johnny; Lucy and pompous old Martin who treated her like a halfwit.

Yes, the walls of the cabin were like paper. She could hear Lucy and Martin in the throes of love-making and conceded that Deborah was right about one thing: the passionate sex life of this unlikely couple. But she wondered anew if hot sex in a hot climate was a strong enough basis for happy marriage.

SIXTEEN

'Did you like the National Park, my dear? The Ambassador and I always enjoy it enormously,' said Helena, settling back in the large sofa upholstered in green and yellow floral chintz. So wonderfully British, thought Lucy each time she came here.

She had been admitted to the private sitting room which, being only about twenty feet long, was more intimate than the grand reception rooms of the Residence, but still hardly cosy. A uniformed maid brought coffee on a large silver tray and began, rather apprehensively, to pour it into gold-crested cups, but Helena waved her imperiously away and completed the task herself.

'Come, Lucy, tell me about your weekend,' she said, smiling in a manner that was almost jolly.

'Well, we didn't see a lot of nature – apart from the insects inside the bungalow, that is.'

Helena seldom recognized Lucy's few attempts at humour.

'Oh dear me,' she said. 'It's very important to take the right sort of binoculars and appropriate reference books. What sort of camera do you use?'

'I don't know. I mean, Martin has something Japanese, fairly basic. Anyway, we didn't take many photographs.'

Helena was horrified. She went on to describe all the wildlife that presented itself to the ambassadorial lens: the rare orchids, the hornbills, the wild pigs, deer, tapir, how they usually stayed in the private lodge of their very dear friend, the Prince, and would go on marvellous safaris where he'd take them to a marvellous hide from which they could see just about everything there was to see.

This led to an enquiry about which members of the Maising royal family Lucy knew. When she confessed to not being acquainted with any of them, Helena launched into a lecture on how important it was for wives to help their husbands make the right sort of contacts by meeting the right sort of people and inviting them to one's home.

'I hope you went on a course at the Foreign Office before you married,' she said severely.

Lucy tried hard not to be intimidated, but her voice began to betray the nervousness that Helena induced. 'No, as I think I told you, I would like to have done, but there wasn't time.'

'One should make time for these things. In your case, it would have been a very good idea. Still, no doubt you have studied the Guidance Notes on diplomatic life. Of course there are some modern versions designed for junior staff, but the older handbooks are so much better – one can learn so much from people like Dame Angela and Sir Harold.'

'Oh.'

'Have you read them, my dear?'

'No, I, er . . . they don't seem to hand them out these days.'

'I will send you round my copies. I think it will help you

to know how things should be done.' Helena pursed her lips and stared hard at the unpromising material in front of her. 'And how are you getting on with the Maising language? Not easy, I know, particularly for those, er, less accustomed to learning.'

'Well, actually I was just on my way to put my name down for some classes at the American Institute,' said Lucy, proud of this resolution. She'd decided to enrol because she wanted to please Martin, and anyway it was frustrating not to be able to communicate, not even to be able to ask the way to the nearest post box.

Helena's eyebrows quivered upwards. 'The American Institute? Oh dear, I think you'd find rather an odd type of person there.'

'But all the teachers are from Maising, properly qualified.'

'What sort of standard, what sort of qualifications, I wonder. You'd be far better hiring a private teacher like Professor Mrs Jaan – the FO will pay, you know. Mrs Jaan is from an awfully good intellectual Maising family. I found her rather a tyrant about verbs and vocabulary lists, but just what one needs. Of course she is used to teaching Oxbridge graduates, such as the Ambassador and me, but I am sure she can adapt to all kinds of people. I tell you what, I will telephone her now, this minute.'

Ignoring Lucy's feeble protests, Helena picked up the telephone and made the necessary, or unnecessary, arrangements.

Eventually Lucy managed to bring the conversation round to the purpose of her visit: arranging the date of the next meeting of the Diplomatic Service Families Association. Eventually she was able to make her escape.

An audience with Helena always left her shaking with mixed feelings of anger and inadequacy. This afternoon she felt the need to work off her tension in the Embassy pool, though generally she preferred to swim in the early morning when the place was uncrowded and when there was no one to stare at her bust.

Today she found a group of wives lounging beside the water and several noisy children splashing about.

As usual, Sandra, the plumpest of these women, was complaining. 'I said to the management officer, I said, what's the point in leaving my nice home in England and my job if

I have to live in a poky little flat abroad. The conditions of service are not what they were, I said. And the furniture, you should see the furniture they provided, cheap and nasty teak units. I haven't even got a cabinet to display my crystal.'

She wiped some of the sweat off her freckled chest and continued. 'I mean, in the old days there was always the duty-free fags to console you, but now, what with my health, the doctor says I should stop smoking. But I don't want to put on weight, I said to him, and when your hubby smokes it's hard to give up, I told him. And when you're living in a country like this you need something to cheer you up, don't you?'

The women nodded their heads. After more discussion about the poor quality of Foreign Office furniture in general and that supplied in Maising in particular, another wife raised the subject of maids, always a popular topic among the expats. Though few of them would be able to afford to employ a cleaner for two hours a week back home, some did not treat their full-time servants here that kindly, Martin had told her.

'Do you know what my maid did the other day? She put the kettle on with no water in it. She does it time after time. I said to her, I said, if you do that again, I'll dock your wages. You've got to be firm with them,' said Sandra.

Lucy sat and listened, waiting for the children to come out of the water for crisps and drinks, allowing her space to swim a length or two. It occurred to her that in some ways she sympathized with these women living this unnatural life so far from home. For instance, she knew she'd enjoyed the national park weekend because she'd been able to cook and play house with no maids about. However, she could not bear the gloomy atmosphere around the pool created by the endless stream of complaints. It made her feel all the more depressed – would she end up just like them, or worse, just like Helena?

Thank God that tomorrow she had half-planned to see Deborah, who was always cheerful and positive, who actually appeared to like living abroad, possibly because she had no real home anywhere else. Deborah had been preoccupied with children at the weekend, but maybe now she'd have time for a chat. Abandoning the idea of a swim, Lucy went home to telephone her.

Deborah's voice was warm and friendly. 'Sure, Lucy, we're

going on a trip tomorrow. I have a plan to visit those ruins we saw when we went with Beth on the bus. You remember Ravi, the place with all the Buddhas and the village that had the statue of Queen Victoria?'

'Yes, I remember. I'd love to come.'

'Great. Well, er, I also planned on taking Alex, he's the son of the Manager of BP. I promised his stepmother I'd show him around. So it'd be great if you'd come along. I'll pick you up at a quarter of nine. Not too early for you, is it? Only it gets kind of warm out there at this time of year.'

When they reached the Ravi ruins next morning, it was already more than kind of warm. Lucy had slept badly the night before. She felt the sweat trickling down her back as soon as she left Deborah's air-conditioned car. The monsoon rains that everyone droned on about must come soon.

As they walked haphazardly around the dark-red ruins, Lucy knew she was meant to be absorbing the past, but her mind was on the present. She had hoped to have the opportunity to confide in Deborah, but the boy Alex stuck close to them.

Deborah in turn paid him a great deal of attention. Lucy thought it kind of her to show so much interest in a teenager. He was a tall thin boy, handsome in a blond sort of way, but scruffily dressed in torn jeans. He spoke little but smiled a great deal. Lucy thought he probably had a bit of a crush on Deb.

Deborah, surprisingly elegant in flowing cream cotton, was even more animated than usual. 'Let's go see if we can find that Meng guy. Maybe he even started the dig. You'd like to meet a genuine live local archaeologist, wouldn't you, Alex? He was working way over in that direction last time.'

They found Meng standing over a group of workmen in coolie hats. They were digging within a square marked off with twine and putting the earth into cone-shaped leather bags. They emptied the bags into a barrow for Meng to examine and then pushed the barrow to a mound some feet away. Just watching them made Lucy feel hotter still.

Meng recognized them immediately and, without much prompting from Deborah, began to expound on his work. Nothing had been found so far, he said, but his coolies were well enough trained to stop the moment they struck stone or brick instead of earth.

Deborah asked a series of intelligent questions while Alex and Lucy looked on. But Meng made the effort to include Lucy in the conversation. Indeed he seemed to want to give her the answers to Deborah's questions. Lucy tried to concentrate, but it was so hot that she began to feel peculiar. Her head swimming, she sat down suddenly on the hot stone steps and closed her eyes. She heard voices around her, far away. She had the sensation of being carried somewhere and then no sensation at all.

SEVENTEEN

When Lucy opened her eyes again she was in a car, but it was not Deborah's comfortable red station wagon. It was a small elderly green vehicle with hard sticky seats and Meng was at the wheel.

'Hello,' he said. 'Welcome back.'

'What's happening? Where's Deborah?' To her own ears, her voice sounded peculiarly weak and strained.

'Well, you see, you passed out and I offered to take you to the doctor because I know the way to the nearest surgery and Deborah doesn't.'

'Oh.'

'Anyway, the digging had more or less ended for today so I was free, but Deborah still hadn't finished showing Alex around.'

'Oh.'

'But she made me promise to ring her to tell her how you were as soon as possible.'

With a great effort, Lucy finally managed to express herself. 'I feel fine, honestly. Just the heat. I don't need to go to the doctor. Please don't take me. I hate doctors. I'll be fine at home. Can you drop me somewhere I can get a taxi?'

'My house is near here. You can rest there until the evening. Then we won't get stuck in a hot traffic jam.'

'I'd rather go home,' murmured Lucy faintly. It really was too bad of Deborah to dump her with this man.

'My maid will look after you – we'll soon be there.'

She had no further strength to protest, and stared out of the window at the suburban maze of houses. She had no idea where she was.

Meng turned down one unmade lane after another, all exactly the same, it seemed. Eventually he stopped the car beside a high concrete wall and unlocked a solid iron gate. Once inside this unpromising boundary, she saw a traditional wooden house with a small well-kept garden. She was slightly reassured. If he lives in such a sweet little villa, he must be all right, she said to herself.

Meng was obliged to help her out of the car and up the steps on to the verandah. Supporting her with one arm, he pushed open the fly screen and unlocked the front door calling loudly for the maid. There was no reply.

'She must be out,' he said in a worried tone. 'Stupid old woman, I told her I'd be home for lunch.'

'I'm not hungry. Can I just have some water?' Lucy sat down suddenly on a rattan day bed with a pale blue cover.

When he had gone in search of refreshments, she looked around. The shutters were drawn against the heat, but she could see clearly that the room was full of treasures, like an antique shop but not as well organized. Every surface was covered in objets d'art, pottery, porcelain, bronze, jade and ivory statuettes and carved animal figures. No wonder the maid had taken the morning off – she was probably exhausted from trying to dust all the items. Lucy was always interested in domestic problems.

Meng returned with a jug of fresh lime juice and some biscuits on a tray. With elaborate care, he placed them on a small lacquer table beside her and then announced that he was going out to look for the errant servant. After drinking two glasses of juice, Lucy began to feel better. The ceiling fan rotated above her. She closed her eyes, listening to the whining whirring noise it made.

She didn't know how much time had passed when she next heard Meng's voice. 'Aha, the sleeping beauty.'

She sat up quickly, straightening her skirt.

'I'm sorry, but old Bin has disappeared entirely – she is somewhat unreliable,' he said.

'I think I'd better go home. My husband will be worried.'
This was untrue as she was not expected back until the evening.
She stood up but was obliged to sit down again.

'See, you are still unwell.' He smiled at her, crinkling his
fine black eyes. 'You are not nervous about being here alone
with me, are you?'

'Well, I . . .'

'You needn't be concerned about me. I am no threat to
women. You see, I am celibate.'

'Oh,' faltered Lucy.

'Yes, you know it is normal for a Buddhist to spend a while
as a monk. Well, I decided that monastic life was not for me,
even for a short time. So I made a vow to renounce as many
earthly desires as possible. I couldn't live without my art
treasures, so I renounced both love and meat.'

'Oh.'

'Actually, my sex drive was never strong and I found it
easier to give up pleasures of the human flesh than to become
a vegetarian. Interesting that the phrase "pleasures of the flesh"
should encompass so many earthly desires, isn't it?'

Lucy was not sure what he meant. His conversation was
far too frank for her taste, but his manner was serious and
entirely unflirtatious. She must have imagined the admiring
looks he had thrown her way when they first met. Nevertheless,
she couldn't help being aware of the fact that he was a very
good-looking man.

She decided to change the subject. 'I love your house,' she
said.

'Thank you. I'll show you round later when you feel better.'

'This room is so pretty and so interesting. All these
ornaments and books – and I like that wall of photographs.
Are they pictures of sites where you did your digging? Did
you take any of them?'

'All of them. Photography is one of my hobbies. Let me
show you my albums. You can look at them while I go and
find you something to eat.' He went to a pile of black port-
folios in the corner and selected four. He placed them on the
table beside her and went out of the room.

Each contained some fifty large black and white prints. She
admired the set of archaeological views, then some scenes of
village life, followed by a set of sea pictures. In the last folder

she found portraits of several different oriental women, all young, all beautiful. Lucy studied them, envying their hair and their skin. Then she put the folder down quickly for the remainder of the shots were male and female nudes, or part nudes of buttocks and breasts, artistically photographed in discreet non-pornographic poses, but still quite naked.

When he returned with a tray of small sweet cakes, she made polite remarks about his photography, concentrating on the landscapes. She did not mention the nudes as he'd probably given them to her by mistake, but to be on the safe side, she decided it best to change the conversation again, this time to a subject that had been on her mind for some time.

'Do your coolies at the dig come from that village you took me and Deborah to when we first met you?' she asked.

'Some of them do. Why?'

'Oh, well, I just, er, was interested in the statue of Queen Victoria. You know the way the village people sort of worship the statue and the spirits and stuff.'

'Yes, Lucy, you're right. These villagers and their customs and animist beliefs are fascinating. I think that if I hadn't been an archaeologist I should like to have studied anthropology. But of course that involves leading an even more uncomfortable life than my own because most primitive tribes worth studying live in the middle of the jungle or up some grim mountain. Easily accessible people like the villagers you met have already been the subject of at least two books, one in French and one in English. Would you like to borrow one?'

'Uh, is it very scholarly?'

He smiled. 'Perhaps a bit heavy. Pity really, because one could make a book of quite readable tales. They're so amusing, those peasants. They are frightened of so many things and so much of their life is spent propitiating the spirits. Did you know that the village elders are afraid of the water spirits and have refused to allow bamboo aqueducts to be constructed, even though they were offered aid to pay for them? So the young women still have to fetch water every day, and it's forbidden to bring it inside the house. All the cooking has to be done outdoors, and those villagers who are not afraid to bathe always use exterior wash-huts.'

'D'you mean to say some of them are really afraid of water?'

'Yes, that's why the older ones smell a bit.'

Lucy laughed. 'What about the Spirit Woman? Does she wash?'

'Sometimes, when the moon is full or the auspices are good. But she is not afraid of the spirits for she uses them to make her lotions and potions.'

'What sort of potions?' Lucy tried to make her voice sound casual.

'Well, she has many kinds, all made from herbs and mysterious juices from trees. She has potions for diarrhoea, constipation and skin rashes. In fact, to cure your heat exhaustion just now, I added one of her medicines to the lime juice.'

'You didn't tell me.' Lucy was faintly annoyed, though she had always been interested in herbal remedies.

'But it worked, didn't it? You look much better.'

'So have you got any other spirit medicines?'

'Yes, I bought a sample of a dozen or so. I thought I might get a friend to analyse them. All in the cause of scientific research, you know.'

'Oh.' Lucy let him chat on for a while, then she said, 'Have you got any to spare? I could pay you.'

He smiled. 'Any what?'

'Er, potions from the Spirit Woman.'

'What kind would you like?'

'Well . . .' She stopped, unable to bring herself to say any more.

'Let me guess. You look pretty healthy. I don't think it can be an ailment. And it can't be a love potion because I am sure you are loved. I think a young married woman like you might be interested in fertility.'

Lucy blushed deeply.

'Am I right?'

She nodded.

'I saw you give money to the Spirit Woman and I always have the right instincts about women's problems. I think if I hadn't been an archaeologist, I should have been a gynaecologist.'

'But I thought you just said an anthro-something.'

'Yes, I am a man of many interests.' He smiled. 'It so happens I do have a sample of the fertility potion which I will happily give you, but maybe you would prefer to consult the Spirit Woman directly. That would be best.'

Lucy said she could never be brave enough to do such a thing. Suddenly she found she couldn't stop talking. It was a great relief to be able to discuss her problem with somebody. Meng was extraordinarily understanding for a man. He said it was not unusual for conception to be delayed a few months, even a year or so. She mustn't worry. The Spirit Woman would tell her that it was obvious that the most auspicious time to conceive had not yet come for her. She would have a special child and one must wait for special children, for they were a gift from the gods.

He left the room and returned with a small blue phial. 'I have just one dose remaining. I am told it is quite powerful. You must take it at the time of the month you feel particularly ready for love, just before you go to bed. Would you like something for your husband as well?'

Lucy smiled at the thought. 'No, really, no. Er, how will I know when it is best to take it?'

'I will have to leave that to your female instincts. If you have faith, you will know.'

The conversation turned to the islanders' fertility rituals and to the spirits and their mysterious works. Entranced by Meng's tales, it was with some shock that Lucy realized it was mid-afternoon. She asked to be taken home and to be dropped some distance from the Embassy as she did not want her maids to get the wrong impression.

Relieved that Somjit was not waiting for her, Lucy slipped in through the front door. She went straight to the study and hid the phial at the back of her desk drawer. Then she telephoned Deborah to ask her not to tell Martin she had fainted, so he wouldn't worry.

'It's a relief you're OK,' said Deborah. 'I was worried about you.'

Not that worried, thought Lucy. She said aloud, 'Thank you, but next time we see you, don't mention Meng, will you? Martin might not understand.'

'OK. I felt bad about letting him take you to the doctor without me, but he insisted he could take care of you. I was going to follow in my car, but Alex was on the other side of the ruins and by the time I'd collected him you'd disappeared and then when I got home I phoned, but you weren't back and . . .'

'It's all right. I was fine.'

'But about Meng – he seemed a nice guy, gentle and kind. He didn't get too friendly, did he?'

'Oh, no. He's not like that.'

'Good, that's what I thought. I knew you'd be OK with him. What was the matter with you anyway, Luce? You aren't pregnant, are you?'

'Oh, no. No way. It was just the heat.'

EIGHTEEN

The private letters bag arrived on a Friday morning at the British Embassy. As usual, Lucy sat on the terrace before lunch waiting for Martin to return with her mail. She watched as he crossed the lawn, avoiding the sprinklers left to play all day by the languid gardeners. He looked tired and crumpled, and older than usual, but he smiled so happily when he caught sight of her that her heart jumped a little. She had been reading *Woman's World* on the subject of marriage vows and had decided that most of the time her marriage was definitely for better rather than for worse. Worse: she was not pregnant and had still not discussed the fact with him. Better, no, best: he seemed to love her more and more.

She kissed him rapidly. 'Any letters?'

'More interested in the mail than in your husband, aren't you?'

'Today, yes,' said Lucy. This was their little Friday joke.

She sifted through the letters looking for her mother's spidery handwriting, but there was nothing from her, nor from matron. She opened the most interesting envelope, the one with a round girlish scrawl she vaguely recognized, and began to read.

'Martin, guess what? I've had a letter from Porky Pritchard. She says her husband Jazzer wants to come and stay.'

'Oh, when?' Martin never sounded particularly enthusiastic about her friends.

'Quite soon, in three weeks' time.'

'Oh, dear,' he said. 'I'll be rather busy liaising on the bus contract. That is to say, matters should be coming to fruition.'

'What contract?'

'The contract to supply new local buses. I told you it was coming up – the Embassy is keen that British Coachworks should win rather than the Japanese. In fact, we've even got a Minister coming out from London to wave the flag. But you won't be involved so I suppose it's all right to have a guest. You can look after this Jazzer person yourself.'

'Funnily enough, Porky mentions something about buses and her husband is an MP, you know.'

'Really? What sort of an MP? Tory, Labour, Raving Loony Workers for Freedom?'

Lucy smiled. 'Well, he used to be Conservative, but he changed to Labour, though he isn't the Labour type at all, of course. Maybe you could call him a lefty toff.'

'I can't think of anyone called Pritchard.'

'That's her maiden name, sorry. I always call her that because we were at school together. Jazzer, her husband, is James Jamison-Smith. I don't suppose he's at all important, but maybe you've heard of him.'

He raised his eyebrows. 'My God, of course I've heard of him, Lucy, he's the bloody Minister of Export Trade, the one we're expecting. But he's a VIP – he'll be staying with the Ambassador.'

'Oh, yes, Porky put some sort of PS about that. Let me read it. This is what she says: "Jazzer doesn't want to stay with the Ambo because he is a boring old fart married to a vicious old tart." Quite a poem, but a bit strong, don't you think?'

'For God's sake, Lucy, keep your voice down.' Martin was trying not to laugh.

'I'm only reading out what Porky says.'

'Nevertheless, it is practically *lèse-majesté*.'

'What does that mean?'

'It means treasonable talk. Good God, does she really say that?' Martin began to laugh so loudly that his face, even his ears, turned quite red. Finally he said, 'Anyway, I am sure Helena won't approve of his staying here.'

'Apparently his office is going to send the Ambassador an email saying that Jazzer has made up his mind to stay with us and that's that.'

'Then it seems we have no choice. Hope you'll be able to cope with a ministerial guest, Lulu.'

She smiled. 'Well, it's only Jazzer. He's small and fat, if I remember rightly – bit like Porky herself.'

'He may be Jazzer to you, but to the rest of us he's a major VIP and we have to treat him accordingly.'

'I expect I'll manage.'

Last month *Woman's World* had had a feature on confidence building and she was trying to follow the advice given.

She received the expected summons to the Residence later that afternoon. Helena was pacing angrily around the terrace, shouting at the servants about a pot plant that had been incorrectly watered. As soon as she saw Lucy, she stopped berating the maids mid-sentence and turned her fire.

'Lucy, I don't think it is at all suitable for a Minister of State to stay at a Counsellor's house.'

'No, well, er, perhaps not, but . . .'

'The Ambassador tells me he has received rather a peremptory message on the subject stating that Mr Jamison-Smith wishes to be your guest.'

'Well, his wife . . .'

'I am afraid that I do not regard it as a point in your favour that the Minister has disregarded protocol. However, it would appear that there is little one can do about it. I think I had better come over to your house just before the Minister arrives and check that the arrangements you have made are in order. It will reflect badly on the whole Embassy if everything is not as it should be.'

'That really won't be necessary,' said Lucy, stung into some sort of response at last. She paused in shock at her own daringly defiant remark. 'Jazzer, I mean, James is quite an informal person.'

Helena sniffed and ran her hands through her damp black hair revealing that the roots needed retouching. 'Obviously he must be.' She gave Lucy another severe look. 'I do feel you should call him Minister rather than Jazzer.'

Lucy breathed in and out. Then she tried to be tactful. 'Anyway, since we would have to look after official visitors when you and the Ambassador are on home leave, maybe having Mr Jamison-Smith to stay will be good practice for me.'

Helena sniffed again. 'Well, at least you have a well-trained maid, thanks to your predecessor. I suppose I shall just have to let you carry on, but please come to me if you have any problems.'

As Lucy walked home across the compound, she was aware of having won some sort of minor victory in the battle of life. She had asserted herself and Helena had capitulated, even tried to help.

Despite her brave words, she did become rather nervous during the weeks leading up to Jazzer's arrival. Martin came back every day with a new version of the Minister's programme, neatly printed out on pale azure crested stationery.

'He'll be having most of his meals at the Residence or out, Lucy, so you will only have to do one dinner party and a working breakfast.'

'Entertaining people to breakfast? Oh goodness, Nee is hopeless at cooking eggs and things, she fries everything in smelly oil. I mean, her idea of a hot breakfast is fish soup with chillies. I suppose I could get some of that local bacon, but it's so fatty. And there hasn't been any cereal in the shops for weeks apart from soggy out-of-date American cornflakes. Are you sure Jazzer will approve of the working brekky idea? I don't think he's the sort of chap to eat much in the morning and you have made such busy days for him he won't have any spare time at all.'

'Don't be silly, darling. He's not meant to have much spare time. It's not a holiday, though I admit he is going on to Bali afterwards. This whole programme is agreed with his office in London in advance. If the Minister doesn't like any of the arrangements, his Private Secretary will let us know.'

Jazzer was very short, about Lucy's height, with thin mousy hair slicked straight back. His face was round and unlined and his bright blue eyes confident, his manner extremely friendly. He wore a smart pale grey tropical suit and pungent aftershave. One could almost touch the charm he exuded, a charm which could be turned up and up to an exceedingly warm glow.

When he was settled in the corner of the drawing room sofa, drinking Earl Grey out of one of Lucy's best wedding-present cups, she remembered that she did not like him very

much. He was one of those men who stared at her chest in a
not particularly nice way.

'Dear old Luce, Porky sends you lots and lots of hugs and
kisses. Can't wait till we're alone so I can deliver them direct,
straight from the stallion's mouth, as they say.'

Lucy decided to ignore the stallion aspect. 'How is Porky?'

'Oh, she's a bit bogged down by the sprogs. Jolly tricky
when they're at different schools.'

'Do tell me about them, what are they all up to?' She hoped
that by concentrating on his children, she would deflect Jazzer's
attention from the top button of her blouse.

'Well, Henry has just started at prep school, poor little chap.
It was rather a wrench for Porky. One knows in theory that
one's sons are going away at eight, just as one did oneself,
but when the time comes it's quite a blow.'

'Poor Porky.'

'Yes, and Nanny was frightfully cut up too.'

'But Sophie and Persephone are still at home?'

'Yes, Soso's going to the village primary school at the
moment. Porky wasn't keen on the idea, but it's good for the
image to be democratic in these matters.'

'And is she going to the local comprehensive after that?'

'Oh, no, Porky wouldn't wear that. We thought Godolphin,
just like you and Porkers. I'm sure you approve, even if my
cabinet colleagues don't.'

'And the baby?'

'Yes, darling little Persie. Not really a baby now – goes to
some sort of nursery school run by one of Porky's chums.
Haven't seen much of any of the kids lately. You know old
Porks prefers to stick in the country. She loathes my pad in
Westminster and everything to do with politics. Can't blame
her . . . Oh, damn the fellow, there's young Simon making
signals.'

The Private Secretary, serious and shining, knocked on the
glass door and wafted in. 'Do excuse me. Minister, there are
some urgent messages from the Office.'

'Sorry, Luce my love, no peace for the wicked, duty calls
and all that.'

The working breakfast, for men only, was not as difficult
to organize as Lucy had feared since no foreign dignitaries

attended, but the dinner for Jazzer was another matter. As well as the Ambassador and some important local British businessmen, a member of the royal family and the Chief Transport Minister of Maising were invited, plus their wives, who didn't really count, Martin said, but one had to invite them.

Lucy changed her mind about the menu so many times that Nee, the fat old cook, became confused. Then Lucy had to ask Somjit to reorder the food to be on the safe side.

When the great day of the party came, even Somjit became nervous and kept ordering Boo, the number two maid, to dust and redust all the furniture, arrange and rearrange all the flowers, sweep and resweep the floors, lay and relay the table. She made beautiful water lilies with the table napkins and then Boo was forced to re-iron some of them because a crease was found in the wrong place. Lucy watched all this, just as she watched Nee waddle backwards and forwards to the shops for items she had forgotten, her fat face running with sweat. Lucy did not dare to intervene amongst her three servants in case she made matters worse, so she just paced about in the drawing room becoming more and more edgy.

Martin spent hours working out the placement at the dinner table. All very complicated, he said, because of the seniority of the people present.

'Please don't put me next to the Prince or the Maising Minister – I won't know what to say to them,' begged Lucy.

'But you're the hostess. Actually, I might put Jazzer and the Ambo in the middle, then we can have some guests of honour in the middle and some at the end. Of course, Jazzer has got to have a chance to talk to the Trade Minister, so I'll put him in the middle too. It's terribly difficult. I'll have to check the book.'

To calm her nerves, Lucy had two gins and the party itself passed like a not particularly pleasant dream. Before dinner the women huddled in a group and whispered to each other while the men Exchanged Views in loud voices. It was clear that none of the guests noticed the food, let alone the flowers, except that one wife was semi-vegetarian and had to have an omelette instead of the overcooked beef. This caused such confusion amongst the maids that they forgot to serve the special sauce which Lucy had spent hours making the day before. But the efficient wine waiter hired for the night kept all the glasses topped up.

During the dinner, the Prince on Lucy's right said nothing at all, and the dignitary on her left talked almost exclusively to the pretty Maising woman sitting next to him. Even if Lucy had wanted to join in their conversation she could not, for they spoke in their own language. Still, the meal was passable and everyone except Lucy and the Prince appeared to be having a good time. As was normal in Maising society, they all left immediately after coffee had been served, an excellent custom in Lucy's view.

When they were alone in their bedroom afterwards, Martin congratulated her, saying it had all gone extremely well and Jazzer had told the Ambassador what an excellent job Martin was doing and if British Coachworks did get the contract to supply Maising with new buses then much of the credit should go to him.

Lucy decided not to say how much she had hated the party. Now it was over, she felt enormously relieved and happy that her husband was so happy. He took her into his arms and kissed her passionately. 'Come to bed, my darling.'

Lucy hesitated. She said she had to fetch something from downstairs. She didn't say what. She was feeling distinctly amorous herself, so it must be the right night to take the blue fertility potion that was sitting at the back of her desk drawer.

The potion was revolting, like stale fish laced with chilli, and she was obliged to drink some juice to take the taste away. As she was replacing the juice in the refrigerator, she noticed that Nee had failed to cover some of the leftover food, so Lucy fetched the foil and completed the task herself. By the time she returned to bed, Martin was already asleep.

Poor lamb, he's exhausted, she thought tenderly. Never mind, there's always tomorrow. She lay down beside him. But all of a sudden she felt restless, as if she wanted to go for a long walk, hardly possible in Maising in the middle of the night. After tossing and turning for a while, she crept downstairs again to find some brandy to soothe her nerves.

In the neat but still smoky dining room, she opened the sideboard and took out a bottle of Rémy Martin and a brandy glass. As she unscrewed the cap of the bottle and poured herself a small tot, the verandah door opened.

'Secret drinking, eh, Luce,' boomed Jazzer. 'Better watch it.'

'Oh, Jazzer, er, would you like some brandy too?'

'Yes, please, old thing. A large one. Must say, you look rather luscious in your negligee.'

'It's just a cotton dressing gown, nothing fancy.'

'Maybe it's the shape inside that makes it look so pretty,' he said with a leer. Lucy did not want to ruin a successful evening by being rude, so she sought to change the subject. As she had used up all her questions about Porky and the children, she asked him about the House of Commons. This was an excellent choice as Jazzer found plenty to say on what a den of intrigue it was. Once in full flow, he talked well and she found him rather amusing. They both had another brandy.

'I say, Luce,' said Jazzer eventually, 'I've still got some files to read and I can't get my bedside light to work.'

'Oh dear, I am sorry. What a bad hostess I am! The electrical layout in this old house is very weird. You have to switch it on behind the curtain as well – the maid must have failed to check.'

'Which curtain?'

'The right-hand curtain near the bed, you know.'

He smiled innocently. 'There are so many curtains and doors in that room. Could you just come up and fix it for me? I do have to get the work finished tonight so Simon can send a telegram back to London first thing in the morning.'

They climbed the wide stairs together and went along to the end of the house to the guest bedroom which now smelt strongly of Jazzer's aftershave. In order to reach the switch behind the curtain, Lucy was obliged to stand on the edge of the bed. She had drunk rather too much that evening, however, to be entirely steady on her feet. Jazzer caught her as she was about to fall.

But he didn't let go. She started to pull away, laughing a little, but he pushed her back on to the bed laughing too. When he put his hand on her stomach and stroked it downwards, a normal Lucy would have slapped his face, but instead she gasped and lay still. Clearly encouraged by her passivity, Jazzer pressed on. And on.

It must have been three in the morning when Lucy opened her eyes. Due to the security lighting outside, the bedrooms in her house were never very dark so she could see quite clearly that she was not in her own room and that the man lying naked beside her, his hand on her left breast, was not her husband but Jazzer, Her Majesty's Minister for Export Trade.

He did not stir when she wriggled away from him. She gathered up her nightwear and slipped out of the room and along the balcony to her bathroom. Shaking with misery, she thanked God for the fact that the air-conditioning would drown the noise of the water and any other noises that had occurred in the night. Everything she'd worn smelt of Jazzer and his vile aftershave. When she had washed herself she flung her nightdress into the bath so that the maids wouldn't notice the unfamiliar scent.

She was angry and confused. Though he'd murmured something about *droit de seigneur*, Jazzer hadn't raped her. When it came to the point to say no, she'd just lain there in a trance. If she had screamed or torn his hair, he might have stopped, but she had kept silent, yielding. Why, oh why? She didn't like him, he wasn't attractive, she had been a little merry but certainly not blind drunk. She blew her nose and threw the tissue into the waste-paper basket. It landed next to the empty blue phial.

Oh God, the fertility potion – it must have caused her crazy behaviour. What if it also did what it was supposed to? What if she became pregnant with Jazzer's child? Weak and nauseated, she crept into her bedroom and lay down beside Martin who continued to snore contentedly.

NINETEEN

Deborah had noticed the large silver Embassy Jaguar waiting beside the dusty pavement, but when she entered Maising's smartest gift shop she was surprised to see Lucy rather than the Ambassador or his wife. Lucy, looking pale and strained, was accompanied by a small, fat young-to-middle-aged man who was talking a great deal. Deborah could see from the expression on her face that Lucy disliked this small, fat man.

'Hi, Lucy,' she called.

Lucy made the introductions. 'Er, Mr Jamison-Smith is a visitor from England. He's trying to buy a china or bronze cat for his wife who collects them. Do you think this is a good place?'

'Sure, a great selection, but did you try Jata's? They have more antique things there.'

'Doesn't have to be antique,' said Mr Smith. 'Just authentic Maising stuff. Poor Lucy, she has already taken me to at least five shops and now we've come back to look at the first cat I saw. What a marvellously patient hostess she is, a perfect FO wife.' He smiled at Deborah appraisingly. 'I must say, there are some stunning women in this country. Would you care to join us for a drink, Mrs Case? How about the Hilton just across the road?'

'Jazzer, we have to buy the cats and get back or you'll miss your plane,' said Lucy.

'Oh dear, well, if you come to London, get my address from Lucy, Mrs Case, or may I call you Deborah? I'd be so pleased to show you around the Houses of Parliament.' He gave Deborah another meaningful stare.

With maximum drama and confusion, he purchased three life-sized china cats and arranged for them to be sent to England. She noticed that as they left the shop, he was attempting to massage his hostess's bottom.

Deborah turned her mind to her mother-in-law's birthday present. She looked around at the display of brassware, china ornaments, silver filigree, woodcarving and wickerwork – goods and souvenirs that were exactly the same as in all the other stores in the town. She sighed. Muriel had everything that could possibly be purchased in Maising. She would wait and suggest that Johnny buy his mother something suitable in Hong Kong next week.

Nowadays Deborah found herself longing for her husband to go away. Every time he left the house in the morning, she mentally sighed with relief, and every time his key turned in the lock at night her heart sank. And when he left the country for a few days, she felt liberated and happy – not just because his departure left her free to spend more time with Alex, but because she had begun to detest Johnny.

Perhaps she had never liked him much in the first place,

and now that the sexual attraction between them was dying, there did not seem to be much remaining to hold them together. Apart from the children.

If she took the children and left, where would she go and what would she do? Could she support them and herself by teaching English or French? Probably not, not without a home to live in. She didn't have the courage to leave her comfortable expatriate existence and return to Europe or the States to live alone in poverty with two small children. Nor could she go back to her parents and admit the failure of the marriage they had been so against. She wondered how other couples survived and compromised once they fell out of love. Maybe some perfect marriages existed, but then some must be more imperfect than her own.

For instance, if her poor cowed father-in-law could endure Muriel, she could put up with Johnny – at least for now.

Deborah was dismayed to find herself sitting next to Jock at Muriel's birthday dinner. She had always tended to avoid Poppy's husband. He was a difficult man to talk to, never initiating a subject of conversation and always giving monosyllabic answers to attempts at small talk from females. He could become quite eloquent on the subject of money, but that was not a topic that interested her. Now that she was sleeping with his teenage son, she found it difficult to meet his eye, let alone make polite party conversation.

Fortunately Muriel claimed his attention during most of the meal. She was at her most flirtatious in a black lace gown which showed rather too much of her crumpled breasts. Now in her mid-sixties, she never forgot the fact that she had once been a beauty. Indeed her eyes were still round and fine, but her thin brows were redrawn into an exaggerated arch of surprise and her leathery cheeks over-rouged, giving her the air of an elderly doll. Her hair, newly tinted by Maising's premier hair salon, was now the colour of Victoria plums and she had applied matching purple-red lipstick which ran into tiny rivulets around her pursed mouth.

'Have some more, Debbie dear,' she said as the servants appeared with a second dish of fried duck.

'No, thanks very much, Muriel.'

'I understand – we girlies have to watch our weight, don't

we? Mind you, Jock, when I was Deb's age I was ever so thin. My admirers used to be able to span my tiny waist with their hands – and even when I had my little Johnny, I was slim as a reed only six weeks after.'

As Muriel continued to entertain them with stories about herself, Deborah was able to remain silent. From time to time she glanced at Jock's tombstone face, wondering how he came to father the sensitive, artistic Alex. Alex never mentioned his mother, and even Poppy was relatively reticent on the subject of her predecessor. She recalled Poppy's résumé of Alex's mother – 'A large cushion of a woman, messy and maternal, a painter of watery watercolours.'

Perhaps that's why he likes me, thought Deborah. He has an infant memory of cosy cushions of flesh.

'You're like a woman from an Old Master painting,' he'd remarked one day after they'd made love. 'No, I don't mean Rubenesque – more those women who picnicked naked on the grass, you know. Wonderful paintable powerful thighs and a delicious rounded stomach.' She had been immensely flattered that he had managed to make a virtue of her pear-shaped figure.

Sipping her wine absent-mindedly, she smiled at the memory. At that moment she caught Poppy's eye down the other end of the table and found herself flushing. It seemed that the returning smile from Poppy was cooler than normal.

When the elaborate meal was finally over, she was dismayed when Jock followed her on to the terrace. His expression was serious. 'I've been wanting to have a wee word with you, Deborah. Poppy was going to say something, but I gather you haven't been swimming with us lately.'

Oh Christ, they know, she thought, feeling sick with guilt. Her face white, she stared down, digging her fingers into the palms of her hands. Of course, it was bound to come out sooner or later. She was astonished that they had gotten away with it for so long in this small community. Especially when Alex stared at her in public the way he did.

Then Jock's words began to penetrate. 'We're very grateful to you for taking young Alex in hand, getting him out of the house. I hope he hasn't been a nuisance at all.'

She looked up. 'Uh, no.'

'He's a difficult boy. Talented but lazy. Spends too much

time lying in bed.' Deborah's face remained blank. Or rather
she hoped it did.

'The trouble is the boy has no ambitions. I'm very concerned
about his future. He's talking about giving up the idea of
university. He says he wants to live the simple life, paint,
blather like that. Poppy seems to think there is a woman
involved, perhaps an island girl – we don't know. He's very
secretive. Always going off and refusing to say where he is
going.'

She gulped and said nothing. Then she managed an
enquiring 'Oh?'

'Anyway, I'll get to the point. Poppy says the boy thinks
very highly of you – in fact, she thought at one point he had
a wee bit of a crush on you.' He smiled in a kindly way and
continued. 'We were just wondering if you would be willing
to try and persuade him that he must take up his place at
Oxford. He won't listen to us. But you are nearer his age. He
might take advice from you that he wouldn't take from us.'

Immensely relieved that they knew nothing about the love
affair, Deborah found herself gushing. Sure, OK, definitely,
she would do absolutely anything and everything she could
to help.

A few days passed before she could be alone with Alex.
He sat on the sofa looking expectantly at her.

Avoiding his arms, she took the chair opposite and said
casually, 'Shouldn't you be thinking of going back to Europe,
Alex? Surely the semester at Oxford must begin in September.'

'October actually. But I've more or less decided not to go.'

'What do you mean "not go"?'

'All that sort of stuff, dons and colleges and dreaming spires,
it doesn't seem all that relevant to real life.' He kept rubbing
his hands together. Then he stood up and began to pace around
the room. 'I thought,' he said, 'that we could all go somewhere like Bangkok – somewhere where no one knows us.
You could teach and I could get some sort of job – we could
take it in turns to look after the children.'

'Hey, wait a minute, you mean that we should go away
together, is that what you're saying?'

'Well, I love you.' He spoke as if that were the end of it.

'But Alex . . .'

'And you love me – or you seem to. In bed you, you couldn't be that passionate if you didn't love me. That's the way it seems to me, anyway.'

'Yes, I did, do love you, but . . .' She took a deep breath. 'It may be perverse, but I don't think I could ever really love the kind of guy who would give up his future, everything, for me.'

'I'm not giving up Oxford for you. I just don't want to go any more. I don't even want to talk about it. Dad and Poppy have moaned on and on about it.' His voice was tense.

'You're crazy. You have to think it over. Reconsider. But whatever you decide to do, you do alone. I can't go away with you. I'm a married woman, for God's sake.'

'Lots of women leave their husbands. And you don't even like yours, do you? Or you wouldn't have bothered with me. Everyone says Johnny is a—'

'Whatever I feel about him, I don't want to leave him right now. There's the kids, two kids.'

'We can take the children with us, as I said.' He smiled briefly. 'I like them too.'

'Yes, but Johnny is the father they know,' she said gently. 'And I guess I ought to stick with him for their sake.'

'But you don't love him.'

'No, I don't love him, but I can't leave.'

Alex turned angrily towards her 'Then you don't love me either. You were just playing games.'

She stared at him for a moment and then she spoke. 'I was unhappy before I met you – more unhappy than I realized, and you made me happy. You restored my faith in myself, made me feel female and desirable again. I hadn't felt that way in a long while and I'll always be grateful to you and always remember you. But I knew it was kind of a temporary thing and I guess I thought you did too. I can't exactly say what sort of love it was we had, but . . . but if we went away together you would start to hate me, and the kids too – no, let me finish – we'd hang round your neck like, I don't know, heavy burdens. You'd soon resent us all. You don't know what it is to have small children around all day, every day. You should be free at your age, young and free. I can't tie you like I got tied.'

'Why can't we be free together? I don't see why—'

'We just can't, not with kids and no money.'

'Money! You're as bad as Dad. I can earn money, you can earn money.'

'You and I won't earn freedom kind of money. Anyway, I'm too old for you. You know that.'

'What does age matter? In the papers you read about people who—'

'It matters. Alex, I'm sorry, but I know I'm right and when you're older you'll agree with me.'

'No, I won't. I'll just stay here in Maising till you change your mind.' He grabbed her by the shoulders.

'No, Alex, no. I don't want to be lovers any more. It's over. If we go on, everything will be spoilt. We have to end it now, when it's good.'

She pushed him away and took a step back. She could hardly bear to look at his face. He seemed puzzled and wounded, like a small child that doesn't understand why it is being punished.

'So you really don't love me. You were just pretending.'

'Oh . . . I can't explain. You must know I wasn't pretending, you must – but now I have to tell you that it's over.'

'So you don't love me enough to come away with me.'

'No, I mean, yes. I mean I like you too much to come away with you. You must go alone. I must stay here with my family and not act like some crazy lovesick school kid.'

'So I'm acting like a crazy school kid?'

'No, no. I didn't mean that, but it has to end.'

'You told me before, more than once, lots of times, that you wanted to end it and then it started up again,' he said, on the edge of breaking down.

'Yes, but now I'm serious, truly. Do you understand, I want to stop now while it's still special and not have it peter out, drag on to some terrible slow quarrelsome end – which it surely will. This way it'll finish when it's good and we'll remember it that way.'

He went to the drinks tray and poured himself a large whisky which he drank all at once, like medicine. She had never seen him drink spirits before.

'I need to make love to you one last time,' he said suddenly.

She smiled a little. 'If you want to, but it really does have to be the last time. Promise.'

'All right.'

He watched as she took off her clothes and then he made love to her, fiercely, peremptorily, with passion, but without tenderness, digging his hands into her back so that she thought she would cry out in pain. Then it was all over. As he lay above her, she felt his tears fall on her face.

Three days later he telephoned briefly to say that he was leaving the country and could they meet. As tactfully as she could, Deborah said this would not be a good idea. Johnny was around all the time at the moment.

'Come to the airport to see me off, then. Jock and Poppy will be there so I won't make a scene or do or say anything that will embarrass you. But I have to see you one more time.'

'OK.'

'Promise?'

'I promise.'

When she set off for the airport that evening, it began to rain heavily. Cursing, she reduced her speed. The rainy season was always a problem. Maising's inadequate drainage system could not cope with the sudden prolonged downpours and lakes of water formed at the sides of the road, making the crowded streets impassable. Suddenly the truck in front of her stopped. She came to a halt. Rain poured down. She could see nothing beyond the truck except a long blur of red tail-lights. Half an hour later she had moved no more than thirty metres. Trying to remain calm, she could do nothing but wait, hoping that the plane would be delayed. But it was another twenty minutes before the traffic began to move.

Eventually she arrived at the airport. She abandoned the car in a no-parking zone and ran through the puddles to the Departures building. Soaking and dishevelled, she bumped into Jock and Poppy on their way out.

'Sorry, my dear, you are too late. Appalling weather, we'll have floods soon, I dare say,' said Jock with a pleasant smile. He explained that contrary to all expectations the London flight had left on time.

'Alex asked me to give you this present – he said he was sorry to miss you,' said Poppy, less pleasantly. There was something hostile about her manner. If she had guessed the truth, it seemed she had not told Jock, but she did not smile when they said goodbye.

Deborah felt instinctively that their friendship had come to an end and that it was, of course, her own fault – another painful casualty of this crazy affair. She had behaved like a shit, betrayed a good friend and hurt a young man. All because she wanted to get back at Johnny.

Once she had returned to the car, she unwrapped the parcel and found a small framed pencil drawing of herself, well-executed, flattering. She recognized it as Alex's favourite. He had shown her only a few of the others, saying this was his only successful attempt, where he had really captured her face and her soul. It was the portrait that he had vowed to keep beside him for ever.

As she drove home through the rain, Deborah could not stop weeping.

TWENTY

The flood water was deep in the outer suburbs of Maising. Claire became increasingly nervous as she drove back from work that afternoon. It was a mistake to be driving in these conditions. She should have left her car at the office and taken the bus home. She lectured herself: must keep the engine running, drive slowly and steadily, but not too slowly. She tried to ignore the fact that the water was slapping against the bottom of the car. It was like being in a boat, a boat with no rudder, a very unpleasant sensation.

Then water started to seep through the doors and a small pool formed around her feet. She drove on past several cars which had broken down. She could see that the islanders were making desperate attempts to shore up shop doorways with sandbags. Unlike her, they all looked cheerful and in high spirits.

Fighting down a feeling of panic, she contemplated turning around while her engine was still working. She could return to Jean-Louis' compound where the land was higher and as yet unflooded. But she didn't fancy staying at his house overnight.

With a bang, one of her wheels struck an invisible pothole in the road. Her car stalled and refused to start again. Grinning delightedly, two small boys who had obviously been waiting for just such an occurrence waded through the water with cries of 'We help, madame.' Brandishing a can of water-repellent, they opened the bonnet of the car and sprayed the oil liberally around. She tried the starter again and to her immense relief, the engine turned and fired. Thrusting a generous tip into the hands of her rescuers, she set off again.

Her mistake was to take a side road with the idea of turning round. The car died again in a narrow lane where there was nobody in sight. On the verge of tears, she sat for a moment in her wet skirt and very wet shoes. Who could she ring? The local garages would be hopelessly busy. There must be cars broken down all over Maising. Howard probably wouldn't want to risk bringing out his precious BMW.

Then she thought of Drew and the Land Rover, the all-weather vehicle. He lived quite near to where she now found herself. That's probably why she had turned down this stupid lane, because she'd recognized the name and knew it led into his road. She'd never been inside his house, but once or twice, or even three times, she had driven past it out of curiosity. (Not that she approved of driving past the houses of potential boyfriends – that was the sort of thing teenagers did. Well, anyway, it was a long time ago, when she thought she might have been falling in love with Drew.)

A small truck went by at amazing speed, creating a wake which caused the flood water in her car to cover her ankles. At that point, she made up her mind. She could not stay in her car all night so she would have to swallow her pride and go to Drew's. At least he was the practical sort of man who would know what to do. She prayed that he was in the country rather than overseas.

The water in the lane didn't quite reach her knees, but it was mid-brown and murky. She thought of insects, especially cockroaches, then she thought of sewage, never very reliably dealt with in Maising, and then she thought of snakes. She waded on, as fast as she could, holding her briefcase over her head. The faster she walked, the wetter she became. Now and then she stumbled into a hole but managed to keep her feet, until finally she arrived at Drew's gate.

His Land Rover was parked on a raised piece of ground by the front door. So he must be there, at home. She stood still for a moment to catch her breath, smiling in relief. Like most of the dwellings in this low-lying area, the house was raised on high foundations. Only the bottom steps were submerged by the flood. She would only have to take a few paces across the garden and she would be out of this vile water.

She rang the bell on the white gate. A pretty young maid came wading to unlock it, holding up her sarong and laughing at the adventure. She led Claire up the steps into the house calling, 'Sir, sir, come quick. Flend come.'

Drew stood at the top of the stairs. A stab of excitement went from Claire's throat to her stomach and back again.

'Ah,' he said, 'I see it is a very nice "flend" indeed. What a surprise! Long time no see. You look a bit wet. Swim here, did you, Claire?'

She couldn't stop smiling. 'I'm sorry,' she said, 'I'm dripping filthy water all over your clean hall. It's a bit smelly too. You see my car . . .'

'Yeah, I know, it broke down. Like every other damn car in Maising. Now, first things first. Min, take madam upstairs for a bath. She can use the guest room to change.'

Drew's white bathroom was very much like any other basic old-fashioned masculine bathroom. Claire was pleased to find nothing female amongst the razors and bottles of aftershave, not a trace of scent or face lotions. Not that she approved of searching men's bathrooms, of course.

After a quick soak, thinking about Drew and wondering if he was really as pleased to see her as he'd seemed, she stepped out of the bath and stared at herself in the mirror, an old uneven mirror that had cracks on the edge like the bath. What a sight, drowned rat sprang to mind. Telling herself she felt perfectly calm and controlled, she combed her hair with Drew's comb and put on a white towelling robe that was hanging behind the door. It was far too big for her and trailed on the ground.

She went to find her clothes which, in the hope that they might dry a little, she had left on a chair in the guest room. But she could find only her briefcase. Even her underwear had disappeared.

'Min!' she called hopefully, standing at the top of the stairs.

'Can I help you, madam?' Drew asked in a polite tone.

She grinned down at him. 'I was wondering what your maid has done with my clothes.'

'Sorry, she's gone home. I sent her back before it got too dark to see her way through the floods.' He walked halfway up the stairs and smiled at her. 'Nice dressing gown. Looks good on you. As for your own gear, I guess she washed it. She likes to wash everything she can lay her hands on. An absolute fiend for laundry. Your stuff 'll be dry in the morning, I hope. I told her you were staying the night. She said you had a suitcase.'

'Just a briefcase full of papers, actually. Drew, you're very kind, but I wasn't thinking of staying. I suppose I was vaguely hoping you'd take me home in the Land Rover.'

'Sorry, it's a bit crook at the moment – doesn't like the weather either. Anyway, they said on the radio everyone should stay put unless their journey was really necessary. Only the foreigners'll take any notice of that, mind you. But please stay. It's the safest thing to do. The guest room is all yours.'

Finding it hard to believe that the Land Rover was really out of action, Claire was far from sure it would be safe to stay, but she could only smile and agree. 'You'll have to find me something else to wear. I keep tripping over,' she said, still maintaining what she hoped was a serene and friendly manner.

Drew took her into his bedroom and, murmuring something about food, left her alone to choose whatever she wanted. It was a large dark room, quite bare except for a great many books piled up beside the double bed. She glanced at the titles and found mostly history and biography plus agricultural subjects. Again she looked around for something female, but there was no sign, not even a photograph.

Though it was tempting to search through all the drawers and cupboards, politeness compelled her to confine herself to the shelves he had shown her. After some thought, she selected a blue shirt and a pair of striped swimming shorts. The shorts had a drawstring, so she could tighten them to fit her narrow waist, but they were still far too big. Drew's huge shirt covered the shorts like a frock. Examining the ensemble in the bedroom mirror, Claire thought she looked like a clown.

Drew whistled admiringly as she came down the stairs.
'Nice legs!'

'I thought there'd be some female clothes.'

'Why did you think that?'

'I thought Liana lived here.'

He raised his eyebrows. 'Well, she doesn't.'

'Has she moved out?'

'Didn't move in.' He smiled. 'Claire, why are you cross-examining me?'

'Sorry . . . not my business. I'm too nosy. People are always telling me that.'

They began to talk of other things. Drew poured drinks and they talked some more, easy light-hearted talk, but Claire was acutely conscious of every gesture he made, his every glance in her direction. And it seemed to her that his awareness was as intense as her own.

Oh dear. Just be careful, she told herself. Play it cool.

When he went into the kitchen, she asked to use the telephone. She rang Howard to say that she'd been caught in the flood and was staying with some friends. She didn't feel she could explain about Drew over the phone. Anyway, maybe there would be nothing to explain.

Drew made dinner for them both – fried pork and mushrooms, mangetout peas and baby corn. He swore noisily about not being able to find any utensils because Min kept everything in bloody weird places, but the result was surprisingly good. Unfortunately nervous tension prevented her from eating much, but she had several glasses of wine.

'Didn't you like my cooking?' he asked afterwards.

'I loved it, but I wasn't very hungry for some reason.'

'Nor me.' He put his arm around her.

Wondering if she should pull away, Claire closed her eyes for a minute. Then she opened them. 'Did Liana teach you how to cook island food like that?'

'God, no, she can't even cook rice. She's had maids all her life.'

'So did you cook for her when Min wasn't here?'

'Sometimes. Just like you cook for old Howard, I expect.'

They were silent for a moment. Drew still had his arm lightly round her shoulder. Then he said seriously, 'I was disappointed you didn't want to come to Bangkok that time.'

Claire flushed. 'But I did want to . . .' She stopped, fearing she had given herself away. Then she plunged on. 'Actually, actually I phoned to tell you I'd come, but Liana answered the phone. It was very early in the morning. I thought she must have spent the night. So I changed my mind about Bangkok.'

'I see.'

'Was she?'

'Was she what?'

'Staying the night?'

'Claire, what is all this? I don't ask you about your sex life with Howard.'

'You did once, sort of.'

'Yeah, so I did. I guess I was jealous.' He began to stroke her arm gently. She could feel his fingers through the thin cotton shirt.

'But Liana is just a friend,' he continued. 'She was kind to me when I broke up with my wife. Liana is the sort of woman who's very warm and friendly and if she likes a man she sleeps with him, just in friendship, nothing more. Actually she stopped coming here because she said I wasn't a very enthusiastic lover after I met you. She said she required a certain minimum amount of attention and I didn't provide it. She even accused me of fantasizing about you when I was with her.'

'Was that true?'

'You mean, did I fantasize? Yes, I did, thought about you the whole bloody time, as a matter of fact.'

Her heart jumped unevenly. 'Then why didn't you ring me ever?' She moved away so she could see his face.

'Why didn't *you* ring me ever? You sent me a pretty negative email. I thought it was a put-down, telling me to back off, so I did. Thought you'd decided to go for good old Howard.'

'Why d'you always call him that?'

'Suits him – Hooray Howard. Let's leave him out of it. Another bloke hanging around doesn't usually put me off. I guess I'm too cautious these days. And you're pretty cautious too. Maybe I was afraid. I was afraid I might start to like you too much and you'd say you didn't want to get in too deep with a guy who spent all his time travelling.'

She put out her hand to touch his, and then thought better of it. 'I was only cautious because I thought you were too . . . too attractive to be reliable or trustworthy. And I'd made a resolution to be sensible and mature about men. Go for the steady type rather than . . . Well, bitter experience, I suppose.' She decided not to say too much about newly divorced blokes being the worst of the lot.

He raised his eyebrows. 'How do you mean?'

'Well, in my idiotic past I always seem to have fallen for womanizing phoneys or men who were in love with someone else. Like my last love in England – he was a divorced man who was still in love with his wife. It was all very painful.'

'Poor old world-weary Claire. Is that why you left the UK? I remember you said something about him when we first met.'

'He was one reason.'

'And what category of dud bloke did you put me in? Unreliable, untrustworthy, a womanizer, a phoney?' He smiled. 'Don't know why you're here really.'

She smiled in return. 'Well, not a phoney, but, there was all that Liana business, and you were pretty damn casual.' She took a deep breath. 'And do you mind my asking, Drew, what about your wife?'

His voice became more serious. 'She thought I was unreliable in some ways too. She wanted me to give away my foreign trips and work in Canberra as an administrator.'

'She didn't want to travel?'

'No, and she didn't want me to travel either. You see she has her own career in the civil service back home in Oz.'

'So you went your separate ways?'

'Yes.'

'Is she pretty, your wife?'

'People seem to think so.'

'What does she look like?' Claire could see that her line of questioning was making him unhappy, but she couldn't stop herself.

'Sort of red-blonde and skinny. But I really don't want to talk about her.'

He got up and stared out of the window. Behind him the flood water was dark and shiny, all around the house. He turned and smiled. 'We won't talk about anybody else, to hell with them all.'

She went towards him and then stopped, constrained by the thought of Howard. 'I'm not sure I should stay,' she said.

'You have to. Look out of the window.'

She took another deep breath. 'You see, if I stay, I think, well, things may get a bit, well, kind of out of hand or . . .'

He smiled a large and happy smile. 'You could be right. What a good idea! Of course, being a delicately brought-up Australian, I would never have dreamed of suggesting it myself, but . . .' He made to take her in his arms, but she pushed him away gently with both her arms against his chest.

'And if, if we do, I'll have to give up Howard because I can't cope with two lovers. It's a rule I have,' she whispered, looking at the floor. 'And he loves me and I shouldn't be unfaithful.'

He pulled her towards him again. 'Just ditch him.'

'I'm not sure I should.'

'You're not engaged to him?'

'No, but, thing is, we're together and he loves me. I don't want to behave like a shit.'

'Better to end things sooner rather than later, before he's too involved.'

'He's too involved already,' she said, full of guilt. Oh God, why had she made such a mess of everything?

'What about me?'

'I don't know how I feel about you or how you really feel about me except that . . .' Except that she longed for him and she knew she could not stall much longer. She said aloud, 'Except that it's very late and maybe I should sleep alone.'

'Maybe, or maybe you should have the guts to do what you want for a change. You're such a polite English person. Maybe you should break your own bloody rules.' He took her in his arms, pulling up the loose shirt so that his hands touched the bare skin of her back. 'Either way, you have to kiss me goodnight,' he whispered in her ear. She kissed him on the cheek.

'Rotten Pommy prude,' he said.

So she kissed him on the lips. They kissed again and again. No longer trying to hold back, she was aware only of Drew standing so close, his desire, her desire for him. His body, hands, mouth. He pushed her away a little and began to unfasten the buttons of her shirt one by one, kissing the brown and then the white skin.

She didn't really notice that outside the torrential rain had begun again.

Some time later, as they lay peacefully in each other's arms on the rug by the window, Claire opened her eyes. 'It's raining very hard,' she remarked.

He smiled, tenderly caressing her face. 'Is that all you've got to say, after all that passion?'

'You know we Brits like to talk about the weather whenever possible. But it is sort of vaguely relevant. D'you see, look, the Land Rover's wheels are covered in water now.'

He peered out of the window, leaning across her. 'So they are.'

'It means I'll have to stay a day or two.'

'I can live with that idea,' he whispered. 'Come on, let's go upstairs. It's more comfortable. I didn't mean to make love downstairs, but you overwhelmed me.'

She smiled as he pulled her up. 'You were the overwhelming one,' she said.

'How about we try overwhelming each other all over again?'

He took her by the hand. When they reached his bedroom, he picked her up and carried her across to his bed.

'Wow, caveman, why didn't you carry me all the way up the stairs?'

He lay down beside her. 'Thought you'd be too heavy and I was right,' he murmured.

She laughed. 'Very rude.'

Just then the telephone rang, loud in the silent house. 'Answer it,' she said.

'No.'

'You must.'

He let go of her and picked up the telephone. 'Hello . . . Oh, it's you . . . I see . . . All right . . . OK.' It was not a long conversation.

'Who was it?' she asked.

His voice was different. 'Someone from Australia. About a meeting.'

'Funny time to ring.'

'Yeah,' he said absently.

Suddenly Claire realized how little she knew about him. All her doubts returned. Surely a business colleague wouldn't ring in the middle of the night. It must have been another woman and Drew was lying to her. All her instincts told her so. Taking a deep breath, she said, 'Actually, I'm going to my own bed now, alone if you don't mind. Goodnight, thanks for dinner and . . . everything. I hope you understand, but maybe it would be better for us if, if we were just friends. I don't think it will really ever work out otherwise, you and me.'

As she walked towards the door, she did not dare turn to see the expression on his face. 'Come back. I want to tell you something important.'

She turned. 'What?'

'Can't tell you unless you come here.'

'Oh, all right.' She went to sit on the edge of the bed.

He smiled. 'Lie down. You'll be more comfortable.'

'I can hear perfectly well sitting up.'

He moved to sit behind her and ran his fingers down her backbone. 'I wanted to tell you that you look terrific from the rear,' he whispered. 'That bottom of yours. I thought you were skinny, but you're really quite plump when you're naked and beautiful.'

'Plump! Where am I plump?' She was trying not to laugh.

'Here . . . and here.'

'But . . .'

'And here.'

Claire was stranded at Drew's house for another day and another night. They made love again and again, with a desperate yet tender passion. Occasionally they talked and sometimes they ate, but mostly they stayed in bed. There was no time for anything else. In a way that she had not done before in her over-anxious life, Claire abandoned herself to love and lust, and Drew. It's never been like this, she thought, not straight away, not ever really. Not such wild extraordinary shattering joy, hour after hour.

'Why, oh why is it so good?' she asked in a mindless daze of gratification.

He smiled down at her. 'Because you're generous, lusty and bloody wonderful.'

'And because you're a fantastically sexy skilful lover. You turn me on like crazy, you know that.'

He grinned. 'I know, I know,' he said, stroking her cheekbone. 'But the turn-on is mutual, oh boy, it's mutual.'

Because we're in love, she wanted to add, but didn't. It was too soon.

Later, over breakfast, he said, 'You asked me about my marriage, but you never talk about yours, all those years ago.'

'No, I don't.'

'Why not?'

'Well, I suppose I'd wrapped it up carefully in tissue paper and put it away. Sometimes you don't want to share private personal memories. You can't really explain all the nuances of a marriage to somebody else.' She smiled. 'Or perhaps I didn't really want to re-examine it in case it didn't turn out to be as blissful as I remembered.'

'So tell me now. Might be good to air it.'

Claire was silent for a moment before she began. 'Well, you know, a few years after you've been widowed, you tend to look at the past through rose-tinted glasses, pretending to yourself that your marriage was perfect. Which, of course, it wasn't because it didn't have time to be. We were too young. It was more like a lovely, sexy fling with lots of quarrels.'

'What was he like?'

'Oh, handsome, funny, a very strong character. That's why we rowed, I guess, fighting for supremacy.' She smiled and took another sip of coffee.

'But you were happy?'

'Yes, yes, I was. Most of the time. But it, the marriage, made me pretty cautious about men.'

'Why?'

'I don't know . . . Maybe because I realized they're pretty damn difficult to live with, even if you are madly in love.'

He grinned. 'Can't live without 'em though.'

'That's just where you're wrong. I learnt, the hard way, that you can. You can manage without them very well. I had to at first anyway. People, anyone, not just young blokes treated me strangely.'

'How d'you mean?'

'Well, they were embarrassed by the tragedy. They would walk on the other side of the road to avoid me. It's a weird state, widowhood, weird word, especially if you're young. People are afraid to say the wrong thing. Sometimes I'd take my ring off and pretend to be a divorcee or just a single woman. Seemed easier than going through the whole rigmarole of explaining and upsetting people.'

He looked surprised. 'You were afraid of upsetting other people?'

'Odd, isn't it? When people hear the word widow they take fright and think of weeping black-clad old crones, and you don't fit the picture so they feel awkward.'

'But you don't wear your wedding ring any more.'

She sighed. 'No, gave it up eventually, though I felt disloyal doing so.'

'But after a while?'

'Yes, after a while I began to see another bloke. Quite the wrong type for me, quiet and unassertive, but opposite to my husband. When he didn't work out, I went for a totally different sort – a brash City type. Boom and bust, that was me. That's why I now think it's probably best to remain serenely single.'

'Not you, Claire. You're not the single woman type.'

'Oh, yes, I am. I'm pretty self-sufficient now.'

'But you may want to step off the shelf one day.'

'Rude bastard. I'm not on any shelf – well, if I am I can probably dust myself down and step off it any time I want.'

'With good old Howard?'

'Will you please belt up about good old Howard?'

'OK, OK, how about we stop talking altogether. Hm, now what else could we do? Come to think of it I rather like your boom and your bust.'

At the time Claire didn't really notice the change of subject. Eventually she made another telephone call to Howard to say she was safe 'with friends'. She hated the deceit, but she preferred to wait until she could tell him face to face that she was in love with another man. Oh shit, poor Howard.

The rains stopped and the flood waters began to retreat. The maid returned, giggling sweetly behind her hand when she saw that Claire was still there and that the spare bed had not been slept in.

'I'll take you home now,' said Drew. 'We should be able to make it.'

Claire felt that it should have been she who suggested leaving. She would like to have been invited to stay longer, but Drew's mood had changed. He seemed quiet and pre-occupied that morning.

The Land Rover showed no signs of being 'crook'. As they drove slowly along, she stared out of the window at the muddy streets. Cheerful as ever, the islanders were trying vainly to mop up the remaining pools, but in parts the water was still knee deep. When they reached Lotus Court, Drew turned off the engine.

He turned to her. 'Claire, I have to tell you. I'm going back to Australia.' His face was serious, his voice different, formal.

'Oh, when?'

'Next month. As soon as I've sorted out my office and things here.'

'When will you be back?'

'I don't know. Might be a long time.'

A feeling of dread settled in the pit of Claire's stomach. 'How long?'

'Several months, maybe longer.' There was no suggestion in his bleak tone that he was about to invite her to go with him.

She tried to keep her voice even. 'Have you been posted home then? I thought your contract was for another year.'

'I have asked for a few months' leave of absence, to sort out a family problem. My wife wants to talk.'

'Oh.' Claire gazed hard at her hands.

'I'm sorry. But I have to go and see her.'

It was very warm and humid, but she began to shiver. 'You're still in love with your wife. I didn't know that.'

Drew spoke sharply. 'Christ, no! I'm not in love with her.'

'Then why are you running back to Australia the moment she summons you?'

'How the hell should I know? But I feel I have to go, to make sure. Sort things out.' He was staring out of the window, not looking at her.

'But you're divorced. Deborah told me you were divorced.'

'No, only separated. Legally separated.'

'For God's sake, why didn't you tell me? I had a right to know,' she said angrily. She was on the verge of tears but determined not to show it.

'I thought you did know.'

'No, I didn't.' Claire was silent for a moment and then said suddenly, 'Was it her on the phone the other night very late, the call you answered?'

'Yes.'

'And you didn't tell me. Oh God, you were probably thinking about her all the time we made love.'

'No, I was thinking of you, only you. You must know that.' He took hold of her arm roughly. She pulled away. 'Then why are you going back to her?'

'I just have to sort it out finally. And then . . .'

'Then what?'

'I'll come back.'

'But you might decide to stay in Australia.'

'No, I don't think so.'

Her voice grew higher. 'You don't think so. You're not sure.'

'I'm almost ninety per cent sure I won't stay. But I guess I can't ask you to wait here for me, Claire. I can't ask you to give me time.'

'You're damn right. I'm not going to wait around in case you should deign to show up again. You didn't level with me. You weren't honest. You strung me along – your wife, Liana, everything.'

'You're wrong. I was straight with you. Wait, I thought—'

But Claire opened the door of the Land Rover and slammed it behind her. Without looking back, she ran up the stairs to her apartment.

TWENTY-ONE

Six weeks after, Lucy began to fear that Jazzer's visit had born unwelcome fruit. Every morning she became more and more convinced that she must be pregnant. And it wasn't the joyful happy sensation it should have been. It was all very wrong. She tried drinking gin in a hot bath and then jumping off the bed – and all the other tricks she had read about in Victorian novels – but to no avail.

At times she considered the option of pretending that the child was Martin's. It wasn't impossible that he was responsible for her pregnancy. But she had taken the spirit medicine on the evening she had slept with her ministerial guest and Lucy believed in the potions. In her heart of hearts, she knew the child was Jazzer's and the thought of long-term deception was repugnant to her. She loved Martin and could not envisage living such a lie.

Nor could she tell him what she perceived to be the truth. It would, she was certain, spoil everything. She understood instinctively that Martin had been attracted by her sensible country-girl naivety, that he liked to guide and instruct her, and for their marriage to be her whole world. If she told him about Jazzer, he would never trust her again and their relationship would be irrevocably damaged. She was very unhappy.

In desperation, she decided to telephone Meng. If there were potions to encourage pregnancy, there must surely be medicine to dislodge it. Not wanting to discuss such matters on the telephone, she told him she was thinking of doing a course on archaeology and wished to ask his advice. They agreed to meet at an obscure cafe, which was 'redolent with local colour', according to Meng. She had some difficulty in finding the way, but eventually she arrived at the large outdoor cafe where he was waiting at a small table discreetly situated behind a screen of potted palms. Meng's good looks seemed suddenly ultra-conspicuous in these simple surroundings and she looked around, fearful that someone she knew would see them and wrongly suspect a romantic rendezvous. But the place was almost empty and the only colourful aspect was the rather garish sunshade painted with huge red and yellow flowers.

All through the long afternoon, Meng talked about archaeology. As Lucy sat and listened, she managed to forget her own problems for a time. The fact that an interesting and well-informed man like Meng was prepared to spend so much time on her was flattering and soothing to her ego. He actually talked to her as if she were an equal, an intelligent person in her own right, someone worthy of serious attention. But he wasn't overfamiliar or flirtatious, that's what made him more comfortable to be with than most men, she thought.

He told her stories about his work. He told her of the craftsmen of former times and of the love and reverence which inspired their creations. He explained how the Buddha images were cast using 'lost wax': how a rough figure of the desired measurements was made from clay, how a covering layer of wax was shaped to form the finished image, then how a layer of clay was put on top. Then the wax was melted and the clay baked until it turned into a brick mould. He explained how each craftsman was in charge of a different aspect of the process.

His descriptions were so vivid that Lucy could see the men moulding the wax, she could even see the stamp which created the formal curls of the Buddha's hair. She could visualize the care with which they mixed the metals and the pouring of the molten bronze – and the joy they felt when their creation was complete.

Then he talked about how the islanders melded Buddhism with their animistic beliefs and how the older country peasants worshipped a series of gods and how their lives were influenced by fear of the spirits.

'They believe that even the trees have spirits. For instance, if they gather cloves, then they must be careful to appease the spirits of the clove tree by making gifts to them. I suppose the parallel in England is the corn dolly. I believe they were made to give thanks for the harvest.'

'Oh, yes,' said Lucy doubtfully. She had barely heard of corn dollies, but she felt she must contribute something to the conversation. 'But no one believes in spirits in England these days.'

'I wonder. But of course you are probably right. Here it is a much more serious matter. Sometimes agricultural experts go and talk to the peasants, but they're afraid to try new crops or new strains of rice for fear of offending the spirits of the fields. They say new crops won't grow and, even if they did, no one would eat them.'

Lucy smiled.

'In the same way,' he went on, 'they ignore the medical workers who try to teach them elementary hygiene. If a member of the family is ill, they consider it more effective to sacrifice a chicken than to visit the rural health centre.'

'But what about Spirit Woman's medicines, aren't they sometimes effective?'

'Yes, of course, but that is because of the herbs they contain and also I think there is an element of faith in most healing

. . . That reminds me, how did you get on with the little blue phial?' he asked delicately. 'Did it work? I forgot to tell you that you mustn't drink alcohol with any of the spirit medicines for they are very powerful. Indeed, the fertility drug is reputed to have aphrodisiac effects if taken in the wrong measure or with the wrong foods.'

'I haven't actually used the phial yet,' lied Lucy, uncomfortable that she seemed to have embarked on a new strange life of deceit. 'Er, have you still got any medicines left?'

'What kind are you looking for this time?'

'Any kind. I was thinking I'd like to learn about this sort of thing.'

'I don't have much left, just a few potions for indigestion, but I'll be visiting the Spirit Woman tomorrow, if you would like to come. It is a special evening at the village where they give thanks to the rain gods that have visited them – a most interesting ceremony to watch.'

'Oh, I'd love to come,' said Lucy, before she could stop herself.

Fortunately Martin was away at a regional conference in Bangkok, but for the benefit of her maids Lucy felt she had to invent an excuse to go out in the evening. She mentioned casually to Somjit that she would not be in for dinner as she was attending a Ladies' Club meeting and so all the staff could go off-duty as soon as they liked.

Even as she stepped into Meng's car, she began to have misgivings about embarking on such an expedition. She had the feeling that Helena would not think this appropriate behaviour for a diplomatic wife, however safe and celibate Meng might be.

Away from the city lights, it was growing very dark when they arrived at the Ravi ruins. The rickety poles of the Maising electricity company did not extend much further than the hamlets on the edge of the main road, but Meng was equipped with a powerful torch and seemed to know where he was going. Beyond the glow of the torch she could see nothing, but she could hear loud croaking and grating noises, as if they were surrounded by giant frogs and mammoth grasshoppers. Jumping at every rustle, every jungle sound, she held tightly on to Meng's arm as they walked down the narrow path to the village.

'Don't be afraid, Lucy. These are good people,' he said.
'I know.'
'They won't harm you.'
'I know,' she repeated. But more and more she felt she
should never have come. It wasn't right to be wandering round
the edge of the jungle at nightfall with Meng.

To her relief, they soon came to the village, which looked
welcoming enough in the light of the fires glowing outside
every dwelling. Most of the villages were seated on the ground
eating their evening meal. Obviously delighted to see their
visitors, they drew Lucy towards them and offered her food.
When she whispered to Meng that she was not hungry, he
told her she must eat what was offered or mortally offend her
hosts.

They gave her a small round bowl and a spoon. Then a fat,
grey-haired woman served her some rice from a large
aluminium pan and a helping of what looked like fish bones
and green string. When Lucy had eaten what she could, she
was pressed to have some more. Meng said something to the
fat woman, and Lucy was given a second bowl of rice.

'Take that to Girah the Spirit Woman,' he said.

Girah's dark slanted eyes stared at Lucy in the flickering
light of the innumerable yellow candles that surrounded her.
Instinctively Lucy knelt down on a small rush prayer mat at
her feet. They remained in silence for several minutes.

Then Girah spoke. Her voice was harsh and guttural.

'She says give her your hand,' whispered Meng, who was
standing in the shadows.

Lucy did as she was told. Girah placed a small, sharp green
stone in the palm of Lucy's hand and squeezed until Lucy
almost cried out with pain. Then Girah took the stone and
dropped it first into a jar of colourless liquid and then into a
small fire burning at the feet of Queen Victoria's statue.
Eventually she spoke.

'She wants me to go away,' said Meng. 'She says that you
will understand better if I am not here.'

He backed away into the darkness.

Lucy stared into the glittering eyes as if hypnotized. With
a stick, Girah drew a picture on the ground of a woman with
bulging stomach. Then she took a blue phial and placed it on
the stomach. The phial looked very similar to the one that

Lucy had used already. With her toothless grin, Girah picked up the phial and handed it to Lucy, holding out her fingers to indicate a price of ten rads. Lucy took it and paid. She dared not do otherwise.

Next the Spirit Woman picked up a sharp stick, red at one end as if it had been dipped in paint. She jabbed it into the stomach of the figure she had drawn.

Lucy drew in her breath. Smiling just as broadly, the old woman opened a dark rush basket and took out a bamboo leaf folded into a parcel. She opened up the leaf a little so that Lucy could see it contained a brown paste. She indicated that this time the cost would be twenty rads. As if to demonstrate her point all the more clearly, she pretended to eat some of the paste and then she stabbed the ground again moving the stick about, so that the stomach of ghostly illustration disappeared into the dust.

It seemed to Lucy an age before Meng returned to collect her. He told her the villagers were now ready for the cere- mony. They had dressed themselves in bright red and blue costumes, and braided their hair with beads. Three musicians played a mournful, monotonous rhythm on strange percus- sion instruments. Six dancers made slow stylized steps, hopping from one leg to the other and gazing up at their hands, which they weaved about their heads.

'They use their hands to indicate the rain clouds,' said Meng earnestly. He passed her a drink in a pink plastic cup.

'Wow, this tastes strong, but shouldn't we be drinking out of coconut shells?' she asked smiling.

'All these villagers love plastic. I fear the jungle will soon be covered in it.'

'What is this drink? It's rather nice.'

'Rice whisky,' he said, 'And coconut milk and some secret ingredient. They say it's very good for you. Have some more.'

Lucy had some more and some more.

She was not aware of how she came to be in Meng's house, reclining on a chair, half-naked, covered in a thin silk shawl. In horror she sat up, her head reeling. In the dim light she could see her bra and shirt hanging on the chair. She put them on quickly. As her eyes became accustomed to the gloom, she noticed a dark form lying fully clothed on the sofa on the opposite side of the room.

She gulped. 'Meng, what happened?'

He opened his eyes and smiled. 'Hello, Lucy.'

'What happened? Why am I here?'

'Nothing happened. I just thought you were too, well a little too merry to go straight back to the Embassy. I should have warned you that that drink is rather strong.'

'Yes, you should have, but I mean what happened here? You didn't – did I? I mean why, why didn't I have a shirt on?' Lucy blushed deeply as she spoke.

'I don't know. You said you had to take your top off because you were too hot, but I persuaded you to keep the rest of your clothes on. And I covered you with a shawl, even though you looked so very beautiful lying there.' He smiled sweetly at her. 'I thought it right to cover you in case I was tempted to break my vows of celibacy.'

'But you didn't . . . didn't break them?'

'Of course not. Besides, you were in my charge.'

Lucy smiled in relief, but she felt that she had been tricked into drinking too much, that her drink had been spiked. With Meng around, strange things seemed to happen to her.

'I must go home now. Quick, it's very late,' she said. On her way to the door she tripped over Meng's tripod. His camera was on the bookcase nearby.

'What's this doing here?' she asked, suddenly suspicious.

He smiled. 'You were so peaceful – I had to take a photograph of you. I wanted you in my collection.'

'What do you mean in your "collection"?' She reddened again. 'You didn't photograph me without . . . when I was undressed, did you?'

'Only your bosom, not your face,' he said seriously. 'Your face was in shadow. But I have never seen such magnificence, such generous beauty before. No one but me will ever look at the photographs. I will keep them secret and just take them out now and then.'

His manner was sincere and not in any way suggestive, but she felt sick with shock. 'Meng, you can't do this to me. I thought we were friends.'

'Of course we are. I just wanted something to remember you by. Don't worry. I develop all my pictures myself. I repeat, no one else will see them and anyway no one could tell who it was – your face is hidden.'

'Please, please, give me the film.'

Ignoring her outstretched hand, he said, 'Surely you are aware that artists often paint or photograph nudes.'

'Yes, but the sitters know they're being painted. I didn't consent to be photographed. What you did was awful, almost like stealing. Don't you see that?'

He was momentarily contrite. 'I'm sorry but you were relaxed and at peace. And so lovely. I had to take the opportunity. When a perfect, wonderful shot presents itself, perfect subject, perfect light, an artist has to seize the moment or it is lost for ever.'

'You're mad.' Her voice grew higher and higher. 'Don't you see, don't you see, I hate the idea of being a sort of girlie model!' She made a grab at the camera, but he held her back.

'There is nothing girlie about my photography. It is a work of art. You insult me. Now it is late. Let me take you home.'

Though she wept and pleaded further, he was unmoved, even angry as if she had insulted his artistic integrity. They were both silent as he drove her back through the night streets.

Naturally she told Martin nothing about these events when he returned from Bangkok. For some reason she had never mentioned her acquaintance with Meng, and now it was impossible to speak of him. She brooded about the photographs for several days and then decided there was nothing she could do for the time being. She would just have to trust Meng's word.

An even more serious and pressing problem was her pregnancy. At first she could not summon up enough courage to take the paste, then she caught sight of a photograph of Jazzer in *The Times*. Just the sight of him made her feel ill. She clasped and unclasped her hands time and time again, rubbing them together. The dislike she felt for him had grown to deep hatred. She wanted no connection with him. She'd hate his child. It would look just like him, and worse, would grow up to behave like him.

With the copy of the newspaper in front of her, she took out a little silver spoon from the sideboard and ate some of the paste which she had concealed in her desk with the other spirit potions. It tasted quite sweet, like almonds and honey, but with a tinge of chilli that left a hot, sharp feeling on her tongue.

It was several hours before the pain started, followed by the blood. When Martin came back from the office, she was sitting curled up on the bathroom floor, moaning quietly. He immediately called the doctor.

A Chinese gynaecologist with a round face and gentle hands came to examine her. After an injection of morphine, events passed in a sort of dream. Lucy felt as if she were an observer watching some other woman being placed in an ambulance, then a hospital bed, examined, re-examined, she heard the words 'routine curettage', and she was taken down to the operating theatre where a smiling American nurse held her hand. Then there was the anaesthetic.

Afterwards there was nausea but no pain. It was all over. The hospital was noisy at night. She could hear the cry of newborn babies in the wing opposite. Next morning she was thankful when the doctor said she could go home.

Martin treated her as if she were a delicate invalid. Once they reached the house, he insisted she go straight up to bed. Then he sat beside her, holding her hand.

'Lucy, will you ever forgive me?' he asked.

She trembled. 'Forgive you for what?'

'Doctor Nim said you told him you had taken native medicine to bring about a miscarriage.'

'Oh.' Lucy closed her eyes. 'I don't really remember what happened, but if that's what he said, then that's what I must have done.'

'Darling, what a terrible sacrifice. If I had known you were pregnant, I wouldn't have minded. I know I was negative about the idea when we talked about it, but it's awful, appalling, that you thought you had to get rid of our child. I'm so dreadfully sorry. I realize now I haven't talked to you enough. I've been preoccupied. I didn't realize how you felt. Please forgive me. You see, I'm not good at this sort of soul-searching stuff.' He ran his hands through his hair.

Lucy said nothing.

He went on in a sudden tumult of words, quite unlike his normal measured tones. 'I never told you about Anne, how she was totally obsessed with the children and how cold she became after they were born and how things were never the same. We never made love, you know. She didn't seem to want it after the second birth.'

Lucy put her hand on his.

'The boys,' he said, sounding more and more wretched, 'well, they more or less destroyed our marriage: she always stayed in England with them when they got to school age. Then when the marriage was virtually over, I tried to rescue it. I persuaded her to join me in Africa, and she caught hepatitis and died. The boys blamed me, and still do, in a way. They moved in with her sister, who blames me too, and I hardly ever see them. I know I told you some of this originally, but I didn't tell you the whole story. I know I should have tried to. Then you might have understood. You wouldn't have had to go through all this agony. I'm so sorry.'

Lucy said nothing. She began to weep quietly. She could not begin to explain that she, not he, was the guilty one.

Martin took her hand. 'Darling, if you want a child, I know it will be different. We'll have one, or even two or more, if you like. But Doctor Nim says you must wait a few months. Promise me you won't take any more native medicine, will you? The doctor advises strongly against it. He says it is not suitable for Westerners. Where did you get hold of it, anyway?'

'Oh, please, please, don't ask me any more questions. I just can't talk about it.' Lucy wept more tears.

Martin cradled her in his arms, stroking her hair. 'It's all right, my darling. Everything will be all right.'

TWENTY-TWO

For Deborah everything was far from all right. Alex had made Maising bearable, but now he had gone there was nothing left to keep her in the country, except her ailing marriage. Feeling that it was her duty to try to resuscitate it, she had once suggested counselling.

Johnny laughed. 'Marriage guidance – how bloody stupid you Yanks are! When I need guidance from some half-baked do-gooder, I'll throw in the towel. Anyway, what the hell is wrong with *our marriage*?' He emphasized the words sarcastically, attempting to imitate her American accent. 'I bring in the bacon. You look after the kids. We don't fight much. You have your lovers. I have mine. And we even fuck now and then in between – if I can raise the enthusiasm, that is. It all seems fair enough to me.'

'Just an idea. I suppose, naively, I expected marriage to be sort of different,' said Deborah in as calm a tone as she could manage.

'You read too many agony aunts in those daft women's mags. Christ, marriage guidance!'

'I hardly ever read magazines.'

'Slushy novels then. All you women read sentimental trash.'

Johnny was given to sweeping statements of this type. Recently Deborah had decided to ignore them. 'I think I expected companionship at least and perhaps fatherly attention to your son,' she said.

'You're so damn intense, aren't you? You have plenty of friends, not to mention boyfriends. As for the kids, you've got Pima to help you – most women in the West would give their eye teeth for a maid like her. Paid by me, please note.' He finished his glass of whisky and then turned to look for the bottle. 'I pay for everything. Everything.'

Deborah followed him. 'Hey, wait a minute. I do teach, you know.'

'Part-time, very part-time. Most women in the UK have a full-time job, but you don't have to. But when you do a bit of teaching, English or sex or whatever you fancy, you can just dump the kids with Pima. Just bear that in mind. I've always given you a very good life. Never stopped you doing what you wanted.'

She was determined to remain calm. 'Johnny, you . . .'

'You're just a moaner, never satisfied, like all the other white women here.'

Deborah glared at him. 'At least you should take more notice of the children, especially Sam. He'd like to have his dad around more. It's important for a boy.'

'I do take notice of the children – there you go, moaning again. I'm a bloody good father.'

He poured himself some more whisky, added a few cubes of ice. Mutely, Deborah handed him a bottle of soda, but he waved it away.

Taking a large gulp of his drink, he went on. 'Now have we finished this big talk? Are you having your period or something? You seem in a bad mood. Get yourself another boyfriend, do you good. Anyway, I'm going out in a minute.'

'Do you think you should drive and drink like you do?'

'Mind your own bloody business.'

'In Europe they have strict laws now.'

'We're not living in bloody rule-book Europe, are we? God, I never want to go back there. Much better here. Plenty of freedom. No bureaucrats or social engineers breathing down your neck.' He waved an unsteady arm. 'Make the most of it, Deb. Turned down a home posting the other day – knew it wouldn't suit us.'

She stared at him. 'Run that by me again. You turned down a posting in London without telling me?'

'Well, I don't want to leave the East, so there's no point in discussing it. Our life is here. We'd have a miserable time in London, smaller salary, smaller flat, no maid, ghastly weather.'

'You should have told me,' she said slowly. It was weird how she always managed to sound so outwardly composed when she was raging inside.

'It's my career, my decision. You just don't know when you're well off, do you?'

She raised her eyebrows. 'I'd just like to be consulted about important decisions.' Then she took a deep breath. 'Can we just straighten the record? I don't have loads of lovers every day of the week. I had an affair with Alex – just to kind of cheer me up, to redress the balance for all your women. I thought it might make me feel better, restore my morale. And it did, for a while.'

'So we're even-steven. Don't give me that innocent look – it won't wash. Can't expect me to be faithful to you when you're not exactly Miss Chastity yourself. Damn lucky I didn't divorce you really. It's still a man's world, you know, my dear Deb. Women are supposed to behave themselves. But I'm a tolerant bloke.' He took yet another gulp of his drink. 'Talk about teaching, you must have taught that toy boy of yours a thing or two – valuable lessons, if you passed on to him the benefit of my experience.' He smirked. 'I should have charged him really, come to think of it.'

'My God, you bastard . . .'

'I was extremely reasonable about him. I could have smashed his pretty face in, but I didn't. I felt like it at times when I saw him sniffing around you like a randy little poodle. You were making a bloody fool of yourself, you know, Deb old thing. But I kept quiet and let you get on with it. Soul of patience, really. But it doesn't look good, a mother of two carrying on with a teenager. Letting the side down a bit. Got to set a good example, you know. Hope you were reasonably discreet about it. Don't want too much talk in the British community. It's all right for chaps to have a bit of a fling – a man like me needs a change from time to time, only natural – but their lady wives should appear to be above such things. And I'm very fond of you, you know.'

Deborah finally lost control. 'A bit of a fling?' she shouted.

'Don't start yelling – doesn't suit you. You'll wake the kids. I've got to go out now or I'll be late. Don't wait up. I might not come back tonight.'

During the long evening, she began to understand how brutalized women accepted battering as normal. Not that Johnny attacked her physically. Tonight he had made her furiously angry, but normally it was his neglect that wounded her in a constant irritating hurt, like small, painful grazes. Somehow his neglect was worse than the fight that had just taken place. Most of the time he just acted as if he did not have a wife and family.

In the beginning when they had met and married, she had basked in his total love and attention. His desire for her seemed insatiable and she learned to match him in sensuality. They were utterly happy. The shock of betrayal had made her physically sick when, still in those early days, she'd found out about his extramarital games. After endless bitter rows and bitter tears from her, he promised to reform. But there were more women, more lies and then more rows.

The drinking must have begun around that time. Her fault, he said.

Why hadn't she left him before the children were born? Perhaps because of some old-fashioned feeling that women should be understanding about that type of masculine behaviour. Perhaps she'd thought he would change, grow up, grow out of his womanizing if she remained steadfast. But he never changed.

Now she was beginning to accept as the norm Johnny's

drinking, Johnny's women and the way he now talked about them openly. But she did not approve of her own acquiescent behaviour. Except in as much as she was doing the right thing for the children. But was she? Received wisdom was that a bad marriage was bad for the children. But was even Johnny better than no father? Probably she should get out now when the kids were small or stay till they were too old to care. Alex would probably have some child development statistics to prove which was best, or the lesser of two evils.

She began to think harder about making the effort to leave and, if she did leave, where she should go. It was a choice between Washington where she knew no one except her parents, Geneva where she still had school friends, or London, where her sister lived. London was cheaper than Geneva, especially for childcare and medical facilities. And her sister Susan was a gem. Even her British husband was not a bad guy.

As well as their Georgetown house, her parents maintained a flat in Chelsea so that they could visit Susan without having to stay in the cramped Richmond terrace where she and Brian lived in great disorder with their three small destructive sons. If Deborah went to live in London, she could at least have the support of her relations. She wondered if she could face living in her parents' tiny flat on a temporary basis and if indeed they would agree to her doing so. She knew they would not approve of a divorce.

She had been thinking of how she was going to tell them about the impending breakdown of her marriage when the telephone rang early one morning. Her sister's voice was clear, but small and distant. 'Mom just died, right here in London,' she said.

Seated in the jumbo jet on her way to England, Deborah found herself preoccupied with the practicalities of death, as well as the grief and the disbelief. For instance, she worried about not having anything appropriate to wear to the cremation as she only had one outfit that was not tropical, a blue wool skirt and sweater, and a crumpled white raincoat. This was her travelling gear. She had not thought to acquire something suitable for a winter funeral in Europe. And shoes, she did not have any winter shoes. It was stupid not to have the right kind of shoes for this stupid, wrong, unexpected death.

*   *   *

In the event, she managed to squeeze into an old coat of Susan's and bought, in a hurry and at vast expense, some un-attractive black boots. In her borrowed clothes, she went with her father, Susan and Brian to Putney Vale Crematorium. They were all horribly civilized and brave. While they were waiting for the coffin, they made jokes in bright voices about all the depressing wreaths and morbid cushions of chrysanthemums laid out for other customers in the Garden of Remembrance. Then they attended the short impersonal ceremony in the empty crematorium. Afterwards, they went back to Richmond where they ate a tasteless Chinese takeaway meal as no one wanted to eat out and Susan did not feel like cooking.

Her father, over-calm and over-rational as ever, said he would take the ashes back to the US to scatter at home in the yard. Then he would have a church service for Mom in Washington so that all her friends could attend. He talked about Mom, and his daughters listened. Deborah had never felt close to her father and even now he seemed remote and far away. But that was his way of dealing with emotions. It must be.

Mom had always been the one who dealt with Dad, tact-fully negotiating on behalf of the girls: permission for Deborah to go out with a boy, permission for Susan to buy a new tennis racquet, to go on a school trip. It occurred to Deborah that throughout her childhood she had rarely spoken directly to her father. Mom had always arranged everything. She had been Father's agent for dealing with not only his daughters but with the rest of the practical world. Only international affairs and diplomacy, his profession, were worthy of his direct attention. Now he would have to manage without Mom. They all would. It was hard to comprehend.

As a form of therapy, Deborah played with her nephews, who seemed little affected by their grandmother's death. She said nothing to her family about leaving Johnny. It was not the right time. Nor did she make any enquiries about jobs or housing in London. That bleak November, the city no longer seemed like any kind of home.

After Deborah returned to Maising, Claire took a deep breath and went up to see her. 'I am so terribly sorry to hear about your mother,' she said sincerely, but she felt both hesitant and inadequate.

Deborah's voice was shaky, but she smiled. 'Yes, thank you.'

Putting her arms around her, Claire searched for the right thing to say. 'D'you want to talk about it or not?'

'Seems like I want to talk all the time. It's affected me that way.' She recounted every detail of her trip to Europe, her father's face, her sister's dress, buying the wrong shoes even.

Pima came into the room to pour their coffee. She paused for a minute, seemingly concerned about something, but she went out again without speaking.

Deborah pulled out a small gold cross which was hanging around her neck. 'Dad gave me this. It belonged to her. She was kind of religious. I'm not, not religious, except in emergencies like now. Anyway, I'm wearing this for Mom. There's some more of her stuff I'd like to show you. It's in the bedroom.'

With quiet methodical movements, Pima was making the bed. She spoke urgently when Deborah came into the room. 'Madame, Pima see man on beach wear cross, same like cross belong to madame.'

'What man?'

'Dead man. Man from water. Sam find long time ago.'

'I thought you said he was an Asian man?'

'Yes, Asian man, but wear cross.'

'What are you talking about, Pima?' asked Claire.

'Never mind, Miss Claire.' Pima looked confused, as if aware she should not have spoken to her mistress in front of a visitor.

'She's just remembered something about the body on the beach, at the yacht club – I think I told you. It was a few months ago now. She said it was an Asian wearing a cross. Sounds very strange.'

'Did they find out who he was? I remember you mentioned it at the time,' said Claire, not especially interested.

'I don't know. I didn't hear anything more about it. I suppose if it'd been a Westerner there might have been more publicity. But Pima thought she'd seen the dead guy once before at a party, not here, at the Bank or the Embassy. You know she waits at parties sometimes.'

They had been speaking too fast for Pima to follow the conversation, but she suddenly repeated the word Embassy.

'Excuse me, what did you say, Pima?'

'Pima see Asian man wear red shirt with cross at Embassy, same dead man.'

'Are you sure?' asked Deborah.

She drew Claire out of the room and muttered, 'She's confused, poor girl. It doesn't sound very likely that a man would wear a red shirt to an Embassy party. I mean, they always dress quiet and conservative on an occasion like that.'

Claire felt a strange lump in her stomach. 'Except for Pel.'

'Who?'

'Someone I used to work with. A nice boy. He went away a few months ago. And he hasn't come back.'

'When was this?'

Claire gulped. 'Last August. When did Pima see the body?'

'I think it was around then. I remember because I had just weaned Jojo. Let me get my calendar. Where's my purse?' She went through to the hall and came back with a straw bag. She rummaged around in the bottom and produced her diary. 'Yes, right, August the ninth we went to the club.'

Claire said slowly, 'Well, I last saw Pel in the first week of August.'

'And did he wear a cross, this Pel guy?'

'Yes, yes, he's a Christian, quite devout.' Claire paced about. 'Another thing about him, he was rather a sharp dresser in an informal way. He never wore a tie. And he did go to the Embassy, to Lucy's, once with Jean-Louis, but I can't remember when, except I was there too, and . . . and Howard.'

'Was Pima serving?'

'I honestly can't say. The main thing I remember about the evening was, well, I brought Howard back here afterwards and we, well, we got together, as it were.'

'And now you're two-timing him,' said Deborah, changing the subject with sudden and surprising ferocity.

Claire flushed. 'How do you mean?'

'I'm not blind, Claire. We live in the same block and I saw you with Drew, in his car, early one morning. I guess it's none of my business, but Howard is a good friend.'

'It's over with Drew. I don't really want to discuss it. It's a private matter. Just like your affair with Alex. Don't worry, I didn't say anything to anyone about that.'

Deborah suddenly started to cry.

Claire put her arms around her. 'Oh, I'm sorry. I didn't mean to attack you, not now when you're upset and . . . I don't blame you about Alex. I'm not criticizing. Please don't think that. You deserved a bit of fun. But I wanted you to have someone older, more suitable who could take you away from Johnny, look after you and . . . oh, please, don't cry.'

Deborah said, 'I guess I'm miserable about Mom, and then there was the long flight and the funeral and all that. And Alex is gone. And my life, my marriage is a mess right now.' Her shoulders shook as she held on to Claire. Eventually she was quiet.

Feeling inadequate and out of her depth, Claire patted her. 'Everything will sort itself out. I mean, as far as you're concerned. It'll be OK. As I said, I think you deserve some one much nicer than Johnny.'

Deborah smiled a little. 'You're a good, kind, supportive friend.' A few moments later she said, 'But I guess I should sort out my life myself. I don't know why everyone assumes a woman needs a man to take care of her. I don't need taking care of. I'll manage fine on my own.'

TWENTY-THREE

Claire could do little about Deborah's problems, but she felt there must be some action she should take about Pel. When she considered the matter calmly, it seemed extremely unlikely that he was the body on the beach, and yet there had been no word from him since his departure.

These preoccupations had partially taken her mind off Drew, who had not contacted her since their quarrel after the flood. She waited for an explanation, an apology, a reassurance, but none came. It seemed to prove what she had known all along: he was not seriously interested in her. All that semi-romantic stuff he had dished out was obviously just a line. As she should have recognized. Be realistic, woman, she told herself miserably – it was only lust, at least for him.

Twice she'd started to dial his number but had immediately put the receiver down. Then, swallowing her pride, she tried again on two or three different evenings, letting the phone ring for what seemed like ten minutes. Obviously he had left for Australia, to see his wife, without even saying goodbye. So that was that.

In an unhappy moral daze, she'd continued her relationship with Howard as if the three nights with Drew had never taken place, an episode she was determined to bury along with her feelings about him. But she had major misgivings about her own bad behaviour. She tried to concentrate on Howard, who loved her in a proper steadfast manner. Despite these efforts, Drew was still the first thought to enter her head every morning, and every night she brooded about him until she went to sleep, the bastard. She was in a state of guilty indecision and not at all proud of the fact that, having been unfaithful to Howard, she had sunk back into his arms. She knew she should give up all idea of a future with either man, and remain alone and independent. After all, she'd spent many years alone and independent and all the better for that. But somehow she couldn't bring herself to finish with Howard and hurt him so badly.

Instead she found herself being particularly kind and gentle with him, to assuage her unconfessed sins.

Making an effort to share her problems and thoughts with him – or almost all her thoughts – she decided to ask his advice about the matter of the body on the beach and to tell him about its possible connection with Pel. When she discussed this mystery, however, Howard said firmly that dead bodies were the concern of the local police, happened all the time, she mustn't take it seriously, that there was no reason to suppose it had anything to do with Pel's disappearance. Anyway, it was absolutely not the sort of thing she should become involved with, in any circumstances.

Ignoring this sensible advice, Claire went to see Lucy, who confirmed that she did indeed keep records of every party: it was all part of diplomatic life, entertainment allowance and all that. She remembered the evening Claire had in mind because it was the first reception she had given and some agriculture people had come from England.

Lucy began to look through her files, which were not as well organized as she had claimed. Claire watched impatiently as Lucy picked up one set of bills and papers after another, with lots of sighs and sorrys and oh dears.

Suddenly Lucy gave a cry of triumph. Here was the party in question. Claire was on the list, and so were Jean-Louis and Pel. She remembered Pel particularly because he was wearing a red open-necked shirt without a jacket, highly conspicuous amid the surrounding suits. Claire hugged her and told her she was very clever to remember such things, but what about Pima? Was she on the list to serve drinks? Lucy rifled through the file again and eventually found a set of accounts. Pima's name was down as having received the equivalent of ten pounds for the evening's work.

Claire thought about the matter all night. Next day, before she went to work, she printed a photograph of Pel and took it upstairs to show Pima. The maid looked worried and said she was not sure. Maybe he was the man on the beach, but maybe he wasn't.

All the way to the office in the bus (her car, never the same since the flood, had broken down again) she practised what she would say to Jean-Louis.

She waited until he had had his morning coffee and smoked his second low-tar cigarette, then she took a deep breath and spoke. 'Jean-Louis, I thought you should know that a young Asian man wearing a cross was fished out of the sea near the yacht club last August quite soon after Pel left here.'

A strange expression passed over his pudgy face for a second, and then he smiled. 'Ah, do not make yourself anxious, Claire. I have received word from Pel since then. He is safe in Thailand.'

She smiled happily. 'Oh, what a relief! You didn't tell me.'

'I am sorry, my dear. I suppose I imagined that he would have communicated with you directly since he was so fond of you.' These last words were spoken without any sarcastic overtone, but Claire found herself flushing.

'Well, yes, perhaps he should have sent me a postcard or something. Still I'm glad you've heard from him.'

Friendly and calm, Jean-Louis passed the day much as usual, except that he tended to make most of his telephone calls when she was out of the room.

Just before she was about to go home, she said, 'Can you give me Pel's address so I can send this on to him?'

'What is that?'

'A book he lent me.'

'Ah, he has removed from his present address. When I hear from him, I will forward the book. Give it to me, please. Now is it not time for you to leave? *Au revoir. A demain.*'

Claire left by the front door, as normal, but then she changed her mind and skirted round the house to the garden at the back. She would sit for a minute and relax by the pool before going to the bus stop: one needed to be feeling strong to face public transport in Maising. She lay stretched out on the daybed and pulled down the long fringed canopy to screen herself from the setting sun.

After a little while she heard footsteps. She peered through the fringe to see the handsome figure of Meng walking up the steps to the verandah. He did not see her. Her curiosity roused, she decided not to move. She heard sounds above her: Suni bringing drinks for Meng and Jean-Louis. Then she heard Jean-Louis dismiss the maid.

'Where is your assistant?' asked the suave, educated voice of Meng.

'She has gone home.'

'A charming woman. And so attractive.'

'An inquisitive woman. I am thinking of dispensing with her services quite soon, sending her back to England.' Claire was shocked by the malevolence in his tone.

'Why? I thought you found her work satisfactory.'

'She is indeed extremely competent, but she has begun to ask questions about Pel. She is even talking about a body on a beach. A stupid coincidence, but we don't want any unnecessary scandal.'

She could hear Meng draw in his breath. 'Ah, that is why you wanted to see me.' Jean-Louis said, 'But you have disposed of the evidence?'

'Of course.'

'All of it, I hope.'

'Well, I have got rid of his belongings as you asked. But I've kept a little souvenir of the boy.'

'Imbecile,' snapped Jean-Louis. 'What souvenir?'

'Amongst his possessions I found a small ivory bird – such delicate work, fully articulated, quite enchanting. Japanese, I believe. A collector's item – I couldn't bear to destroy it.'

'And what have you done with this, this souvenir?'

'I have put it amongst my collection of ivory figurines.

It's not conspicuous there. No one save you or I will recognize it.'

'What about Claire, or my maid?'

'You told me that he kept all his possessions in his room. You are not suggesting Claire was in the habit of visiting him there.'

'Not as far as I am aware.'

'And the maid is unimportant.'

'Yes, she is. But . . .'

'Calm yourself, Jean-Louis. I shan't be inviting Claire or Suni to my house. They aren't my type. I see no problem, no risk.'

'You're mad. You must dispose of this ornament.'

'If I try to sell it, or throw it away, I may draw attention. As it is, you may rest assured that among a dozen other pieces of ivory it is invisible.' She could hear the scraping of his chair as he stood up. 'Now the mosquitoes are beginning to bite. Let's go inside, Jean-Louis, so I can examine those papers you wanted to show me. We must ensure that the bus contract goes to the generous Mr Nisaki, mustn't we?'

As soon as they had gone into the house, Claire tiptoed away. Terrified that they would see her from the window and know that she had been eavesdropping, she ducked down low behind the bank of shrubs until she was safely around the corner. Then she ran down the drive so that she arrived at the bus stop exhausted and sweating.

All the way back to the city in the stifling malodorous bus, she wondered what she should do. She was shaking with shock and anger. Pel really was dead, but would anyone believe her if she said Jean-Louis had had him killed?

It suddenly came to her that Lucy's husband would be the best person to take action, so, instead of going home, she made her way to the Embassy.

Far from being anxious to help, Lucy became quieter and quieter as she told her the story.

'Claire, I don't think I really want to be involved,' she said. 'It's really nothing to do with me – or the Embassy. Pel wasn't a British subject. Can't you just go to the police?'

'I'm a young, foreign female, for God's sake. They won't take any notice of me. Jean-Louis is big pals with half the police force – he's always having one of the chief policemen to dinner. I mean it's not really my business either, but they might listen to Martin.'

'No.'

'I think they're bound to,' said Claire, certain that she was right.

'No, you don't understand. I don't want to tell Martin about Meng.'

'What? Not say he's involved in murder?'

'I mean I don't want to mention him at all. He is, was a friend of mine, sort of.' She spoke nervously, staring at the floor, her face flushed.

Claire gazed at her. There was something very odd about Lucy's tone. 'What do you mean?'

There was no reply.

Claire said, 'Surely you don't mean . . .? You're not having an affair with him, are you?'

'No, of course not.'

Claire took her arm. 'What? Lucy, tell me, what is the matter?'

'He could blackmail me. No, not blackmail. I mean, he just has a hold on me that he could use if he wanted.' She could hardly bring the words out.

'What kind of a hold?'

Lucy walked to the window and stood with her back to the room. 'I just can't talk about it.'

After a pause Claire said, 'I can't go to the police with no real evidence. If only I could take a photo of the ivory bird at Meng's or get hold of it, but that would be too risky. Unless you go, maybe. He won't be suspicious of you if you're a friend. You could go to his house and get it. I can describe it.'

'No, I won't go there again. Not ever.'

'Lucy, you must help. Someone's been killed. He's a very sweet, harmless boy who was kind and helpful to me. I have to do something. I don't know if there were any other friends but me.' She gestured towards Lucy. 'Anyway, if Meng gets arrested for being involved in murder, he'll be put in prison and then he can't blackmail you or whatever he's doing.'

Claire did not seem to be able to get through to Lucy, who would not look her in the eye and remained by the window playing with the fraying end of her woven belt.

'Meng couldn't possibly be a murderer, he's very gentle,' said Lucy eventually.

'Maybe he didn't actually do it, but he knew about it,' said Claire. 'I told you about what I overheard. And then there's this mysterious hold he has over you. There is something very peculiar about him.'

There was another long silence and then Lucy said, 'I've changed my mind. I think we could go to Meng's house – in the morning when he's at the dig and look for the ornament – and other, er, evidence. It won't be dangerous, if we go together. I'm sure he'd never harm us.'

'He must have a maid. She's bound to let us in, two respectable-looking Englishwomen, but we can't search the house in front of her.' Claire paced around. 'Perhaps we can think up an excuse. Is she a bright kind of girl?'

'No, an old woman, rather slow-witted, Meng said.'

'Good,' said Claire excitedly. 'You speak enough of the language to communicate, don't you? You can distract her, lure her into the kitchen or the garden, while I look for the ivory bird.'

'But what will it prove? I mean Meng could say Pel gave it to him,' said Lucy, still sounding agitated.

'No, I remember Pel told me it was his most precious possession – the only thing he had that belonged to his parents. He would never have parted with it. I'm not the only person who knows about it. Suni, Jean-Louis' maid, she must have seen it in Pel's room.'

'But . . .'

'Come on, Lucy. If you won't consult Martin about this, then you and I have got to do something. Besides, as you said, we might find other evidence at Meng's.'

'Yes, we might,' said Lucy guardedly.

Two days later, Claire rang the office to say she was ill. Then she collected her car from the repair garage and Lucy from the Embassy. The traffic was heavy until they began to leave the city behind.

'You say you've been here before. Are you sure this is right?' asked Claire, as they found themselves in an obscure northern suburb of Maising.

'Yes,' said Lucy, sounding unconvinced. 'But I can't even see the road signs.' Among the shacks and shophouses, Claire's nerve was beginning to fail and Lucy became agitated, but eventually the road became wider and they found themselves driving past small, solid single-storey houses. At Lucy's instructions, Claire made a series of turns. 'I'm sure we're going in circles. Haven't we passed that noodle stall before?'

'Oh, yes . . . and then there's that poor dead dog again.' A little later Lucy suddenly said, 'Turn left and park here. I think we'd better walk.'

Evidently pleased she had found the way after all, Lucy became relatively composed. She stopped in front of a large iron gate and rang the bell. An old woman in a white blouse and purple sarong opened the gate. When she saw the novel vision of two quaint foreign girls, she grinned broadly. Lucy, smiling back, asked for Meng, saying she was a friend.

The maid admitted them to the house, speaking in a high squeaky voice, throwing in the odd word of English. Extremely ugly with a snub nose and small eyes, like a cheerful pig, she invited the girls to sit down and brought them drinks of Coca-Cola along with some sickly sweet white cakes wrapped in bamboo leaves. She seemed particularly fascinated by Claire's blonde hair and kept touching it, talking all the while. As far as they could understand her, she seemed to be saying that her master would soon be home for lunch.

Claire looked at her watch. It was already eleven o'clock. With a slightly later start than she'd planned and then getting so lost, they were well behind schedule.

'We'll have to go. I can't face him,' hissed Lucy.

'Surely he won't be having lunch this early. Try and get the woman out of the room,' murmured Claire.

The maid smiled and made eating gestures; then she rushed out of the room. Before the girls could move, she came back with a basket. She spoke again, and waddled toward the front door. Lucy smiled back in sudden comprehension and thanked her.

'What are you thanking her for?'

'She says she is sure Professor Meng will invite us to stay to lunch. She's going to the market to get some more food. She'll be back in twenty minutes, she says. I didn't know he was a professor. How grand.'

'I don't give a damn if he's Einstein, he's still a very shady character. But you did well to get rid of her,' whispered Claire, smiling at the old woman.

As soon as the maid had gone, Claire searched the room. The whole house was like a small, cluttered and disorganized museum. Every shelf, every table, was crammed with ancient pottery, ornaments and objets d'art, apparently grouped at random. She was beginning to despair of ever finding anything when suddenly she saw a low shelf full of ivory figurines and right in the middle of it was Pel's bird. Taking a quick photograph of it in situ, she put the treasure into her pocket. Then she hurried towards the desk and began to open drawers at random, but the only papers written in English were archaeological reports. Anyway, she had no idea what she was looking for. Meanwhile, Lucy continued to riffle through some large folders in the corner.

'There's so much stuff, but I can't find anything else interesting,' said Claire urgently. 'I think we'd better go now before the maid gets back – or Meng for that matter. What were you looking for? Did you find anything among those photos?'

'No, nothing. Claire, you didn't see any negatives, did you? I suppose there must be a dark room somewhere.'

'We really have to go. Quick, I'm getting nervous. I've got the ivory bird, that's the main thing.'

'But I need to find something else,' said Lucy, staring around.

'There just isn't time. Come on.' Claire suddenly heard the garden gates clanking open. 'Oh my God. Listen, a car. Quick, it's him.'

Lucy stood transfixed, white in the face.

'Go to the front door, stall him,' hissed Claire, intending to replace the ivory bird.

But it was too late. Handsome and godlike as ever, Meng appeared. He'd met the maid in the road and was delighted to hear that they were staying to lunch. Beaming at them both, he stood in the middle of the room. 'Make yourselves at home. I always take a shower as soon as I get back from the dig, but before I do, can I get you a drink?'

Lucy opened her mouth and shut it and then managed a whispered, 'No, thank you.'

'No, I mean, yes please . . . er, lime juice or water or anything, please,' stuttered Claire, convinced that he was staring past her at the shelf of ivories. While he was out of the room, she rummaged in her pocket and put the precious ivory bird back with the other pieces. She was too agitated to remember whether or not it was in the same position as she had found it.

TWENTY-FOUR

'What a ridiculous, terrifying and pointless expedition,' said Claire, putting her foot on the accelerator. She wanted to get away as fast as possible.

Lucy did not speak.

A little later Claire said, 'At least Meng didn't seem to suspect anything. All that risk for nothing. I didn't even have the guts to carry my great plan through. Wouldn't have been any good as a spy or a private detective, would I? Sorry, Lucy, hope you're OK.'

'I'm OK,' said Lucy, but her voice faltered. 'Um, I've been thinking, was it dusty?'

'What?' asked Claire.

'The shelf where you found the ivory ornaments.'

'Well, no, it was much the tidiest – looked as if it had just been cleaned and rearranged. That's why I noticed it.'

'Good,' said Lucy.

'I can't think what to do next, except I have got the photo. But I've just realized there's nothing to prove it was taken at Meng's house, so it doesn't help much, so stupid,' said Claire, turning the wheel sharply to avoid a stray dog. They were now nearly back in the centre of town.

'Whatever you do, I can't do it with you,' said Lucy in a rush.

When they arrived at the Embassy, she got out of the car and ran to her house, hardly saying goodbye.

Back at her own flat, door locked, windows shut, Claire could not rest although she felt utterly exhausted. She paced about. She would like to have talked to Howard, but he was away on a business trip. She would have liked to talk to Drew, but he had disappeared from her life.

During a long, tense night she formed a plan of asking Deborah to telephone Jean-Louis to say she was still unwell and couldn't go to the office for a few days. At least then she would have time to think.

For three days she sat at home, seeing only Deborah, and discussing the problem over and over again. Eventually, as nothing untoward or unexpected happened, she began to relax a little. Meng must actually have believed Lucy's weak excuse about calling to see him on the subject of archaeology lectures for Embassy staff. In fact, he'd behaved in a perfectly charming manner, and seemed as kind and gentle as Lucy had said.

Claire pondered about the conversation she had overheard between him and Jean-Louis. Could she have misunderstood? Perhaps, but she didn't think so.

'Of course you did. Too much imagination, like all women,' said Howard on the telephone from Singapore. 'Naturally I don't approve of those gay types, but it's quite ridiculous to say they're criminals. Not likely to be involved in bodies on beaches. Ridiculous, as I said in the first place. Be sensible, go back to work, and if you have the slightest problem, give me another ring. But I'll be out of contact at the weekend, going up-country.'

The next day she returned to the office. Jean-Louis treated her with such gentlemanly consideration, with so many kind enquiries about her health, and so many reminders to take it easy, that eventually she was almost, but not entirely, reassured by his unthreatening manner.

Day followed day in gentle routine and in an atmosphere of calm. Then on Friday Jean-Louis reminded her he had made arrangements for her to view the Buddhist art collection of Kim Kwan. Kim Kwan was a millionaire from Hong Kong who had recently bought one of the local islands. Claire longed to see the famous collection which had been transferred to his new home.

That evening as she was packing her bag for the overnight boat trip, she began to have renewed doubts. Jean-Louis said the local ferry only called at Kim Kwan's island every ten days. She must catch it this evening, spend the night on the island, and the following day a private launch would return her to Maising. But Claire wondered if it was sensible to go off by herself on a boat trip organized by Jean-Louis.

Howard was still away – in fact still out of contact – but
he would no doubt remind her that she was being over-
imaginative. As he said, she'd probably somehow misunderstood
the whole conversation she'd overheard between Meng and
Jean-Louis. They could just have been disposing of Pel's
things, even the ivory bird, because he had left them behind,
accidentally or on purpose, when he went away so suddenly.
The body on the beach could just have been the remains of
an unlucky stranger.

Finally she convinced herself that the attractions of the trip
were greater than the imaginary dangers. She might never get
another chance to see the Kwan collection, a collection which
was reputed to be even more extensive than that of Jean-Louis.
The visit would be of great professional interest. She must
think about her career: she might soon be unemployed and
Mr Kwan might give her a job. Then she could stay in this
part of the world.

She did not even admit to herself that she wanted to stay
in Maising in the hopes that one day Drew would return.

Yes, she would make the trip, but, to be on the safe side,
she would tell Deborah exactly when and where she was going.
She hurried downstairs and knocked on the Case's door.

Johnny answered it. His dissolute reptilian face was shiny
and yellowish, his shirt dishevelled. 'Claire! What a treat!'
He leered at her, grabbing her arm and pulling her into the
hall. He smelt of stale sweat and gin. 'What a piece of luck!
Come and have a little drinkie with old Johnny, put a bit of
colour in your cheeks, make your hair curl.'

'No, thanks.'

'Nonsense. Just what you need. G & T, isn't it?' He ushered
her into the sitting room and, turning to the drinks table,
slurped a generous tot of export gin into a tumbler. 'There's
no more ice, damn it. Can't get that fool Pima to make enough.
Always melting too quickly, ice, very unreliable.'

Claire perched on the edge of her chair. 'Can I have a word
with Deborah?'

'Deb's not here. Gone out to some fearful island cultural
evening. Back late, she said. Lucky, isn't it, that I am all on
my ownio? Gather your boyfriend is away too. Wonder what
you and I can do to amuse ourselves? How about a spot of
dins at a nice restaurant, and then we could go to a little

nightclub I know where all sorts of exciting things happen, things a nice girl like you could hardly imagine – most educational for you.'

Claire got up. 'Sorry. I've got to go now. I must really. Have to catch a ferry,' she said hastily. 'But, er, can I write a note to Deb.'

'All rightee – there's paper by the phone. Or should be. Deb's not the most organized woman.'

She found a notepad and a blunt crayon of Sam's and scrawled a few words. 'Where can I put it where she'll see it?'

'Give it to me, darling. Kids tend to mess the house up a bit. Can't find anything these days.' He peered at the note, then put it in his pocket.

'You won't forget to give it to her, will you? You see – it's important. I'm just letting her know where I'm going. To Kwan's island. For the weekend.'

'Where's that?' he asked blearily. 'And which lover are you going with this time?'

'Don't be stupid. Johnny, you will give her the note, won't you?'

'Course I will – now give me a little kiss before you go.'

Claire avoided his outstretched arms and quickly made her escape. Back in her own flat, door bolted, she tried to telephone Lucy, but the maid told her that sir and madame were out for the evening. Before she left, Claire decided to text Deb and Lucy to tell them her plans, not that she had a huge amount of faith in the Maising mobile network. Sometimes messages arrived and sometimes they did not.

After an uncomfortable night on a smelly sluggish ferry, hardly more than a large fishing boat, Claire was relieved to step ashore. Most of the other passengers had disembarked – noisily and disruptively – at other obscure islands on the way and, apart from a sleepy-looking Chinese man, Claire was the only person to leave the boat at Kim Kwan's remote island.

Even though it was only just dawn, she was surprised not to be met. She looked around for reassurance that she had arrived at the right place. Apart from an open palm-thatched shelter, there were no buildings to be seen. Gurgling and thumping, the ferry backed away from the jetty.

The Chinese, whom she judged by his clothes to be a servant, beckoned to her. Claire looked around again. She had no choice but to follow the little man along what appeared to be a newly made path around the rocks. Turning the corner, she stopped in amazement. It was just light enough to see that ahead of them stood a long staircase decorated with green stone snakes and Chinese dragons. At the top of the staircase stood an elaborate red and gold building, a temple-like edifice which looked as if it had been brought piece by ornamental piece from the Forbidden City in Beijing.

The servant, still without speaking, shuffled up the stairs and rang on a large bell-pull. Eventually another man, perhaps the butler, answered the door and greeted her with a low bow, his hands pressed together.

'Wel-come,' he said, and led her through to a courtyard where a table was laid for breakfast, complete with a shining silver coffee set and marmalade in a cut-glass jar.

He pulled a chair out for her and, as she sat down, handed her a typewritten note.

Miss Downing,
Sorry I cannot be with you. Please make yourself at home.
KK

'I didn't know Mr Kwan was going to be here. When are you expecting him?' asked Claire.

The butler, portly and solemn with a pale flat face, bowed low again. 'No unsthand Englith,' he lisped.

Claire spent an absorbing day photographing, making notes and sometimes just gazing at the beautiful statues, vases, fragments of ancient figures and shards of pottery, all displayed and lit with professional expertise around Kwan's extraordinary house. How on earth had he achieved all this so far from civilization? she wondered.

Suddenly to her surprise she saw two Buddha heads that looked exactly the same as those she'd found in the glory hole in her flat. The ones Pel said he would return to their rightful place. She picked them up and examined them – she was pretty sure they were the same. Curiouser and curiouser. Somehow she doubted Kim Kwan was the original owner of these Buddhas. She'd always assumed they had been looted from a temple. Were they stolen goods that he had acquired or what? Feeling shaky in the pit of her stomach, she photographed them anyway.

Was it a wise thing to do? But then she had been invited here.

From time to time, with polite gestures, the butler served her drinks or delicious Chinese titbits on a silver tray. He seemed to anticipate exactly when she was hungry or thirsty. That evening, after a solitary dinner – an aromatic dish of fish with peculiar vegetables – another servant appeared, a thin old woman. She was also Chinese and spoke no English either, but Claire was obscurely pleased to see another female. The amah showed her to a modern air-conditioned bedroom and bathroom, smart and luxurious like an international hotel suite. In these comfortable surroundings, she was soon asleep.

She rose early the next morning in order to complete her studies before the return trip. 'What time is the boat?' she asked periodically of the butler and the amah. Both smiled uncomprehendingly.

Eventually, when no launch appeared by mid-afternoon, Claire went for a long hot walk around the jetty area. She could not find any sort of boat, nor any other inhabitants on the island. She returned to the house.

'Telephone? Is there a satellite telephone or radio system?' she asked, gesturing with her hand and holding an imaginary receiver to her ear. She was met with the usual polite impassive lack of response. Of course she couldn't get a signal on her mobile out here, but there must be some method of talking to the outside world. She began to explore the house. The butler padded solicitously after her, but merely shrugged his shoulders when she came across two or three locked doors. 'Solly, no thpeak Englith,' he repeated now and then.

Eventually, as darkness fell, Claire resigned herself to another night on the island.

It wasn't until her third evening that she began to suspect that, either by accident or design, she was stuck until the ferry returned in ten days' time. If in fact it did return.

As the hours dragged by, she found she was no longer able to appreciate either the charm of the antiquities or the

splendours of the house. She packed her bag and sat watch-
fully by the jetty.

Still polite, the servant brought her food on a tray and placed
it on a small wooden table under the palm shelter. Kind and
courteous, he opened the door when she, tired, worried and cross,
returned to the house at night. She lay in bed more and more
convinced that she had been deliberately lured into this
luxurious prison. No one knew where she was, apart from
Jean-Louis and Deb, if Johnny had given her the note. Perhaps
he intended to keep her there for weeks, and eventually throw
her into the sea like Pel. No, no, such thoughts were ridiculous.
These Chinese servants were gentle people, even if they could
not, would not, summon her a boat.

Eventually Claire became angry. She shrieked at the butler,
'Boat. Must have boat. Telephone? Radio? Computer?' She
led him to the locked doors.

But he merely shook his head sorrowfully, embarrassed at
her lack of control. 'No have key.'

'So you do speak a bit of English. Where is Mr Kwan?'

'Come soon.' But he did not come and as each long day
dragged on in the same uneventful way, Claire's sense of fore-
boding increased. She could not eat much nor could she sleep.
And she certainly couldn't work. She spent her time by the
jetty staring out to sea.

On her fifth afternoon on the island she was dozing in the
shade of a large rock when she heard the sound of an engine.
She stared as a distant white motor cruiser advanced majes-
tically towards them. It grew larger and larger until there was
no longer any doubt. It was heading for the island.

In a panic, Claire began to run down the beach. Flinging
off her dress, she waded into the sea. She would swim out
to her rescuers before any one could stop her. She dived under
the water and began to swim as fast as she could. Now and
then she surfaced and looked back. No one was attempting
to pursue her. Encouraged, she swam on, but still far from
the boat she began to weaken. Gasping for breath and treading
water, she looked back at the shore again. The butler appeared
to be waving or signalling to the motor boat. It dawned on
her suddenly that she could be swimming towards another
trap. Numb with despair, she turned on her back and floated
until eventually the cruiser drew close to her.

Silhouetted against the sky, a uniformed crewman leant over the railings, trailing a lifebelt. As Claire clung to the belt, she was towed around to the stern of the boat where a teak ladder was extended into the water. Feeling too exhausted to care what happened next, she clambered aboard.

The sailor led her around the deck and down into the cabin. There, wearing huge sunglasses, a peaked cap, white jeans and blue sailor shirt, sat a glamorous Maising woman. She gave an order and the sailor departed.

The woman spoke in English with a strong American over-tone. 'It is good you don't recognize me. Please continue to pretend that you don't know me. I must now go ashore and talk. It's best if you speak as little as possible when I am gone.'

Claire stared. 'Is it you? – Liana, what on earth are you doing here?'

'I'll explain, but not yet. Now please keep quiet. I must talk to the servants and make out like I am acting on Kim Kwan's orders. It will be best if you stay in the cabin, particularly in your current outfit.'

Claire was suddenly conscious that she was dripping wet, and clad only in her semi-transparent Marks & Spencers underwear.

Liana smiled again, her lipstick red against her pale cream face and perfect teeth. 'Here, drink this. Then why not take a shower? There are some clothes of mine in the locker opposite the bathroom. Help yourself to whatever you want.'

'But . . .'

'Just do what I say,' said Liana, suddenly adopting a threatening tone as another crew member knocked on the door of the cabin.

Too confused to argue, Claire watched her leave. She gulped down the Coke without tasting it. Then she looked for the shower. She found it amidships: a real shower with real water. The towels were white and fluffy. There was shampoo and soap and scent all neatly slotted into a small shelf. She showered as quickly as possible and then looked for something to wear. In the designated locker, she found a minuscule bikini and a long T-shirt that covered its inadequacies.

When she had dressed she felt temporarily revived, but her misgivings returned as she sat in the cabin waiting for Liana to reappear. She heard noises above and then there was a great roar as the engines started. She held on to the edge of the table as the boat slewed round. Shortly after, Liana's elegant trousers descended the steps followed by the rest of her elegant body.

'Where are we going? What's happening? What about my camera – it's got all my latest photos, and my notes, and my luggage? Where do you fit into all this?' Claire's flood of questions was unstoppable. She had to raise her voice to be heard above the engines.

'Your luggage will be returned later.' Liana smiled. 'Right now we're going to Drew.'

'What?'

Liana spoke more loudly. 'I'm taking you to Drew.'

Her heart jolting, Claire remained suspicious. 'I thought he'd left for Australia.'

'He postponed his trip when he heard you'd gone missing.'

'But how did he know where I was?'

'He didn't. No one did. Apparently you disappeared without telling anyone where you were going.'

'I left a note for Deb . . . and Jean-Louis knew.'

'Jean-Louis is out of the country. Some people were concerned about your whereabouts,' she continued calmly. 'News that you'd disappeared reached Drew and he asked me to make enquiries. He knows that someone in my position can usually find out what they want to know.'

Claire raised her eyebrows. 'Your position?'

'I am a member of one of Maising's major families,' said Liana with pride. 'I have contacts in the Government and one of my brothers-in-law is Deputy Chief of Police. He was able to discover where you were.'

'But why didn't the police come and rescue me if they knew where I was?'

'Some thought you were in danger. Others said you were the guest of Kim Kwan, who must not be offended. The police are not interested in helping those who make unnecessary trouble in high places.'

Claire decided to ignore the implications of that remark. 'But what about the Embassy? Didn't they make a fuss?'

'Your employer's maid said you must be on holiday. Most people saw no reason to doubt her.'

'Not Deb or Lucy. Lucy wouldn't believe that.'

'Who?'

'Lucy at the Embassy. Did she tell Drew?'

'I don't know what she did or did not do. Only Deborah Case seemed really concerned about you and, of course, your friend Howard. But he, too, was inclined to think things should be done through official channels. But your other friend Drew knows that informal methods work best in this country, so he came to me for help.' Liana lit a cigarette and puffed smoke all around the teak-lined cabin.

Claire began to feel slightly seasick. 'But aren't you putting yourself in danger by rescuing me?'

'No, there is no danger, as long as you keep quiet about it.'

'Keep quiet about it? Why, I . . .'

Liana smiled. 'You ask a lot of questions, too many un-answerable questions. Here in Maising, life is colourful but obscure, not clear black and white. Drew understands that, unusually for a Westerner. He's sympathetic to our mentality. Here we go with the quiet discreet flow, the bamboo bends with the wind, as they say. You, too, should be more content to let things pass, then you wouldn't have so many problems.' She waved her languid fingers. 'Now we have a long journey – why not rest? You must be exhausted after such a long and unnecessary swim. Try to sleep a little so that when you meet Drew, you will be fresh.'

Claire flushed at her mildly ironic tone. 'But I still don't understand why you helped me. It's very kind, but you don't even know me.'

Liana stubbed out her half-smoked cigarette. 'Please, enough questions. You must remain below where you won't be seen. Your blonde hair is very conspicuous. Even when it gets dark you should stay in the cabin. You can sleep on one of those bunks.'

Claire stumbled into the forward cabin and lay down. The engine roar was less pronounced, but beneath her the bows of the boat thumped up and down on the water. Everything vibrated, juddered and rattled about. It wasn't a relaxing situation, but eventually, exhausted, she slept.

When the roaring stopped, she opened her eyes. It was night-time. To her astonishment she could hear the sound of disco music. She looked out of the porthole at fairy lights and palm trees.

'Where are we?' she asked when Liana appeared.

'Welcome to Sunny Island. I'll hand you over to Drew. Just make your way to Hut number twenty-eight. He'll be waiting.'

'But how . . .?'

'No time to ask questions. Just walk down the jetty and follow the path round to the right.'

'Aren't you coming?' asked Claire, fearing some kind of a trick.

'No. Now please go ashore. This is a holiday resort for Europeans. You won't be conspicuous here.'

'What about your clothes? I'm wearing your clothes.'

'Keep them – as a souvenir. And take these shoes too.' She took out an elegant pair of black leather sandals.

'Thanks, very kind, but . . . I couldn't.'

'Don't be silly – you need them.'

Claire put the sandals on her feet and then held out her hand. 'Thanks, and thank you very much for rescuing me.'

Liana shook hands politely. 'My pleasure. But you must say nothing to anyone about what I've done to help you. All right? If the wrong people find out, there may be trouble. Do you understand?'

'Yes, of course.'

'Now hurry. I cannot wait here.'

One of the crew handed Claire on to the jetty and then the cruiser went astern, turned and roared off. She felt abandoned. Would Drew really be here?

She walked to the end of the jetty.

TWENTY-FIVE

'Welcome to Sunny Island Resort Hotel' said the sign, just as Liana had promised.

Huts 18-36 were indicated to the right. Slowly Claire followed the curving path amongst coconut palms and thatched huts, neat and pretty. The holidaymakers could be heard in the distance, laughing and talking; the disco blared away. She thought of going to join them, to find help. But she walked on.

If only she could be sure Drew was really here.

Eventually she arrived at no 28, identical to all the other small round huts. The light was on inside. Her heart thumping, she crept round the back with the idea of peering through the window, but the sand was decorated with small seashells which scrunched beneath her feet. She started in fear as the door of the hut opened and a tall dark figure appeared.

'Claire? Is that you? Oh, thank God you're all right.'

She ran into Drew's arms and burst into tears of relief, burying her head in his shoulder.

He held her tight for a while and then he said gently, 'Hey, come inside. Don't cry. You're OK. But what the hell are you wearing? That T-shirt looks a bit small for you.'

'It's Liana's,' she said with a watery smile.

'Yeah, I guess you're a bit fat compared with her.'

'Fat!' spluttered Claire indignantly.

'That's better, made you laugh.' Taking her face in his hands, he kissed her gently and then with increasing passion. She clung to him tightly, her knees almost giving way beneath her. They remained holding each other for some moments. Then he peeled off her T-shirt, and his hands began to caress and explore, gently but insistently.

Head reeling, she pushed him away. 'No one said anything about sex being part of the deal,' she said breathlessly.

'Afraid it's obligatory for the rescued female to sleep with the rescuing male. You must've seen it in all the movies.' He pulled her to him again.

'But that's just so corny. Aren't you going to let me recover a bit?'

'Mm, no, can't wait any longer, waited too long, always waited too long for you.'

She smiled, her eyes closing. 'I repeat, you're supposed to . . . do the rescuing personally . . . but if you insist on your so-called rights,' she murmured between kisses.

'You bet I insist.'

Later he said, 'Now, have a drink and I'll tell you the plan while I serve dinner.'

'Sorry, I'm not very hungry.'

'Just sit down and shut up and listen. Do as you're told for a change.'

Claire looked around. 'Don't you want to hear about everything, about what happened? I certainly want to ask a few questions.'

'Yes, of course, but first things first. Just sit down and belt up. The food's ready, not very exciting, a kind of takeaway, but the best I could do. Sorry it's got a bit cold, but you would insist on sex. Eat up now, like a good girl.'

'Yes, my hero,' said Claire with a grin.

She sat down at the table and helped herself to a small portion of lukewarm fried rice.

'Liana's the heroic one, not me,' he said.

'Yes, she certainly is. Tell me, d'you always get women to do the dangerous dirty work for you?'

'Of course. They're so good at that sort of thing. Though Liana claimed it wasn't going to be that dangerous.' He smiled, and then sat down opposite. 'Now I thought I told you to drink and eat and be silent.'

'Yes, sir.'

'That's better. You women today don't have enough discipline. That's why you get yourselves in trouble. Now, listen, this is the plan for getting you back to Maising. We'll sail back on a Hobie Cat tomorrow.'

'A catamaran? Why can't we go on an ordinary passenger boat?'

'(A) There's no ordinary passenger boat leaving tomorrow and (B) no one will notice a blonde on a Hobie, that's why. Then I'll take you straight to Lucy's on my way to the airport.'

'The airport?'

'Yes, I have a flight to Australia tomorrow.'

Claire was silent for a moment and then she said quietly, 'Oh. And what about me?'

'Lucy says you can stay at the Embassy. You'll be safe there.'

'Oh.' She was still quiet. 'So you're going back . . . to your wife.'

Drew spoke gently. 'Like I told you, I'm going to Canberra to *talk* to Meredith. That's all.'

Pulling herself together, Claire said in a hearty kind of rush, 'Well, it was good of you to postpone your trip so you could arrange to save a damsel in distress.'

He smiled. 'You're bloody lucky to have been rescued at all. You don't sound very grateful.'

'Oh, Drew, I am grateful, truly. But why did Liana do it? And how come she knew where I was? How come nobody came before? What the hell was going on? I just don't know who's on what side. I mean who's on whose side?'

'It isn't a question of sides, but I'm on yours. And Liana likes to help out when she can. She's a great fixer. And she likes to demonstrate the clever and best way of doing things to us poor ignorant bungling foreigners. Always deal through locals with local knowledge, that's my principle. Works best in a country like this, or anywhere else for that matter. You'd disappeared so I asked Liana, a local expert, to find you – simple as that. Ask the right person and you get the right answer.'

'But I just don't understand – why her? What's her connection with Kim Kwan?'

'I don't know. I don't know anything about this great mystery of yours.'

'Well, how did you know I'd disappeared?'

'Deb called me – she was worried. Eventually Johnny remembered you'd left a note, but he'd lost it. He said you'd gone somewhere, but he couldn't remember where.'

'I see . . .' She paused deep in thought and then she asked, 'Are you still connected with her, with Liana?'

He grinned. 'If you mean am I sleeping with her, well, no more often than with all my other twenty girls. You're the best though, by far.'

'Bastard,' she said, punching him. 'Be serious for a moment.'

'Why d' you always have to know everything about everything, little Miss Nosy?'

'I'm not nosy. Only when you . . . when you like someone you want to know about them.'

'So you like Liana, do you?'

'No, you fool, you know perfectly well what I meant. I mean I quite like you, so I wanted to know about you, but you're always so damn secretive.'

He grinned. 'You do talk a lot of bull sometimes, Claire. Now, what d' you want to know about?'

'Oh, I don't know, everything. You, your wife, everything you haven't told me.'

He gestured towards her. 'If you come to Canberra, I can tell you at leisure. Nice place, Canberra, a bit staid perhaps, but it's attractive, good climate, great architecture, intelligent inhabitants like me.'

Claire's heart leapt, but she said quietly, 'Your wife will be there.'

'She won't be at the farm. She lives in town, leads her own life. We've separated. I told you before, but you wouldn't listen.'

'But you also said you wanted to sort things out with her.'

He walked around the room. Then he turned and stared at her. 'Maybe you're right. But it's more that I have to sort myself out.' His tone changed. 'Now, let's clear up this meal and have an early night. We're leaving first thing tomorrow. I'll wash the dishes. You dry and put them away under the sink. And you can tell me all about your crazy and not very successful detective work. Like why a nice sensible English girl got herself marooned.'

Claire smiled, a little sheepish. 'Yessir.'

He grinned. 'I approve of this new subdued Claire.'

While they were washing up she studied him. He was just the same, tall and brown and untidy. His hair was longer and curled slightly on his neck, in a very endearing way.

Later they stood in the doorway gazing at the dark sea. She shivered slightly as Drew put his arm around her.

'This reminds me of when we first had dinner together, at sunset at the restaurant on the pier,' she said.

'Mm. Me too. Boy, I fancied you like crazy.'

She smiled. 'Did you? The way I remember it, you spurned me.'

'Yeah, well, I was too shy. And you were a bit forward, inviting me up to your flat.'

Laughing, she punched him gently in the stomach. 'Forward! I was not forward!'

'Course you were. But now I've got you where I want you.' Nuzzling her ear, he whispered. 'Take off your clothes, slave, and submit yourself to my desires.'

'Again?'

'Mm.'

At one point, in the heat of their passion, she nearly said that she loved him, but she stopped herself, just in time.

During the night she woke up and began to think about all the questions she had asked and how no one, least of all Drew,

had given her any proper answers. Then he put his arm around
her and she found herself embroiled in him and his body and
his forceful, erotic love-making, and so again she stopped
thinking about anything else.

Next morning the wind was strong. Drew did not seem altogether
happy as he rigged the catamaran. 'We should've started earlier,
before the wind got up like this. When we get out there, you'll
have to go out on the trapeze.'

'What? I don't know how to. I mostly just crewed on
ordinary dinghies.'

'It's easy, common sense. You've seen the Hobies at the
sailing club. I was hoping that it wouldn't be necessary for
the crew to trapeze, but in this wind you'll have to. Here, put
on the harness.' He laced her into the blue and red canvas
contraption. 'Quite a good chastity belt, isn't it?' he said. 'This
hook clips on to the trapeze halyard – those wires that hang
down from top of the mast each side. In a strong wind the
large sail area makes the Hobie heel right over. To balance
the boat you need to hang from the trapeze on the windward
side – that's the side opposite the sail, the uphill side as it
were. Here, practise it on shore.'

'OK, I understand. I'm not thick, you know.' Claire clambered on to the trampoline and hooked herself on to a wire
rope. Then she leant back.

'Not bad,' said Drew. 'You're supposed to stand on the edge
of the boat and lean right out. Let the wire support you.'

On the beach Claire had found it quite comfortable, easy
even. Out at sea, however, it was another matter. The Hobie
raced along faster and faster. It was exhilarating at first, but
as they drew away from the shelter of the islands, Drew yelled
to her that she must go out, trapeze. Trembling, she knelt to
hook herself on to the wire rope that danced as it hung from
the mast high above. Then somehow or other, bracing one
foot again his leg, she stood up and leant back towards the
sea. Miraculously she kept her balance. The wind whistled
past her. She felt she was defeating the elements. 'Wow, I did
it,' she yelled triumphantly.

'Great. Now haul in the jib sheet a bit – that rope you're
clinging on to.'

The catamaran bowled along on the top of the waves. Clouds

of spray hit Claire and soon she was soaked. After an hour in the same position on the same tack, she became exhausted.

'Are you all right up there?' he yelled from the deck.

'I'm tired, cold, hungry and terrified. Otherwise just fine.'

'Can't hear. What did you say?'

'I said I'm fine.'

Just then one of the hulls hit a wave and the catamaran suddenly lost speed. Claire did not. She was swung forward like a monkey on the end of a rope, around the front of the mast and back again.

'Shit, bugger it!' She let out a string of expletives as she grazed her arms and bruised her legs on all the fitments placed on boats specifically designed, it seems, to injure the unwary sailor.

'What language! I didn't know you knew such words. Not such a polite little Pommy person after all,' said Drew, laughing as he hauled her back into position. 'Sorry about that: helmsman's fault. Still, we didn't capsize.'

'God, I didn't know there was any risk of that. I should have a wetsuit. I'm not dressed for this type of sailing. Is it much longer?' muttered Claire, rubbing her thigh.

'Only an hour. But you know the first law of sailing?'

'What's that?'

'On a sailing trip the time of arrival is always at least one hour later than the Captain estimates.'

'Oh God. I can't stick this out much longer. I'm not cut out for it, really I'm not.'

'But it's not so windy now. We're drawing near to Maising. Soon you'll be able to sit down and cuddle next to me.'

Claire watched as the shore line grew slowly closer. She began to pick out beach houses, then people and soon they were amongst other boats. She could see the familiar yacht club beach getting nearer and nearer and, at last, they arrived.

No one took any notice of them when Drew beached the boat at the club. Claire was almost too stiff to walk as she clambered down, and her fingers were almost too cold to unbuckle the clips and divest herself of the trapeze harness.

The head boat boy sauntered down to put away the boat. It was all a matter of routine for him, she realized. She wanted to scream and say, 'Look, we've arrived – we're safe,' but she kept silent.

Drew said, 'Just walk casually with me to the car park. Martin was sending an Embassy driver for us.'

'Really? Oh, great. But I'm petrified that Jean-Louis will suddenly appear.'

'I don't think so. Just keep walking.'

A white Ford with blue diplomatic number plates stood parked in the shade. The driver even had a couple of towels to hand. Gratefully Claire wrapped one around herself and sank back into the seat. Looking around, Drew got in beside her, arranging the other towel so that his wet swimming shorts would not damage the official upholstery.

She squeezed his hand. 'So far so good.'

They were silent on the drive back into the city. Claire was still mentally holding her breath, fearful that at any moment they would be ambushed. But eventually they arrived at the tall, crested Embassy gates. The guard opened them and saluted smartly.

'Thank you, Drew,' said Claire in heartfelt relief as they stopped under the portico of the large white colonial mansion.

'That's OK. Look, I have to go as soon as I'm ready . . . I left my gear here. Like I said, when I've changed, I need to get a taxi to the airport.'

'What, straight away?'

'Yeah, sorry. So I'll say goodbye now.'

'Oh, well, goodbye then.'

'I don't know what your plans are,' he said awkwardly.

'I don't know either,' she said, looking up at him.

'See you then. By the way, I left a note of my address and phone number in Oz. Told Lucy to give it to you.'

'Oh,' she said.

'Just in case you ever need it.'

'Right.'

He turned and rang the doorbell.

TWENTY-SIX

Lucy herself opened the door. She flung her arms around Claire. 'Oh, I'm so relieved you're OK. It's wonderful to see you. I've been so worried. Somjit has made up a bed for you. You must stay as long as you like.' She turned and then gave a squeak. 'Oh, Drew, I nearly forgot. I know you're in a rush to get to the airport. I won't hold you up. Your clothes and stuff are in the middle bathroom.'

With a quick apologetic grin, Drew raced up the stairs. Claire gazed after him. 'Come and sit down,' urged Lucy. 'Will you have something to drink?'

'Marvellous, I'd like two huge glasses of water, please – but I'd better shower first. I'm far too underdressed to sit on your smart chairs.'

Lucy laughed, squeezing her hand. 'Rubbish, but if you'd really rather change, I'll take you straight up to your room. I'll find you something to wear.'

After a luxurious bath, Claire dressed in the rather peculiar saggy pink shift-dress that Lucy had provided and, hoping to have a quiet moment with Drew, stood waiting on the wide upstairs landing. But there was no sign of him and so, reluctant to start opening all the grand-looking bedroom doors, she went slowly downstairs to join Lucy on the verandah.

The promised glasses of water had been placed by the side of a comfortable planter's chair. Claire sank down in relief and drank most of the first glass in one gulp.

Immediately Lucy began. 'Martin was so angry when he heard what we'd been up to. But I sort of played down my part in the whole thing. I didn't say it was me who went with you to Meng's. You have to understand, Martin's a lot older and in his job he has to be rather careful – and, without meaning to, I think I've been rather indiscreet. I mean, diplomats' wives are not meant to do silly things.'

'Yes, I'm sorry if I dragged you into it all, but I felt I had to do something about Pel. I expect the Embassy will see justice done now.'

Lucy shot her a quick glance. 'I think Martin wants to talk to you when you've recovered a bit. But you will be careful what you say about me and Meng, won't you?'

Blimey, thought Claire.

'Lucy, you're putting me in an impossible position. You'll have to tell me what he knows already.'

'I said you had reason to believe Pel had been murdered, that you thought Jean-Louis and Meng were involved and that you went to Meng's house to search for evidence, that's all I said. I have to tell you he thinks you've been very silly, acting like some sort of youthful Miss Marple. He says it's far too dangerous in this sort of place. Particularly as you may have overdramatized the situation, he thinks.'

'Hardly,' said Claire indignantly. 'But has anyone been arrested yet for kidnapping me?'

'I don't know. You weren't exactly kidnapped, were you?'

'Well, marooned then, deliberately marooned.'

'You'll have to talk to Martin later. Now, why don't you go and have a rest before dinner – you must be exhausted.'

'Yes, OK, thanks, but I have to say goodbye to Drew first.'

'Goodness, he's already gone – when you were in the shower just now.'

'Oh.'

'I mean, I explained that you were otherwise occupied, and I think he said something about having said goodbye to you already. He was in a terrific rush – I can't remember if he said anything else.'

'Oh.'

When Lucy disappeared to talk to her servants, Claire walked slowly round the garden reliving her last conversation with Drew. Did he care for her or didn't he? Surely, if he had really wanted to, he could have postponed his trip to Australia a little longer? Last night when they'd made love, it seemed as if he genuinely cared for her and yet now, without even saying goodbye properly, he had disappeared.

She stared down at the grass looking in vain for some kind of tropical daisy so that she could play 'He loves me, he loves me not' with the petals – it would be as reliable a guide to Drew's feelings as any indication he had given.

Howard, on the other hand, had always made his feelings perfectly clear. Poor Howard! She suddenly realized that she'd hardly given him a thought until now. He must be frantic with worry about her. She went inside to ask Lucy if she might ring him straight away.

He sounded overjoyed to hear her voice. 'Can I come round to see you?' he asked.

'Yes, of course, I expect Lucy won't mind – I'll just ask her – yes, she says that's fine. Maybe after dinner would be best. I'll have had my little chat with Martin by then. About nine o'clock.'

'Claire, we have to have a serious talk.'

'Oh, I . . . I'll see you later.'

Dinner was served by three maids. Claire sat with Lucy and Martin at one end of an astonishingly long mahogany table. Her hosts seemed quite at ease in these formal surroundings: Lucy, who had always appeared so awkward in her role as a grand lady and diplomatic hostess, seemed to have grown into the job. And she was somehow prettier this evening. Her eyes sparkled and occasionally she touched her husband's arm.

In the candle light, Martin looked distinguished, but younger and less grey than usual, and Claire noticed the tenderness with which he responded to Lucy's quiet, sometimes rather dull, conversational remarks. They really love each other, she thought with envy. Her own euphoria at being rescued had been dampened by Drew's departure, but she talked a great deal and drank an enthusiastic amount of wine.

After dinner, Martin and Claire were left alone. His long face took on a stern and official expression. 'You've caused a lot of trouble, Claire.'

Suddenly conscious of her own unimportance in the scheme of life, she felt like a small naughty schoolgirl in the presence of an authoritarian headmaster. 'I'm terribly sorry,' she said, 'but you see I felt I was doing the right thing – Pel was murdered and Jean-Louis was respon—'

'Lucy has told me all about it.'

Not quite all, I bet, thought Claire.

'You don't have any actual evidence, do you?' he continued. 'No actual proof that the body on the beach was Pel?'

'But I overheard . . .'

'Then it is not certain that any crime has been committed and, if it came to a trial, it would be your word against that of Vandenberg.'

'Yes, I suppose so. But he's such a creep. I bet he's got all sorts of skeletons in the cupboard. There's all his antique smuggling.'

He frowned. 'Do you have any proof, any documents?'

'No, but the police could get some, I'm sure. There was this mysterious locked filing cabinet and then when I got hold of the key, it was empty.' Even as she said the words, she realized how unconvincing this piece of non-evidence sounded. 'And Meng, the archaeologist, is involved,' she added more firmly.

'The man whose house you tried to burgle?'

'We . . . er, I didn't steal anything. I just tried to photograph and retrieve Pel's ivory bird,' said Claire, feeling increasingly foolish.

'And where is this ornament now?'

'I don't know. Still at Meng's, I suppose.'

'So you have no evidence,' he repeated.

'No, I haven't because I left behind my camera on Kim Kwan's island. I don't suppose I'll ever get it back.'

'Oh dear.'

His braying, expressionless voice was beginning to annoy her and the combination of wine and tiredness made her aggressive. 'But I was kidnapped, marooned, made a sort of hostage – I'm a British citizen. Surely the Embassy must take action?'

'I don't think any local court would believe your story. Jean-Louis Vandenberg is highly respected here. As of course is Kim Kwan. Both are very influential people. And your enforced stay on the island is not so unusual. Ferries here are not reliable.'

Claire interrupted, 'But Liana . . .'

'Liana and Drew may have exaggerated the danger of your position. I don't know why. As I said, you're not the first person to have missed an irregular ferry boat in these parts.'

'Missed a ferry boat?' she said indignantly. 'But I was held deliberately – for five whole days. Ask Liana.'

'Liana has already made it clear that her part in this strange matter must be kept quiet, hasn't she?'

'Yes, she has, I forgot, but Drew . . .'

'Drew has gone to Australia,' he said patiently.

So he has, she thought. 'He might come back,' she said uncertainly.

'Perhaps, but he will want to protect Liana.'

'Yes. I don't understand, but I suppose he will.' She felt the ground slipping away from under her feet. She began again. 'But you can't just let Jean-Louis get off. I don't know what you're trying to say. D'you think I made the whole thing up? That I marooned myself deliberately?'

'No, but it may all have been just a misunderstanding. You must realize things are not always what they seem in a country like this.'

Incredulous, she opened and shut her mouth. 'So you don't believe it. You don't believe I was held against my will, kidnapped?'

'Who knows? I'm not a policeman, Claire. I'm a diplomat,' he said suavely, 'And the diplomatic thing to do, just in case you actually were and are still in danger, is for you to leave the country.'

Shaking with anger and shock, Claire stood up. 'Leave the country? Why should I? I'm not the guilty one. It's not me who—'

'It so happens that someone is willing to give you a first-class plane ticket to the UK on condition that you go tomorrow.'

She stared at him. 'Who?'

'If I tell you, will you keep the whole subject confidential?'

She shrugged her shoulders. 'Well, yes, I suppose so.' What the hell was going on?

'You must give me your word, Claire.'

'All right, all right, I give my word. Cross my heart and hope to die.'

'If you leave Maising, your death is unlikely.'

'D'you mean you believe that if I stay I'm still in danger?'

'You may be. I don't know. Now just listen: British Coachworks are in an advanced stage of negotiations. They hope to get the contract to supply the capital with two hundred new buses this year and a further five hundred during the following years, plus a parts and maintenance agreement. You see what this means for future British exports in the area?'

'Yes, I think so, but . . .'

'Jean-Louis Vandenberg happens to be a director and a major shareholder of the Maising Bus Company. He has a great deal of influence with the local Minister of Transport

and is a friend of the Prime Minister. If the British Embassy
makes allegations that he's guilty of various crimes, allegations that we can't prove, then it's unlikely that Britain will
get the bus contract.'

'So?'

'So, if you were to create a fuss and antagonize Jean-Louis,
then British Coachworks would be out of the running and
would have to lay off workers instead of taking on extra men
to cope with the new contract. Men in the North East, a very
depressed area, would lose their jobs and possibly their homes,
all because of you.'

'I see,' she said, subdued. Then she rallied herself. 'But you
seem to have forgotten Pel. We don't even know why he was
murdered. What if Jean-Louis is a dangerous person who
should be stopped, in case he murders someone else?'

'There you go again with your wild accusations. We have
no reason to suppose Pel was the body on the beach. In fact,
I heard that the police identified it as that of a Chinese
criminal.'

'I don't believe it.' Claire marched up and down.

'Why don't you believe it? You just jumped to the wrong
conclusion, Claire, and now you're reluctant to admit it. Could
you go to court and swear it was Pel?'

'No, but . . .'

'You must understand that nothing is straightforward here.
In England when you turn up a stone, you'll merely find a
few harmless woodlice. Here you may find something
poisonous and deadly. So in the East it is best to leave stones
where they are. We Europeans must try to be pragmatic and
sensible, rather than behave like idealistic boy scouts.'

'But . . .'

'I know that on television if there's a body, then the
police or the private eye investigates and the murderer is
brought to justice. It's not always like that in real life.
Especially in this part of the world where accidental death
is a commonplace occurrence. As I said, the police have
made their own enquiries into the drowned man, whoever
he may be, and are satisfied. It's a local matter, though,
nothing to do with us. There's nothing you can or should
do about it. Far better to be sensible. In fact, you are doing
something positive by being sensible. Don't you see that

by leaving the country quietly, you can, indirectly, benefit a lot of unemployed people in England?'

'Oh, and what if I say I want to stay? Stay here and just keep quiet about everything.'

'I repeat, it may not be safe for you to stay, particularly if you may have, inadvertently, questioned the honour of Kim Kwan, who is even more influential than Jean-Louis. And perhaps more ruthless. There is no point in putting yourself at risk for someone who is already dead . . . that is, according to you.'

No longer sure of anything, Claire gave up the battle. 'Then it seems I have no choice.' After a pause she said, 'Am I permitted to go and collect my clothes from my flat? Oh, yes, and my camera – my photos and notes on Kwan's collection and my overnight case – they're still on the island. And what about Grace, my cat?'

'One of our security officers will accompany you to your flat and Lucy can help too. We'll have the cat here, if no other good home can be found for it. Lucy likes animals. You can take the usual large suitcase with you and British Coachworks will also pay for the rest of your effects to be air-freighted back home, along with your camera and so forth, if indeed they are returned.'

'Liana said they would be, though I guess the camera might not show up.'

'I'll speak to her,' he said. 'Now, do you want me to telephone your parents and ask them to meet you at the airport?'

'No, thanks. I'll fix things up myself. You and British Coachworks seem to be tying me up and forwarding me like a parcel, but I suppose I should be grateful.' She took a deep breath. 'Actually that sounds awful – I mean, I am truly very grateful for your hospitality. And for backing up Drew and Liana. It's just been a bit of a shock. I'm sorry, well, I'm sorry if I've been a nuisance.'

'Not at all. We're here to help.' He smiled, suddenly charming again now that she had fallen in with the official recommendations.

'Of course I could sell my story to the *Daily Mirror* when I get back,' she said. 'I WAS ISLAND SEX SLAVE, SAYS BRITISH GIRL, BUT EMBASSY LETS KIDNAPPERS GO FREE.'

Martin looked alarmed. 'You didn't say anything about a sexual attack.'

She laughed, thinking of Drew. 'Just a joke. I'll leave quietly and I won't go to the *Mirror*. Perhaps just the *Sun*, if I run out of money one fine day.'

Martin smiled grimly.

An anxious-looking Howard appeared at the house later that evening. As soon as they were alone, he crushed her in his arms, but Claire gently disentangled herself.

'Let me get you another drink,' she said. 'Lucy said to help ourselves.'

'I've already got one somewhere – just put it down for a moment. Oh, there it is.' He turned to retrieve his whisky from the table. 'So tell me what happened. You look marvellous considering all you've been through. Hadn't the first idea where you were. Did everything I could through official channels. For all I knew, you had stayed out of touch deliberately, but I was worried sick all the same. How did you get back from the island, by the way?'

Claire hesitated for a moment. 'Oh, official channels . . . And now I've been thrown out of the country and I'm leaving tomorrow,' she said in a rush.

He stared at her in dismay. 'Thrown out?'

'Well, not exactly. I'm leaving of my own accord. So we need to talk, as you say.' She took a deep breath. 'Thing is, Howard, I don't know if you still want to marry me, but I don't think I'd make a very good banker's wife.'

'Well,' he said seriously, 'you're sometimes rather restless, well, dramatic at the moment, but once you've settled down and had children, you'll probably be a perfectly normal, sensible mother.'

'But if I remain the wild and reckless woman that I seem to have turned into, and I don't become, uh, normal, it might not be good for your career to . . .'

He did not smile. 'Where is all this talk leading to, Claire? You know I love you, but . . . do you, do you still care for me? What about this Australian that Deborah told me about?'

So he knows, she thought guiltily. 'Just what did Deb tell you?'

He spoke slowly, dragging out each painful word. 'Don't

suppose she meant to tell me anything, but I was talking to her and I was saying it was amazing that a sweet, innocent girl like you had got involved with murderers and kidnappers. Deborah said you were very sweet but maybe not all that innocent. I asked what she meant and, after a bit of humming and hawing, she told me about this other man, Drew.'

'I see.' She did see. Maybe Deb had done her a favour in a way. Claire knew she should have told him all months ago. She'd learnt over the years that some things are best left unsaid, some sins best unconfessed, but this time she was very much in the wrong.

'You, you said nothing about him all the time we . . .'

She put her hand on his arm. 'I'm so sorry, Howard, really I am. I've behaved appallingly.'

'Well, do you want him or me?' he asked miserably. He looked as if he knew the answer already.

'Thing is, it's not a question of who I want. I haven't got him. He's gone. It wasn't a relationship in the normal sense of the word – just a man I bumped into now and then. I knew it was the wrong thing to do, but . . .'

'Pretty explosive bumps from what Deborah said.'

Claire flushed and looked down. 'He's gone now,' she repeated.

'Then is there a chance for me? I could get a posting somewhere else, if I ask to be transferred.'

She walked the length of the drawing room and then turned and faced him. 'I don't think I'd make you happy. Find someone more sensible. Someone like your friend Deb.'

'She's already married.'

'Not so as you'd notice.'

'What do you mean?'

'She's got such an awful husband. I hope she ditches him. Their marriage is on the rocks. Has been for ages.'

He put his hand on her arm. 'But our marriage would be different. I told you, I love you.'

She felt even more of a shit. 'No, you don't. That's what frightens me. You love some imaginary, sweet, ideal Claire that I couldn't live up to. You are very attractive and nice, too nice for me really, and I am terribly fond of you, but . . .'

'Fond! So, so are you, are you saying it's over?'

'Yes, I'm sorry, truly.' Her voice was heavy with guilt. 'I feel

awful about sort of leading you on all this time. I'm sorry I
jittered about for so long. It wasn't fair. But you see, I really,
really wanted it to work between you and me, but . . . but it just
didn't somehow, not for me. I don't know why. You're such a
terrific man.' She faltered into silence.

Picking up his whisky glass again and draining it, he
continued to speak calmly. 'So you're really leaving tomorrow?'

'Yes.'

There didn't seem to be much more to say, and they walked
slowly towards the front door together. As she was shutting
it behind him, he made one final effort. 'What are you going
to do now? Will you go back to Sotheby's?'

'I don't know where I'll go or what I'll do.'

When Claire arrived at the airport the next morning, she took
her first-class London ticket to the British Airways desk.
Fearing that she was making yet another of life's mistakes,
she made enquiries about exchanging it for a flight to Australia.

TWENTY-SEVEN

Bereft and lonely without Claire, Howard went round to
the Cases' flat one evening. He rang the bell and waited,
but it was some time before the door opened. Deborah
stood there, red-eyed and dishevelled in a crumpled denim
skirt and baggy T-shirt.

He hesitated. 'Hello, Deb. Is Johnny in? Just came round
for a chat.'

'No.' Her face expressionless, she pushed her long hair
away from her eyes.

'Do you . . .? Is he expected back soon?'

'No, but come in, Howard.' She waved her arm. 'Sorry the
place is a mess. Pima went to see her folks. We can't seem
to cope too well without her.'

He looked around at the piles of toys and discarded shoes.
Plastic bags full of shopping sat on the floor waiting to be
unpacked. There was a stack of old newspapers in the corner,
and, more significant, a carton full of empty bottles.

He said, 'Oh, bad luck. When is Pima coming back?'

'I don't know.'

'Very unwise to let a good maid go on holiday.' He smiled, attempting to lighten the atmosphere.

'Yeah, you're right,' said Deborah vaguely. 'Have a drink, Howard. You look like you could use one.'

'Thanks. Could I have a whisky?'

'Help yourself. Get me one too, would you? It's in there.' She pointed in the direction of the kitchen and remained slumped on the sofa, unusually quiet.

He was pouring a drink from the half-empty whisky bottle when a postcard of Sydney Harbour Bridge caught his eye. He picked it up and turned it over. With a start, he recognized Claire's handwriting. She wrote:

> Decided to visit Australia. Luckily I got an instant electronic visa. Boiling hot here. Just like Maising. Miss you all. Love Claire.

Sick with misery, he dropped the card back on to the shelf and, hardly knowing what he was doing, walked back into the sitting room.

'You forgot the ice. And the water,' said Deborah.

'Sorry.'

'What's wrong? You look kind of strange.'

He paused and then said, 'I saw the postcard from Claire. I suppose she's gone to that Australian, Drew. I thought she went to England. But she's gone to him.'

'Yeah, took me by surprise too. Drew's in Canberra, but I guess that's quite near Sydney, isn't it?'

'Near enough. I didn't know she was going to him,' he repeated. 'She said there was nothing serious between them. Or that's what I thought she said.' He felt empty, hopeless.

'Poor Howard.' She touched his hand.

'Mind you, she said it was finished, her and me, I mean. But I suppose I hoped she would write from England and say she'd changed her mind. But now . . .'

Deborah went to the kitchen and came back with the whisky bottle, a bucket of ice and a jug of water. 'Let's both get drunk – we're two of a kind.'

Howard had been staring at the carpet. Now he looked at

her, remembering her presence. 'How do you mean? Two of
a kind?'

'Johnny just walked out on me.'

'Oh God. Oh God, I'm sorry. But he's always, always been
a bit outrageous. He'll come back. He usually does, doesn't
he? Nobody in his right mind would leave a woman like you.'

'Thanks, but I don't want him back. I guess I just wanted
to be the one to quit. I've been planning to leave him for
months and now that I'm the one who's been dumped, I'm
sort of upset – it's crazy.' She laughed, slightly hysterically.
Then she took two large gulps of whisky.

'But what makes you think he won't come back anyway?'

'It's different this time. I can tell. You know these things.
Usually he keeps his life in two compartments. Me and the
kids are in one compartment, and his bar girls, or whatever,
are in the other. But this woman has taken him over. He hasn't
been home for weeks. Normally he always comes home, like
he's just been out for a game of squash or something.'

Involuntarily Howard smiled at the idea of Johnny's sex
life being likened to a game of squash. Quite appropriate, he
thought. Fortunately she didn't notice his expression.

She went on. 'But this time he's emotionally involved.
Usually Johnny is not into emotions, but he says this woman's
different – dynamic, intelligent, irresistible, the great love of
his life – I guess that's what they all say, when they leave
their wives. But she can have him. I won't fight for him
because, goddammit, I don't want him. I'm just mad I didn't
leave first.'

Howard picked up his own glass and added some ice.
Deborah continued to talk about Johnny and her marriage. He
began to talk about Claire. Sometimes they listened to each
other. As they talked on and on, they both drank steadily.

He said, 'This bottle's finished. We should go out and eat.'

'I can't. You go. I have to stay with the kids. They're asleep.'

'OK, I'll go and get us some dinner and another bottle and
then I'll come back.'

'Don't bother. You go, eat something good, find a nice bar
girl. A nice bar girl would cheer you up.'

But Howard returned half an hour later with some white
plastic boxes of lukewarm Chinese food. He found some plates,
knives and forks, and arranged the unappetizing meal on the

coffee table near her. She ate little, but she drank yet more whisky.

'Actually,' she said, beginning to slur her words, 'it's my own fault. If you make a mistake – and let's face facts, my marriage was a mistake, oh boy, what a mishtake – then you should be prepared to admit it. I shouldn't have married a shit. Didn't recognize that when I met him. I was young and stupid, kind of rushed the whole deal.'

'Maybe that was my problem. I rushed into things with Claire.'

'But you didn't make a mishtake about her – she's a nice person, very nice. She just fell for someone else. You meet a nice person and they fall for someone else. Life's a shit, but that's life, Howard.'

'Yes,' he said, feeling sure that she had just said something truly profound. 'Yes, that's life.'

'Yeah, I guess so.' She kicked off her sandals and lay back on the sofa. At least two of the bottom buttons on her skirt had come undone, revealing a considerable amount of ample brown thigh. Howard stared at this artless but tempting display. A vision of Claire's slim body came into his mind which he suppressed with difficulty. 'Even though it's better to cut your losses and quit, it doesn't feel good to fail, you know,' Deborah said blearily.

'D'you mind me asking, why did Johnny really leave?'

'Haven't you listened to a word I said? He found someone he liked better. Men do it all the time.'

'He's a fool. If I had a wife like you I'd . . . I'd . . .'

'You'd what?'

'I'd be very sure to love and cherish you.' It was true. He would. She was a lovely woman and so warm-hearted, a kind, generous woman, he said to himself. Johnny shouldn't have treated her like that.

She looked at him, her eyes half-closed. 'That's nice, Howard. You're a good man. Even though you're drunk.'

'I'm not drunk, not yet, not completely. I may be soon. Or at least I'm no drunker than you are . . . That's good. You smiled.'

'Yeah, you cheered me up some. Did I cheer you up?'

'Yes, you did.' He wanted to be near her to reassure her. And to reassure himself. He moved to the sofa and began to massage her ankles. Very nice ankles, all brown, like her long legs. There was a lot of Deborah, a whole lot of woman. 'D'you know what would cheer me up even more?' he blurted out, suddenly reckless.

'What?'

'I want to spend the night with you.'

There was a long pause while she studied his face. 'Like, in the same bed?'

Howard nodded solemnly. 'In the same bed.'

'Oh.'

'You don't sound very enthusiastic,' he said.

She smiled, focusing on his face again. 'Acksherly – no, that didn't sound right. I'll try to say it again. Actually, I could be. Maybe even quite, very enthu . . . enthusiastic. But . . . that time at the beach, way back, do you remember?'

He continued to massage her ankles with great concentration, then his hands strayed a little higher. 'Course I do. How could I forget?'

'Maybe you didn't like it. Turned out to be a one-night stand.'

He looked up, smiling. 'I liked it, I liked it a lot, too much even, but you were married.'

'Yes, I was married then. And even if I'm nearly not married now, I don't want to get involved in casual sex. I mean sex without love, isn't right.' She put her hand on his. 'I like you, but 'tsn't right, casual sex.'

Howard pulled her to him. 'It wouldn't be casual. We're friends, you and me. We need each other.' He stroked her hair. 'It'd be friendship sex, that's different, quite different.'

'You reckon? Yeah, that's nice.'

As Deborah sank into his arms, his head reeled. It was comforting to hold her, to caress her, to keep her safe from her dark thoughts, and to be safe from his, safe from his thoughts of Claire. He closed his eyes and mind to let his body take over.

Deborah awoke at five thirty the next morning with a terrible thirst and a severe headache.

'Oh God,' she moaned to herself when she saw Howard lying beside her. 'You blew it again, Deb.' She shook him awake and told him to leave before the children got up.

'What does it matter if they do see me?'

'I can't cope with complications, Howard.'

'When will I see you again?'

'I don't know. Right now I have one hell of a hangover. And I need to be alone to sort out my life.'

He made to take her in his arms, but she pushed him away. 'No, I'm no good to anyone. I feel as bad as I look.'

'You look fine, a lot better than I do, I'm sure.' Running his hands through his hair, he got out of bed and ambled off in the direction of the bathroom.

Deborah closed her eyes again. A naked Howard was not a bad sight, if you liked a whole lot of man, but she just did not want to get involved.

By the door he turned. 'I'll phone you when I get home. But can I please have a coffee first – to recover a bit?'

'No, just leave quickly, Howard.' Then she saw his face. 'Oh God, I'm a bitch. Listen, I'll call you when I get my act together. OK?'

'All right . . . Deb, don't forget I'm a friend.'

Her mother-in-law, however, was distinctly less friendly. Deborah held the receiver away from her ear as Muriel's vowels whined down the telephone line.

'You're a selfish girl, Debbie. Both of you, you and Johnny. Both very selfish. Trevor and I were looking forward to Christmas with little Sam and Jojo. Trevor has been all the way to Bangkok to buy a new tree. It was ever such a job to get it back on the plane. Oh dear, and now you've made me spill my tea all over the bedspread. It's all very upsetting.'

In spite of herself, Deborah grinned. She could picture Muriel breakfasting in her frilly pink bed on the other side of the city.

'A genuine living Christmas tree?' asked Deborah.

'Of course not. Japanese and plastic. But it's ever so realistic. And Trevor was going to dress up as Santa. He's hired a costume from the drama group. And I've ordered the turkey from Singapore. Someone's got to eat it. They're not cheap, after all.'

'Muriel, I guess I'm sorry about the break-up. But we'll come to your Christmas lunch, me and the children. If you'd like to have us.'

'But Johnny will be there.'

'So what? He and I are grown-ups. We needn't fight on Christmas Day. As long as he leaves his woman at home.'

'What woman?'

'The woman he's moved in with, Muriel.'

'I'm sure you're exaggerating, dear. It's just a little tiff that you and he are having. You young people are just not prepared to try at marriage. It's a matter of give and take. Even Trevor and I used to have our little problems now and then.'

'Just tell your son I'm not coming to Christmas lunch if he brings his whore along.'

In the event it was much like any other of Muriel's plastic tropical Christmases, except that this year the fake bonhomie was even worse than in the past. Trevor and Johnny drank a lot, Deborah and Muriel drank little and the children behaved quite well.

Sam did not make any embarrassing remarks about his father as he was far too busy playing with all the heaps of flimsy Hong Kong toys with batteries and wires that would all be broken tomorrow. Jojo crawled about, exploring as far as she was allowed, trying to reach up to Muriel's collection of dainty china figurines.

One day, before I finally leave the country, I'll let her smash them all, thought Deborah grimly.

Then taking a deep breath, she made her announcement. 'I'm leaving for the States as soon as I can arrange it. I'm going to stopover with my sister in London on the way. And I'll probably visit Geneva.'

'When will you be back?' asked Muriel.

'I don't know. Maybe I won't come back at all.'

Later Johnny said, 'My mother was very upset by all your talk of leaving the country.'

'To hell with your mother.'

'You can't think only of yourself, Deb. She's a granny and she loves the kids. And so do I.'

'Neither you nor she wants to take care of them, though.'

'Hell, no. You can have custody. And I'll pay a generous allowance for them. You can stay in the flat and I'll pay the maid, of course. But I'll only cough up if you stay in Maising.'

'I don't want your damn money. I can support myself.'

'I think you'll find you do want it. The pittance you earn teaching English won't keep you in the nice comfortable manner which you've become accustomed to. There are such things as bills, you know, lots and lots of big, big bills.'

'Then I'll have to move downmarket, won't I?'

Johnny went on as if she had not spoken. 'By all means go and visit your father. But you know you can't stand living with him and you can't afford anywhere else. It's a big, bad, expensive world out there. I expect you'll be back before long.'

'Johnny, don't you think we'll both be happier if I'm living in another country? A big legal battle won't do your reputation any good – this is a small place. Talk to your new girlfriend. I'll bet she wants me to leave.'

The day after, Johnny telephoned her. His manner was friendly, almost appeasing. 'I talked to Liana.'

'Is that her name? I seem to have heard it before some place.'

'Maybe you have. She's quite a girl.'

'I'll bet.'

'Liana seems to think you're right. That you and the children might be happier in another country, though of course I'd like to see them from time to time.'

Deborah smiled grimly. 'OK.'

'Liana thinks I should pay reasonable expenses for the kids wherever you are. Do you want some sort of official legal separation? Liana thinks it's a good idea.'

'You bet. I am so glad your friend and I have so many ideas in common. But I don't want your money.'

She could hear him whispering to someone. 'Liana thinks that's balls. She advises you to get a lawyer and take what you can. She says . . .'

'Unusually generous, your friend. Sounds too good to be true. Maybe she did do me a favour, but just tell her to butt out of my life or the breaks around here won't be so damn clean.'

After checking her bank balance, Deborah rang Howard to consult him about cheap flights to Europe and the States. He offered to bring round some brochures that evening.

When she opened the door and saw him standing there, Deborah felt a pang of something, she was not sure what. He looked spruce and handsome in a pale cream shirt, and also a little uncertain of his welcome. Putting on her friendly social manner, she offered him a drink.

'How are you feeling, Deb?' he asked, half-sheepish, half-hopeful.

'I feel good, thanks. Well, not exactly good but OK.'

They chatted for some time.

She found herself inviting him to stay to dinner. 'But, just to make it quite clear, tonight we're not going to get smashed – or get laid – the other night was a one-off, sort of mutual first-aid,' she added.

He smiled. 'Pity.'

After dinner he listened patiently while she told him about her travel plans and how she wanted to go to Switzerland, London and New York.

'How long will you be in Switzerland?' he asked.

'Oh, I don't know, I can't afford to go for long, but it would be so great to just stop by, to see friends in Geneva.'

He smiled at her. 'How about stopping by with me? You see my uncle offered me the use of his chalet in Wengen. I don't particularly like the idea of being there on my own, so how about you and the kids coming too? Just as friends, no strings. Then you can go on to Geneva.'

She stared at him, smiling in amazement. 'Run that by me again. You are offering to share a chalet in Wengen. I didn't even know you were due for leave. It sounds like my sort of heaven, but, Howard, I just can't afford a ski holiday.'

'It wouldn't cost you anything. You'd be my guest. No strings, though, as I said.'

'By no strings, d'you mean no friendship sex?'

'You do like to put things bluntly, don't you? I mean, I shan't expect anything from you except companionship.'

'Really?'

'No strings, no pressure.'

'You're crazy, Howard. I'm sure there are all sorts of juicy bimbos who'd just adore to go skiing with you. You can't really mean you want to take a mum with two kids.'

'You want to visit Switzerland. I want to go skiing. You and I get on well, as friends, and you're a pretty yummy mummy too. So it's logical to go together. If you feel worried about the whole thing, you can pay me back some day when you're rich.'

'I don't know what to say.'

'Say yes.'

She hugged him. 'OK. Thank you. I accept. You're a great guy. I can't tell you what this means to me. I feel sort of different, more human. But are you sure you don't mind if we leave sex out of the deal? I'm just not ready for it yet.'

'I understand,' he said gently. Then he said, 'But you haven't opened your Christmas present.'

'What present?'

'I left it in the hall so it would be a surprise. Sorry it's so belated.'

He went out of the room and returned with a plastic bag from which he took a red crêpe paper parcel, stuck up with a great deal of scotch tape and a crumpled green ribbon.

Deborah opened it and laughed. 'A ski hat. How ever did you find a ski hat in tropical Maising?'

'You can buy anything here if you know where to go.'

'It's wonderful. I love the colour and the bobble. I'll wear it in Wengen. But how did you know I'd be coming skiing? How did you know I'd accept?'

'I just hoped,' he said, looking extremely pleased with himself.

'Sometimes you're really very cute,' she said and kissed him on the cheek. 'I just adore my Christmas present. What can I get you? Is there anything you need?'

'Just you,' he said, with a certain amorous look on his face.

Deb felt obliged to take him seriously. 'Howard, darling, sorry to repeat myself, but you do understand I'm not ready for any kind of relationship. I'm not looking for a new man, not right now. Right now I need to learn to take care of myself and my kids.'

'But maybe I could take care of you, and them too. Maybe I could get a job somewhere else — then we could share a house.'

She spoke slowly. 'If we had any sort of love affair, it would be on the rebound, you from Claire, and me from my marriage. A moment ago you were in love with Claire, crazy about her.'

He rubbed his nose thoughtfully. 'I know, but I think she

was right when she said I was in love with the idea of her rather than Claire herself. She was my ideal woman, or rather I thought of her that way. But a long time ago, before I met her, I was very attracted to you, but you were married. So I looked for someone else, and she came along. It's quite possible to be attracted to more than one person, isn't it?'

'Yeah, it is – I accept that because one time I, well there was someone else in Maising once,' she began slowly. 'But that's all in the past.' She paused, looking down at her hands. Then she said, 'But, thing is, you just feel sorry for me.'

'I told you to stop saying "but". Deb, I meant it when I said I liked the way you look. And I like your voice and your fizzy personality. And I like being with you and your children.' He paused. 'And those two nights we've spent together, I liked them too, rather a lot.'

She smiled. 'We were drunk.'

'I know, but I can remember everything.'

'Me too.'

'Might be even better sober.'

She smiled again.

Obviously encouraged, he went on. 'Maybe, just maybe, we might . . .'

Deb shook her head and smiled. 'Forgive me if I've got it wrong, but it looks like you're not that interested in "just good friends". See, I just can't slide from one man to another. Doesn't seem right. I have to prove I can manage on my own. And I definitely wouldn't want to be lovers just because you feel sorry for me and it's convenient – I have to tell you that.'

'All right, if that's the way you want it, but why don't you just stay with me for a while, no strings, until the kids are a bit bigger. Then you can go off and be independent and conquer the world.'

'Howard, listen, I'm not a whole person at the moment. When a marriage breaks up, you're torn in two, all torn and sore on one side, and you need to grow a new skin before you're ready for another relationship. It's just too much too soon.'

'But you weren't happy in your marriage.'

'That's not the point,' she said slowly. 'It was a part of me and now it's gone.'

'Well, yes, and of course you need time. I see that. I won't put any pressure on you. But, please, consider it.'

'No, it just won't work. I've just made up my mind to go to Washington and live with Dad. It'll cheer him up, and it's the only place I can afford.'

There was a circular and confusing argument.

Finally Howard pleaded, 'I don't understand this feminist stuff, but I give in. I accept your decision, you're off to London and then the States, but come skiing en route, just for two weeks. Absolutely platonic, cross my heart.'

She paced around, then turned to face him. 'It's very tempting, but I've just realized I can't, I'm so sorry.'

Howard hunched his shoulders and sighed. 'All right,' he said miserably. 'I'll have to let you go. But promise to stay in touch.'

'I promise I will stay in touch. Please, please don't be too sad, Howard, you'll be fine in the end. You'll find someone else some day.' She smiled gently. 'A nice, kind, single, eligible man like you will never be past his sell-by date.'

TWENTY-EIGHT

Lucy could tell from some yards away that Martin was in a bad temper. He plodded across the lawn like a crumpled bear and flung himself down on the verandah chaise longue without kissing her hello. She called for tea and went to find the McVitie's digestive biscuits, a rare English treat she had been saving for just such an emergency. After tea, when Somjit had cleared away the tray, Martin revealed the cause of his despondency. 'The Japanese got the bloody bus contract, after all that work we did. Stole it from under our noses. Can't imagine how they managed such a low tender.'

'Oh dear,' murmured Lucy sympathetically. 'Is the Ambassador upset?'

'Not half as upset as the chaps from British Coachworks.'

'And poor Claire, making her leave the country, all that was unnecessary.'

'Well, she had to go anyway. For her own safety. Talking

of Claire, you remember that chap she used to work for, Vandenberg? Well, he's suddenly upped and moved to America, health problems, needs a heart operation. Sold up all his business interests and his house here. I saw it in the local rag.'

Lucy seldom read the *Maising Recorder*, a dull and badly printed English-language newspaper, but now she went in search of it. 'Oh, yes, there's a picture of Jean-Louis – amazingly flattering considering how ugly he was – and quite a long spiel about him.' She read the half-page article and stared at the smudgy photograph. Then she said, 'I wonder if his health problems were due to natural causes.'

'Why on earth shouldn't they be?'

'He had lots of enemies. His so-called heart disease could have been induced by native medicine.'

'Lucy, please, we've had quite enough of your amateur detective work and the less said about native medicine the better, don't you think?' He stood up and stretched out his long arms. 'Now, what are we doing this evening? Oh God, the universities dinner. I must have some sort of siesta before we go.'

When they arrived at the crowded private room in the Hotel Splendid, Lucy began to feel depressed. Even though she had learnt to have low expectations of official social functions, she found that the biennial dinner for British university graduates provided new dimensions of boredom. Traditionally, there was a long lecture after a long formal dinner and one couldn't expect to escape before midnight.

This evening she felt tired even before the dinner started. The meal was indifferent, cardboard international cuisine, elaborately presented but tasting of nothing. Lucy sat silently as the five other members at her table talked about the beauties of Cambridge and what a wonderful time they'd had in their day.

She gazed at the elegant buffet table. In the centre was a life-size swan carved out of ice, its beak dripping into a huge bowl of fruit. She wondered idly how long it would take to melt and if it would still be there the next morning. She wondered if anyone would notice if she herself melted away. While she sat staring at the swan, she folded and refolded her table napkin.

Suddenly she thought of a topic of conversation. 'Who's the

speaker this evening?' she asked loudly, addressing the table at large.

'He is an archaeologist,' began an earnest young man in thick round glasses.

His explanations were drowned by applause when Johnny Case staggered to his feet. 'As secretary of the Dining Club, I have to announce that our original speaker, Dr Kim Zar, is ill, but we are very fortunate in being able to find a superb replacement. I have great pleasure in introducing the well-known archaeologist and art historian, recently returned from a long stay in Bangkok, Professor Meng Li Sang.'

Lucy stared in astonishment as Meng mounted the rostrum. He began to talk about the influence of the Ramayana on art throughout south-east Asia. She was mesmerized. He looked handsome as ever, charming, powerful, dark like a fallen angel. Suddenly he saw her and it appeared that he addressed the rest of his talk only to her. She found it hard to concentrate on what he was saying. Sometimes, however, the words penetrated. 'Princess Sita was lured away from her husband by the demon king.' Lucy shuddered. Later she heard, 'Her chastity was called into question and she was forced to undergo an ordeal.' She felt it must be obvious to everyone that his eyes were fixed on her face.

When he had at last finished his lecture, he came straight towards her. 'Lucy, I am so very happy to see you.' He took her hand.

Flushing, she snatched it away. 'I thought you were abroad.'

'I have returned. Come, I would like to introduce you to someone.'

He led her to a small side room where a young man was sitting alone. She thought she had seen him before somewhere.

Meng said, 'May I present my friend Pel? He is from Cambodia. But maybe you know him already? He says he came to your house one evening.'

The young man, as beautiful as Meng, but paler, thin, more delicate, held out his hand. '*Enchanté*, madame. I believe you are a friend of Claire. Do you know where she is? I would like to write a letter.'

Her head reeling, Lucy shook hands automatically. 'She . . . I thought . . . you can't be the Pel who used to work with Claire.'

'The very same,' said Meng, smiling.

'But . . .'

'Pel, Lucy looks as if she would like a drink. Please would you be so kind as to fetch one. I'd like a cognac, Rémy Martin or whatever they have – and for you, Lucy?'

'Oh, water, orange juice, anything soft, thank you,' she said. Pel moved away towards the crowded bar.

Meng was looking rather smug. 'You thought he was dead, didn't you? Well, now you can write to Claire and say he is not.'

Lucy stared at him. 'I don't understand. Claire thought you . . .'

'She thought I killed him or had him killed,' he said more seriously. 'What did you think?'

She hesitated. 'Well, I found it impossible to believe you were a murderer, but Claire overheard a conversation you had with Mr Vandenberg. She was certain you were responsible for Pel's death. I didn't think she'd invent a thing like that . . . not Claire. So I just didn't know what to make of it all.'

'You are both right. I am not a murderer, but I did tell Jean-Louis that Pel was dead. I wanted to protect the boy. You see he and Jean-Louis had quarrelled and Jean-Louis has a vicious streak if things don't go his way.'

'What did they quarrel about?'

'Jean-Louis has gone now. His quarrels went with him. It is best not to ask too many questions, Lucy. You Westerners expect answers when no answer can be given because no question should be asked. That is why your friend Claire got into trouble.'

'But it's all very peculiar. Who was the body on the beach Claire talked about, the one with the cross?'

'I don't know. A coincidence. Probably just a criminal or a refugee.'

'And what about the ivory bird?' Suddenly she wished she hadn't mentioned this.

'Lucy, Lucy, I explained it was necessary to deceive Jean-Louis. And it was most unfortunate he chose to have Claire marooned. It was just to scare her, a warning. Still, she will be pleased to know the truth.'

Lucy was still suspicious. 'How can I prove to her that your friend is the real Pel?'

'I will take a photograph of you both together to send to her. You know I am an excellent photographer,' he said, with a glittering smile.

She blushed scarlet.

'Ah, my poor Lucy, you're still concerned about my portraits. You need never have worried. It was my secret. But now Pel has forced me to destroy all my nude studies, all the prints and negatives. He is a very jealous boy in some ways. I am surprised he has left us alone so long.'

'Jealous?'

'Yes, I have abandoned my celibate state. When we were together in Bangkok, Pel persuaded me to come down off the fence. Or should I say "come out"?' His arch expression made his meaning clear.

Lucy smiled in sudden understanding, feeling a little foolish. 'Oh, I see. You mean that you and Pel are together, a sort of couple.' She was relieved that Meng's attentions towards her had been deflected, but at the same time faintly disappointed.

'As you say, a sort of couple. And we are very happy. Especially now that Jean-Louis has left. Now, let's talk about you. I have to say, Lucy, that you're looking especially well this evening, positively blooming. If you were not married and I were not spoken for, I'd tell you that I find your figure even more impressive than ever.'

Suddenly a familiar voice croaked in Lucy's ear. 'Ah, Professor, I have been looking for you.' Helena loomed over them like a tall black crow. 'May I join you?' she asked. 'What are you talking about?'

'Good evening, Mrs Blackerstaff. We are talking of the impressive figures at the Ravi ruins. Mrs Williamson is most interested in art history,' said Meng.

Lucy suppressed a giggle.

'Is she?' asked Helena doubtfully. 'Now, Professor, I'm organizing a little gathering of international ladies and I wonder if you would come and speak. Perhaps a talk similar to the one you gave this evening, maybe a little more populist in flavour and subject.'

'I should be delighted,' he said. 'But I wonder if I could ask you to arrange the details through Lucy. She is familiar with my work and she could advise about what might appeal to a group of ladies. Ah, my friend is signalling. If you will excuse me, I must go now. Goodnight, Mrs Blackerstaff, Lucy. I enjoyed talking to you.'

Helena stared after him. 'Well, it appears that you have made some of the right contacts, Lucy. Most encouraging. Did you know that the Professor is a minor member of the royal family?'

It was after midnight when Lucy and Martin finally sank into bed.

'Where were you all evening? I couldn't find you after dinner,' said Martin as he turned off the light.

The darkness hid Lucy's blush. 'Oh, just chatting to the lecturer.'

'I was surprised to see that Meng chap back in the country. What did you find to talk about for so long? I didn't know you even knew him.'

'Oh, we discussed all sorts of things. I'll tell you in the morning. I'm very tired now.' She yawned. 'But I'm very happy.'

'That's nice to hear. It appears you're beginning to enjoy diplomatic life a bit, are you?' he asked sleepily.

'Oh, yes, darling.'

'Not too dull?'

'It has its interesting moments, like tonight.'

'Yes, it was an excellent talk. But I didn't know you were that keen on art history.'

'You don't know absolutely everything about me, Martin.'

'Oh, but I think I do, my love. You're such a nice open creature,' he murmured. 'Part of your charm.'

Lucy smiled in the dark and changed the subject. 'I talked to Helena too.'

'Yes, I know. I met her when she was in full flow. She actually said how well you had adapted to life out here. Glad you've been getting on better with her lately.'

'Well, we coexist. Like I coexist with Somjit. She more or less does what I say now, if I'm tactful. I think she and Nee were impressed with the mince pies I made for the Christmas party. "Look more pretty than Missus Belinda make," she said, believe it or not.'

He laughed. 'What an accolade!'

'In fact, all my Christmas preparations seemed to impress them, for some reason.'

'They admire people who take trouble about things, like you do, darling,' he murmured. 'Even heard Somjit boasting about you to one of the other maids. She said, "My madame speak Maising language good. Say words better than Madame Helena."'

'Really?' said Lucy delightedly. She snuggled up to him. 'Hope Helena doesn't hear that. Don't want to spoil a beautiful friendship. But you're right – Helena's quite civil to me now she thinks I know some of the right people, silly old bag.'

'Mmm. But you know lots of nice people too.' He was almost asleep.

She took a deep breath. 'Except I miss Claire and Deborah. I wish Deb was going to be here when the baby is born.'

'Mmm.' Martin suddenly sat up. 'What baby?'

She put her mouth to his ear and whispered, 'Mine, ours, the tadpole in my tum.'

'You're pregnant?' he stuttered happily.

'Mm, yes.'

He turned and hugged her tight. 'You are so, so clever.'

'I was thrilled to pieces when Dr Nim said the test was positive. I was going to keep it secret for a bit longer, but I just couldn't resist telling you. You don't mind, do you?'

'Darling, I'm absolutely delighted.'

After another hug, Lucy said, 'What's more, I think we should introduce the baby to your sons when it's old enough to travel. They'll want to meet their new brother or sister, I'm sure.'

'I don't know about that.'

'Yes, they will.'

'If you say so, darling. You're such a wonder, anything is possible.'

Lucy could tell he meant it. She smiled in the dark and put her arms around him. She was lucky, she knew. At any moment she had expected retribution to strike, but retribution had held off.

She would now have to be sure to keep her marriage safe. Nothing would ever be allowed to destroy her family.

At the foot of the bed Grace the cat began to purr. She was happy in her new superior home.

TWENTY-NINE

Far away in Australia Claire was talking to a different cat and gently lifting it down from the kitchen table because she was cutting up slices of chicken and arranging a small portion on each plate. After adding some cooked frozen peas and rather soggy oven chips, she called her charge. She and the child ate their lunch in companionable silence under the sunshade by the back door, while Thomas the cat regarded them sulkily from the window.

It was very hot that day in Canberra. Claire sat in an absent-minded daze, wondering what Drew was doing, wondering when she was going to contact him.

'I want ketchup, Claire,' said Ned, patting her arm with his sticky little fingers.

'Ketchup doesn't go with chicken.'

'I like some.'

'Oh, all right, but don't forget the magic word.'

'Please, Claire, I want ketchup.'

Though her days were full of conversations of this type, she enjoyed looking after the child. Besides, it was the only job she could find when she arrived in Canberra without any legal permission to work. Not exactly a career move but never mind.

Sydney had been humid and beautiful: the dramatic bow of the bridge, the magical white opera house on the edge of the harbour, the Paddington streets with iron railings, the leafy suburbs and the long, long beaches, but she couldn't stay there. She wanted to be with Drew.

Then, when her plane landed in Canberra, she lost courage. She checked into a quiet hotel near the lake, intending to wait a few days and then telephone him. But she kept postponing her call, reminding herself he needed a proper amount of time to sort out his affairs with his wife. And besides she couldn't just fling herself on him like a lovesick dependent bimbo. She must find somewhere to live and some way of supporting herself temporarily.

While she looked for work, she explored the city. Canberra, too, was beautiful, like a vast park, but she found sightseeing too hot. She visited the air-conditioned museums and galleries, the parliament building, the war memorials, the interesting modern architecture. A natural tourist, she read all the guide books and studied the circular patterns created by the American architect who designed the new capital city in the thirties, and she sat by the man-made lake, watching the boats. She would like to have visited the blue Brindabella mountains, but she had no way to reach them.

Her days in the hotel seemed long and expensive. When one of the male guests started to follow her about, she decided to take the first residential job that was offered, however unsuitable.

Diane, Ned's vastly pregnant mother, had been ecstatic when Claire answered her advertisement for an emergency housekeeper. 'Lucky to find you, Claire. Everyone goes away for Chrissy and after. It's our summer holiday time.' She explained that her husband was working in Indonesia. Grandma had originally promised to look after the household during the confinement, but had now been taken ill. So Claire was desperately needed, for a month at least, to look after Ned while Diane was in hospital for a planned Caesarean and then afterwards.

A month of concentrated domesticity would probably be enough, in Claire's view, but she promised to stay as long as she was needed and she was touched to find that even her clumsy amateur help was welcome. The newborn baby was fretful in the summer heat and Ned was jealous of the attention his brother demanded. Claire was astonished by the sheer hard work generated by this tiny helpless creature.

To allow Diane to rest, Claire would bundle the children into the stroller and go for long walks around the streets. She liked to observe the single-storey houses with their tidy shrubs and neat unfenced front gardens, dry and parched in the heat. Flocks of large, brightly coloured cockatoos and crimson-headed parrots added a touch of exotic glamour to the suburban scene. She avoided the sinister giant magpies, because they were reputed to attack unwary passers-by. With their round watchful eyes, they reminded her of Jean-Louis.

Sometimes it was too hot for walking. She filled the paddling pool in the garden and sat watching Ned splash naked in the water while the baby slept in his wicker basket in the shade of the wattle. All the time she walked and watched the children, all the time she cooked, shopped and cleaned, she thought about Drew. And whether he loved her and, if he did, would it ever work out between them? Whether a modern woman should chase a man halfway round the world, and, though she loved him, were they suited, was he more important than her so-called career? Of course it would be wrong, anti-feminist, to admit that he might be.

Eventually, after three weeks of exhausting and unaccustomed domesticity, and three weeks of inner debate, Claire asked for the afternoon off. She drove Diane's Holden south out of the city. The suburbs stretched on and on, with houses growing smaller and newer, built more closely together, gardens becoming brown and bare. Finally she reached the open countryside, the bush.

Then, after driving several more miles, she took a sign marked Barwah. She drove along a red, unsurfaced road. The midsummer countryside was all the same, red and parched. She stopped to drink some water from a bottle stored in the cool box and studied the map. Then she drove on for a while, more and more slowly until she found a small faded sign reading 'Raidwood': Drew's place.

She looked down across the valley but could see nothing but unwelcoming dry beige land dotted with a few gum trees. With the inevitable swarm of repellent blowflies buzzing persistently around her, she thought of turning back. What if Meredith were there? Time and time again Drew had said they were legally separated and would never again get together, but people could change their minds.

Come on, you've got this far, she said to herself. She opened the rickety gate, drove in and shut it behind her. The drive was steep and rutted. Afraid of damaging the suspension of her borrowed car, she drove slowly, negotiating bends and cattle grids.

Then, at the bottom of the valley, she saw the pretty little white clapboard house with a wide verandah all around it. There was a small brown-green lawn and a dusty flower bed, with several large gum trees providing a few patches of shade. She parked the car outside the house. When she turned off the engine, she noticed the quiet. There was no sound apart from the hum of the insects.

Heart pounding, she rang the doorbell. No answer. Wandering around the back of the house, she couldn't see a car.

Oh, hell, he's out, she thought. What a fool I am not to have phoned. Driving all this way for nothing – absolutely crazy thing to do.

She sat down on the hot steps. After a while she stood up and, pulling back the fly screen, tried the door handle. It opened. He could be there asleep inside. She called his name.

Nothing happened.

She tiptoed in and crept around. The single-storey house was neat and tidy, plainly furnished with cane sofas and chairs, symmetrically arranged. Two of the bedrooms looked unoccupied. In the third stood a double bed, covered with a patchwork quilt. Some of Drew's clothes, familiar to her, were lying on the chair. She picked them up and held them close to her, inhaling the smell of him.

Then she heard a car. She looked out of the window – an old utility truck was coming down the drive, throwing up a cloud of dust. She ran to the sitting room and sat demurely on the sofa. Then in a panic she rummaged around in her handbag for some scent. When the door opened, she was pretending to read a magazine about cattle.

'Strewth! Claire! What the hell are you doing here?'

'I just dropped by,' she began, trying to sound casual, but she was unable to stop herself from running towards him and falling into his arms.

'Thought I'd lost you, thought I'd lost you,' he murmured. He held her tightly, kissing her hair, her eyes, her mouth.

Eventually, she pushed him away a little. 'Drew, I . . .'

'Don't talk,' he said. 'We'll talk later. Let's go to bed.'

She smiled. 'Straight away?'

'Yes – unless you'd prefer afternoon tea?' As he spoke, he propelled her towards the door.

'Is there any cake?' Her voice was light, breathless.

'No cake.' They had reached the corridor.

'What, no lovely chocolatey coconut Lamingtons – no great Australian delicacies?' she asked.

'Not even Lamingtons,' he said as they stood outside his bedroom door.

'No biscuits either?'

His hands held her. 'No, sorry, no bickies. If I'd known, I would have bought some.'

'Well, then, I suppose I won't bother with tea. Drew, what are you doing? It's all a bit soon.'

'D'you want to wait?' he murmured.

'Mmm . . . no . . . I don't . . .'

After they had made love, Drew held her tight in his arms.

'So are you pleased to see me?' she asked, stupefied with gratification and happiness.

He grinned. 'Think I've just shown you that I am.'

They were silent for a while, then, taking a deep breath, she asked, 'What about your wife?'

'Meredith? Oh, she's calling in on her way back from work to discuss the divorce – should be here any moment,' said Drew casually.

'What?' Panic-stricken, Claire leapt out of bed and began to hunt frantically for her clothes.

'Stop, only joking. She's not coming here. Never does.'

'Bastard!' she said, sitting down suddenly. She shook her fist under his nose. 'Don't do that to me. My nerves are in shreds as it is.'

Laughing, he held on to her hands. 'Sorry – but you looked so pretty and sexy jumping about in the nude like a demented grasshopper.'

'Shut up or I really will punch you,' she said with a grin. 'So, it's over, you and Meredith?'

'Yes, she wants a quickie divorce. Which suits me down to the ground. Easier to get through all the legal stuff if you're both in the same country. She's marrying a parliamentarian and good luck to the bugger, I say.'

With a huge inward surge of relief and joy, Claire put her arms around him. 'So how do you feel about it?'

'Bloody good. Like I've just got rid of the biggest pain in the arse in the southern hemisphere.'

He sounded as if he meant it, she thought.

'Only trouble was,' he continued, 'that I thought I'd lost you in the process. I rang Lucy to speak to you and she said she didn't know where you were, that you'd gone walkabout again. Scared the hell out of me. So what have you been up to?'

She told him.

'You've been in Canberra all this time without calling me?'

'I didn't know what you wanted. I didn't know what the situation was. I couldn't just fling myself on you, could I?'

'Claire, you can fling yourself on me any time you like.'

'I'm not talking about sex.'

'Neither am I,' he said.

Later they walked down to the creek and stood side by side, skimming stones into the calm water in smiling silence. It was marginally cooler as the sun set behind the hills and the evening was still and quiet.

Drew's tall figure was dark against the silver-grey bark of the gum trees. He turned to her and took her hand. 'Claire?'

'Mm?'

'What are we going to do next?'

Her heart beat faster, but she said casually, 'I'd better be getting back to Canberra soon. Told Diane I might be late, but . . .'

'No, I mean, in the future.'

'Haven't really thought.' What a lie, she said to herself.

He grinned mischievously. 'Well, I think you need some country air. How about a job as a jackaroo? Or a shearer? Just right for a nice big tough girl like you. Could do with some help on the property – shearers usually camp out, but you could live in the sheep-shed and even come into the house now and then.'

She laughed. 'Don't know if I have the right qualifications.'

'You're the only candidate I have in mind – so I think you might get the job, if you apply.'

She picked up another stone and threw it into the water. Then she whispered into his ear, 'So if I accept the job as a shearer, when do I start my training?'

They kissed with gentle passionate little bites.

Then slowly he drew back. 'Seriously, Claire, we can go anywhere. Don't have to stay here. I'll put a manager on the farm. Just choose somewhere in the world and we'll go. I'll try to fix up a job or a project. But it's got to be together. On a permanent basis. That's what *I* want, at least. And I guess you wouldn't have come all this way unless you quite liked me.'

She smiled. 'Yes, I quite like you.' She held him close. Eventually she said, 'Could we go back to Maising one day?'

'Yes, maybe, but wherever we go, you must still do what you want, your own thing. I'm worried about your ancient gods, all those statues and old stones of yours. Mustn't neglect them.'

'I've been thinking. I might write a book about the old stones actually, but I can do that anywhere in the world. And you know something?'

'Mm?'

'They've been around a long time, the gods and their statues. Hundreds of years. I can leave them alone for a bit and they won't mind. They'll wait as long as I want. I'd rather concentrate on the living right now, the present.'

'So is that yes?' he asked after a while.

She kissed him again. 'Seems to be.'

'So let's go for it,' he said, with a wide happy smile.